A Surgeon and a Spy

Hearts and Sails Book 3

Alina Rubin

Publisher: Hearts and Sails Author Services

ISBN: Paperback 979-8-9855378-7-1

Cover Design: GetCovers

Editor: Marthese Fenech

Leave a Review!

I would love to know what you thought of A Surgeon and a Spy!

You can write a review at:

Amazon

Goodreads

BookBub

Be the first to know of new releases by subscribing to the newsletter at alinarubinauthor.com

I love hearing from my readers! Please connect with me!

Instagram: Alina.Rubin.Author

Facebook: Alina Rubin Author

Email: alina@alinarubinauthor.com

Dedication

To the courageous veterans in my family: my grandparents, Leonid and Oktyabrina Fridman, and my father-in-law, John Leach. Your bravery and sacrifice will be remembered, as well as your wisdom and love.

Prequel Hearts by the Sea

Ella's and Jamie's first meeting occurs in the prequel novella
Hearts by the Sea
Read for free!

An innocent game brings unforeseen consequences

In the idyllic setting of the English coast in 1800s, Jamie Flowers experiences his first infatuation when he meets Ella Parker, a mysterious girl with a troubled past. As the two rehearse *Romeo and Juliet* together, they decide to sneak out for a midnight swim. But their plans are abruptly halted by a shocking revelation, and Ella is soon gone. Left with a broken heart, Jamie searches for her... and himself. With unexpected twists and turns, Hearts by the Sea is a story of first love, secret codes, and self-discovery.

Read Now for Free!

Contents

Chapter 1

April 1812, Seatown, Dorset, England

"Ma, you can't hold me prisoner in my own bedroom!" Jamie Flowers rattled the knob handle, but the door didn't budge.

"I will not let you go." His mother's voice quivered with sobs. "I'll stand guard here if I must. No meals. No rest. But I will ensure that my son won't join the war and lose his life."

Jamie drew a long breath to calm the mad beating of his heart. It hurt to defy his beloved mother. "I'm not a child anymore. You can't tell me to stay in my chamber if I decided to go."

This room is only one floor above ground, he reminded himself. Ella Parker had little trouble climbing up here one summer evening years ago. Surely, he could jump out of the window without getting hurt.

A long sigh echoed through the door. "Eighteen is a child in my eyes. And you..."

He had not felt like a child since one fateful day when he was twelve. When Dr. Miller walked out of the Flowers' home with a confident gait, the family's carefree life and happiness left with him.

His mother continued to sob. "Why are you robbing us of the little time we have left together? Think of your sisters! They are crying in their bedroom."

This is why I must leave, he thought.

Her lilac perfume flowed through the door. Jamie inhaled it, trying to fix it in his mind. "Ma, I know you've been weeping with every friend you have—"

"No... only to... oh God... did you hear?"

He slid to the floor and leaned his back against the door. "I heard you tell Nora that if you see me cold and dead, you will perish with me. I won't allow it. My sisters need their mother."

"We all need you. For as long as we can have you." The door banged from a punch. "I will not let you do this."

"You must. Julia and Audrey cry to their friend Clara. I know this from her brother. And while Caroline would never show her tears to anyone, I bet her pillow would drain puddles if you wrung it. I'm doing this for my sisters and for you."

His gaze fell on his bookcase full of adventure novels about brave seafarers and warriors. The men who found solutions to terrible situations, who led men into battles. These men would've made the same choice that he did.

"If I die far away from you, the loss will be easier to bear." *And I may do some good before I die.*

Mama's wails ebbed to a whimper. He wanted to reach through the door and wrap his arm over her shoulders.

"Please, Ma. Enough of this. Unlock the door."

Her feet shuffled. "Your father is calling me. I will see what he needs. And when I return, you will unpack that trunk and forget everything about the warship, the recruiters, and that wild girl, Ella Parker. Jamie, she was your friend for only two days. I wish she'd never appeared here."

Her heavy footsteps and uneven breaths resonated from the corridor.

This was the moment to escape. April morning sunlight bathed his face as he opened a window to judge his jump. Not high at all, and he would land in the grass. His older sister Caroline was standing a short distance away, tending to the apple tree. Despite what their mother said, she did not appear to be crying.

He thought to yell to her that Ma needed her and make her go away, but his older sister's eyes locked with his, and she nodded to him. No doubt she predicted his plan and approved of it. Caroline understood him better than anyone else.

Jamie's mind told him that such a jump was safe, yet his stomach lurched. Taking risks was new to him. For six years since his diagnosis, his family watched him closely, ensuring he didn't overexert himself.

He raised one leg, and then the other and perched on the ledge. Closed his eyes to stop his head from spinning.

"Jamie, wait!" Caroline's voice made him grip the ledge with his sweaty hands. "Your trunk."

He slapped himself on the forehead. His trunk with all the baggage the recruiters suggested to bring for the voyage, including clothing, books, even a blanket and a pillow, still rested on his bed. He spent the last few days purchasing things for the voyage with the money his father saved for Jamie's education. The thought of his father putting away the money for a degree Jamie did not have time to complete made a lump form in his throat. But that money came useful to order the uniform and equipment, and there was still a handsome sum packed inside the trunk.

"I knew you would forget." Caroline's voice rang with laughter.

His cheeks heated from his folly. "Blimey! Ma will return any second."

"She won't. Father has her distracted in his study. Throw your trunk here."

He climbed back inside and gave his bedroom one last glance. The books that wouldn't fit into his luggage. His desk where he composed stories and poems to amuse his sisters. The drawings of ships and animals made by him and his sisters decorated the walls. His shell collection... but thankfully, the most treasured member of that collection was in the pocket of his breeches. The shell he found with Ella. Perhaps she would remember it.

The memory of the thirteen-year-old girl with raven curls and eyes that had the color of his mother's emeralds made heat spread from his neck to his belly. Despite the six years passing since, he remembered her laughter when she played with his sisters and him.

He shook himself and forced the memory to vanish. With some luck, he would see her again, now as a grown woman. But first he had to leave his home and family behind.

"I spread a blanket as a cushion," Caroline's voice came from the window. "Is there anything fragile inside?"

"The quadrant and the telescope. I packed them under my clothes."

"You are taking the telescope?" She crossed her arms, but then bent down and folded the blanket to protect his luggage even better. "I suppose you need it more than I do. Toss."

The trunk landed with a quiet thud. He threw on his new uniform coat. Determined not to show fear in front of his sister, he climbed over the window ledge as quickly as he could and pushed himself off. His feet hit the ground hard. He shook them to relieve the pain that shot up his shins and knees.

Caroline's arm grabbed his shoulder. "Did you hurt yourself?"

He stepped with care and made himself ignore the pain. "No. I'm going, sister."

"I'll walk you to the coach station."

Jamie limped next to her as they passed the seaside homes. Spring colored the apple and cherry trees white and pink. The sea air tickled his nose.

Caroline was chewing her lip as she walked. Her head shook as she watched him hobble.

"You must think I won't last a day on that warship," he said.

Her hazel eyes stared into his. "You need to get away from us, so you can learn to decide for yourself. Our parents, our servants, and even I watched you from morning till evening, ensuring you did not injure or overtire yourself. No young man should live such a stifled life. Everyone dies, but not everyone gets to live. So find that warship the *Neptune* and our friend Ella. Prove to everyone and yourself whatever you want to prove. Then bring me back that telescope. I do love studying the stars."

"I will leave instructions to have it sent to you when..." His head dipped.

"No." She straightened his collar. "You will return it personally. That's the only reason why I'm not crying or locking you in your room like Ma. You will come back to us."

His eyes twitched, ready to burst with tears. He blinked hard. "Caroline. You know I will not return. Dr. Miller said that none of his patients with a heart defect like mine lived past the age twenty. I have two years at most."

She shook her head. "But he couldn't *see* your heart. He couldn't know for sure that you have a hole there. Even the most famous physician and surgeon in England may be wrong."

"Other medical men confirmed my diagnosis."

"That's because they do not know how compassionate and kind my brother's heart is." Her shoulders squared. "Surely such a heart will keep on beating longer than twenty years. Too many people need it to keep going." Her arms wrapped around his shoulders.

He kissed her cheek and tasted salty tears. She must've cried earlier but kept a brave face for him.

When they neared the coach station, she stopped. "This is a goodbye for now, Jamie. One thing I don't quite understand in your plan. Won't there be a surgeon on the ship? He may examine you when you board. You look healthy, but if all those doctors believed you are ill..."

He rubbed his chin. "I asked the recruiters about a medical exam. They laughed and said a tanned and rosy-cheeked man like me will pass with no problem. Perhaps a ship surgeon would not be as knowledgeable about heart defects as prominent physicians."

"That's likely." Her eyebrows knitted. "And what exactly is Ella Parker doing on the warship? What kind of job could a young woman possibly have there? Seamen are supposedly superstitious and think that women bring bad luck to the ship."

Jamie tugged at his coat buttons. "The recruiter said that Captain Grey of the *Neptune* believes in giving people opportunities. He would take me as a volunteer even if I don't have naval experience. The recruiters mentioned that he even gave an opportunity to a woman, Ella Parker, and she is still there with his crew. That's when I knew what I must do."

"Mysterious Ella Parker." Caroline smiled. "Well, if there's a girl who lives by her own rules, it's her."

Chapter 2

Next day, Plymouth, England.

The judge, wearing a black mantle and a powdered wig, studied Ella with a furrowed brow as she placed her hand on the Bible.

She raised her chin. "I swear by almighty God that the evidence I shall give shall be the truth, the whole truth and nothing but the truth."

"State your full name."

"Ella Parker."

From the corner of her eye, Ella saw Veronica, Marietta, and Henrietta shift on the bench and give her side glances. It dawned on her that she didn't tell the whole truth, and her childhood friends knew it. Ella Parker wasn't her birth name, even though she had used it for the last four years. She was born Lady Eloise Parker, daughter of the Earl of Greenwoods, but preferred to forget that name and the life that came with it.

Before she could explain, the judge continued questioning her. "How do you know the defendant?"

Ella gave a warm look to Matilda Pesce. The changes in her friend made her throat thicken. Matilda's gray hair, normally tucked into a neat braid, was a mess. The face of the fifty-five-year-old woman had thinned, and wrinkles wrapped it like a spider's web. But Matilda's eyes shone like torches.

"I know her as an excellent midwife, an expert in medicinal herbs, and a friend. For a brief time, I was her apprentice. She shared with me the knowledge she gained from delivering hundreds of babies, and occasionally, she had me assist her."

Ella recalled those deliveries trying not to wince from bitter bile creeping up her throat. As a ship surgeon, she could amputate shattered limbs without hesitation, but attending to a woman in labor brought back the memory of her mother's dead eyes. She scanned over the packed courtroom, and her gaze lingered on Marietta, who beamed and lifted her newborn. From what Ella heard, the delivery of her second child was a horrible ordeal, but Matilda saved her and the baby's life. Earlier, Marietta gave an impassioned testimony on the midwife's behalf.

A group of people seated on the other side of the courtroom glared at Marietta, as a woman dressed in black bombazine dress and a veil gave a heart wrenching sob. The man in an expensive-looking jacket with a crepe armband patted her shoulder and dabbed his eye with a lace handkerchief.

Ella's heart went out to them, especially the grieving mother, who didn't testify. Her husband spoke on her behalf. A lawyer by trade, he evoked many tears as he spoke of their loss. But blaming Matilda for the death of the infant was unfair.

The judge narrowed his eyes. "Miss Parker, did you attend Mrs. Lee during her labor together with the defendant?"

"No. I was not in Plymouth at the time."

"You assisted in only a handful of deliveries, and Mrs. Lee's was not one of them. I don't see why you wished to testify." He pursed his lips.

Ella's cheeks heated. "The coroner's conclusion was inaccurate. He said the infant strangulated from the cord around his neck. That's no fault of the midwife. The death was from natural causes. She should not be charged with manslaughter."

Her friends clapped, while grieving parents and their supporters hissed among themselves as they withered Ella with furious glares. The coroner who testified earlier, Mr. Thomas, rose and clenched his large fists. His face turned red.

The judge silenced the audience with a bang of his hand. "Who are you to challenge the coroner's conclusion? You cannot have the medical knowledge to make this argument."

Ella bit the inside of her cheek. Part of her wanted to get off the stand and run. But she had to save Matilda—even at the cost of her secrets.

"I have medical education. Four years ago, I disguised myself as a man and attended medical school. After graduating, the defendant's brother, Joseph Pesce, helped me secure a position as a ship surgeon." Her heart squeezed at the memory of her mentor, who perished two years ago.

Gasps from the audience drowned out the claps of her friends. The coroner approached the father of the deceased infant and whispered something in his ear. The judge scoffed and yelled for silence then stared with a disbelieving gaze and rubbed the back of his neck.

"Do you have proof of graduating from medical school?"

No, she did not. Ella's stomach tightened. Swallowing, she scanned the audience for a friendly face. Veronica and Henrietta nodded encouragingly, but they would not be able to verify her attendance at the university. She wished for her school friend, Oli Higgins, to be here and confirm her words. But she returned only yesterday from her voyage and was lucky she made it to the trial at all. There was no time to write to Oli, who may be away in Chatham with his family.

The judge peered at her and turned a large ring on his finger. "I asked you a question, Miss Parker."

Matilda raised her head with a jerk. *Ella, don't tell them*, she mouthed.

But Ella could not see how else to save her friend. "The exam committee learned I was a woman. Despite my answering every question, they denied me a medical school degree. But I successfully passed the Naval Board exam for a surgeon."

She removed the document proving her qualifications and gave it to the bailiff who brought it to the judge.

The judge studied the document. "This says 'Alan Parker.'"

"My alias in school." That name was also written in the ship's book since the Admiralty frowned on hiring women.

The judge groaned. "You are not a midwife, and you have no proof of your medical knowledge. You wasted my time. Step down."

Matilda's shoulders slumped as if all hope escaped her soul.

Ella's knuckles turned white as she gripped the stand. "Hundreds of seamen can confirm that I'm a skilled surgeon." She wished she brought them to the trial, although they were busy with the ship repairs, and Captain Grey were unlikely to give them leave.

"I asked you to step down. Would you prefer to be removed by force?" The judge slapped his hand on the table.

Realizing that annoying the judge might hurt her friend's chances of a favorable outcome, Ella stepped down and sat between Veronica and Henrietta.

The judge called Matilda to the stand. The midwife's red-rimmed eyes scanned the courtroom, lingering on Ella.

Sweat ran down from under the judge's wig. With the afternoon passing, the room seemed to get hotter by the minute. "Do you have anything to add to what was said today?"

"What is there left to say?" Matilda's voice quivered. "As several of my clients told you, I dedicated my life to midwifery and healing. Assisted any woman who wanted my help and accepted whatever she could pay in return. I did all I could to save Mrs. Lee and her baby."

Matilda sighed and nodded to the woman in black, who hid her face behind her palms. "Her grief and anger are understandable, but there was no fault on my part. But her husband, Mr. Lee, wants to see me sent to the gaol."

Her accusatory stare focused on the husband, who maintained a blank face, except for tightness of his lips. "Perhaps he wants to grow his reputation as a lawyer or help his cousin who is a popular accoucheur."

"That's a lie!" Mr. Lee shouted.

"I love how she always speaks her mind," Henrietta whispered to Ella.

Yes, that's Matilda. But her sharp tongue may be her downfall.

As if proof of Ella's thoughts, Matilda glowered at the judge. "I can tell you have already decided what to do with me. It's well-known you play cards with Mr. Lee every Thursday and your wife drinks tea with his mother."

The judge's nostrils flared. "This has nothing to do with the case. I've heard enough. After the break, I will announce the verdict." With thundering footfalls, he left the courtroom.

"Matilda vexed him." Marietta sighed and kissed the baby who fussed in her arms. "He will jail the best midwife in Plymouth. If not for her, I would be dead."

"We need her." Veronica crossed her arms. "Or who will assist me?" Under Ella's gaze, Veronica blushed and added, "I didn't get a chance to tell you, Ella."

Ella's gaze shifted towards her friend's slightly rounded middle. A lump constricted Ella's throat.

What if Veronica's delivery will be as tragic as Mrs. Lee's? Or as dangerous as Marietta's? Or like my mother's?

"Are you sick, Ella?" Henrietta whispered. "Your face went white."

"I thought you would be happy for me and Ernest." Veronica pouted.

"I'm sorry." Ella patted Veronica's arm. "The trial upset my nerves. I wish you an easy delivery."

"Well, that's not for a while..."

If this baby were inside my womb, I wouldn't sleep until the birth. How can women think of anything else for all those months? Ella wondered. *I will not fall in love, get married or have children. Suitors lie and betray, husbands take away their wives' assets and freedom, and childbirth is an awful ordeal that often results in death.*

Marietta caught Ella's eye and shifted her baby onto her shoulder with another. "Ella, it's all worth it," she mouthed. "I know that after your broken betrothal you think you are better off without a husband and children. But I would do it all over again. The births, my babies, my dear husband Jack... all worth it."

"Love!" Her sister Henrietta murmured as her cheeks pinked. "You will find it one day, my friend. Or it will find you."

Ella rolled her eyes. Her mind snapped back to Matilda and her situation. While her revelation cast a shadow on the judge, she made the case personal and would likely suffer his wrath.

Since the judge was still absent, Ella wedged her way between the benches and approached Matilda, who hunched over the stand. The bailiff tried to hold Ella back but relented under her pleading gaze.

She took her friend's wrinkled hands. "Matilda, don't worry. We'll find a way out of this."

The older woman's shoulders shook. "You shouldn't have said so much about yourself. Or argued that the coroner was wrong. This will get you into trouble."

Ella waved her hand dismissively. "I'll be away on my ship in a few days. And when I get you out of this mess, you will come with me."

"Stop it, Ella! We both know I won't see the light of day for a long time. What's to happen to the women who need me?" Matilda lowered her voice and gestured for Ella to lean in. "Wendy is staying in my house. Her mother learned she was working for Madam Moss and threw her out."

"Wendy, the bosun's daughter? She returned to the brothel after all you did for her?" Ella's heart sank. "What does she need? Money?"

"Not this time. She's with child and due any day. Please check on her right away and stay close to deliver her baby. Perhaps it's my own misery, but I have a bad feeling about her. Since I was arrested three days ago, I can't get her off my mind. I told the constables that I'm needed at home, but they made me stay in the cell before the trial."

Ella pushed down her worry. "Of course. I will take great care of Wendy and the newborn."

Matilda clasped her hand, and they embraced.

"If the ruling is not in your favor, we'll hire a lawyer. You are innocent!"

"Everything had been decided before this trial." Matilda's hands went limp.

"All rise!" the bailiff commanded as the judge entered the courtroom. The spectators broke their conversations and stood. Ella moved back to her seat.

"I've reached the verdict," the judge announced. "From the testimonies and the expert's conclusion, it's clear that the defendant committed manslaughter during the delivery of Mr. and Mrs. Lee's child. Therefore, I sentence Matilda Pesce to eight years in jail."

"Eight years!" Matilda exclaimed, waving her hands. "I won't live that long in that rathole!"

That's the point, Ella thought as tears ran down her cheeks.

Matilda spun to Ella. "Goodbye, my girl. Go to Wendy. As soon as she and her baby are well, go aboard your ship and don't come back for a while. Forget about me." The constables grabbed her and led her away.

Chapter 3

Ella's path to Matilda's lodging took her through the busiest part of Plymouth, crowded with taverns and inns. Even though it was still early afternoon, the streets heaved with drunk sailors.

"Where are you in such a hurry to, sweetheart?" one man called as he walked with an unsteady gait, leaning on another man in his group.

"That's Miss Parker, you dolt." His friend glared at him. "Don't you know her? She's a ship surgeon on the *Neptune*. Saved young Robert Weston and many other men."

"Do you need any assistance, Doctor Ella?" a tall man behind them, one of her crew, called her by the affectionate name she preferred. He was with the ship boy, twelve-year-old Tobby. "We could walk you to wherever you are in such a hurry. You don't need trouble."

Ella shook her head. "I can take care of myself, Olson. But I would appreciate it if you gave a message to Captain Grey that I may be occupied for a few days. If anyone needs medical services, they can see my assistants."

"I can take a message for you, Dr. Ella!" Tobby cried and his eyes sparkled with eagerness. The boy looked taller each time she saw him, and the clothes she bought him last summer barely fit. Hard to believe that he was the same child who came to her sickbay with a severe stomachache two years ago.

"That would be wonderful, but perhaps you could assist me with another errand."

The boy bobbed his head.

"Could you stop by the Cooked Goose and retrieve my medical bag from my room? Then bring it to Matilda Pesce's house. Do you know where that is?"

"Aye, Doctor." Tobby brought his fist to his forehead and sped away with a slight limp in his step. His leg never fully healed after the wound he received.

She turned away from the men and kept on walking, her skirts bringing up the dust.

As she passed by a noisy tavern, her stomach rumbled from the aroma of fried meat. She hadn't eaten much this morning, too nervous for Matilda and her court testimony. Thinking of food, Ella promised herself to visit Matilda to update her on Wendy's condition, and to bring her friend fresh food. She'll ask Veronica and her other friends to visit Matilda as well.

Matilda's home was a small cottage a couple of streets beyond the main one. The cheerful dwelling boasted medical plants growing around it. Ella's heart pinched as she admired Matilda's effort to create a place for women of any standing to confide in their problems and receive advice or a cure.

Matilda, you will return soon, she vowed.

***

Jamie's stomach growled as the enticing aroma of roasted lamb floated around the inn's dining room. The cheerful atmosphere of the Cooked Goose was more pleasant than the dining room of the inn where he rented a room. He was glad that he took the coachman's advice and came here to sate his hunger before meeting Captain Grey.

A serving woman passed him with her tray loaded with tankards of ale. As Jamie sat in the corner and waited for his dinner, he contemplated what he would say to the captain. His volunteer uniform was well-ironed by the inn maid, and he hoped he looked appropriate for the position.

"Miss Jenny! Miss Jenny! Pardon me please." A thin voice rose above the clank of utensils and the hum of conversation.

The boy, about twelve, stood in the middle of the room, holding his straw hat. His face was dirty, and his clothes too small. When the serving woman turned, he made a small bow.

The boy's polite manners contrasted with his lowly appearance. The serving woman, or Miss Jenny as the boy called her, placed the food in front of Jamie, but his fascination with the boy delayed him digging into the appetizing meat.

"What do you want, Tobby?" Miss Jenny groaned as the boy bowed to her again. "You know I cannot feed you without pay. Or did Miss Parker give you a coin?"

"I forgot to ask Miss Parker." Tobby hung his head. "She sent me here to fetch her medical bag. I'm sure she'll give me a coin once I bring the bag to her. Will you feed me then?" He rubbed his belly.

"You should've said something about the bag first." Jenny threw up her hands. "Someone must be ill or injured. I'll get the bag from her room, and you'll carry it to her without dilly-dallying."

When the serving woman hastened upstairs, Jamie called the boy over. "Did you say you are fetching a medical bag for Miss Ella Parker?"

The boy cocked his head. "This is... what's the word... something you don't tell strangers."

"Privileged information? I approve of your discretion." He gave the boy his hand to shake. "Jamie Flowers. A future volunteer on the *Neptune* and a friend of Miss Ella Parker."

"Tobby Hill. A shipboy on the *Neptune*. And also her friend." His handshake was as hardy as a grown man's. Callous palms spoke of arduous work.

"As a shipmate, I beg a favor of you. Would you finish all this food while I bring the medical bag to our mutual friend?" When Tobby furrowed his brow, Jamie added, "I will also give you coins to order a pie."

The boy's head jerked to Jenny, who was descending the stairs with a bag in her hand, to Jamie's heaping plate. "Is this a trick?"

"No trick." Jamie put his hand on his heart. "I haven't seen Miss Parker in a few years and wish to surprise her."

"Fine." The boy sighed. "My leg has been bothering me lately. You can run to Mistress Pesce's herb shop faster than me. Here's how you get there."

Chapter 4

The door to Matilda's house was unlocked. Ella entered and scanned the small sitting room. The familiar chamber no longer had the fragrance of chamomile or lavender, but rather, it exuded the stench of dust and spoiled food. Any other time Ella was here, women perched on the sofa, shifting in the seat from some discomfort or holding their swelled bellies. The absence of clients gave the room an abandoned atmosphere, and the withered plants on the windows augmented that feeling. Ella frowned, thinking of Wendy. Even in the last month of pregnancy, a seventeen-year-old girl should be able to dust, water plants, and throw away the rotten food. Unless...

"Wendy!" Ella called. Not hearing an answer, she hurried to the bedrooms in the back. The furniture there looked untouched, the bed neatly made.

Did the girl leave? Perhaps returned to her mother's?

"Wendy!" Ella called again. "I'm a friend of Matilda's. I'm here to help you."

With no audible answer, the next place to check was the herb shop. When Ella entered Matilda's sanctuary, a gasp caught in her throat.

The overturned tables and chairs. The broken vials and bottles. Powders and liquids poured on the floor. Perhaps Matilda resisted her arrest, and the constables retaliated by destroying her shop. Poor Wendy hid or ran away, terrified by the ruckus.

Ella checked the kitchen. The soup burned into black cinder on the bottom of the pot. A mouse darted away from it. It was fortunate that the fire didn't ignite.

There was still no sign of the girl. Ella returned to the herb shop to tidy it up. In a search for a broom, Ella opened the closet in the corridor. It held linens. She opened another one, and there was a ladder leading up. The house had an attic! Did the girl climb up to hide from the commotion? Probably not, because she'd have come down after everyone left. Still, Ella had to check.

"Wendy?" she shouted, peering into the dark at the top of the ladder. "Are you up in the attic?"

No response. Ella inhaled a deep breath and clambered up the ladder.

Enveloped by the darkness, she scolded herself for not bringing a lantern. As soon as she stepped off, her head hit the ceiling. Wincing, she crouched to her knees. Her eyes could hardly distinguish anything. And she could hardly breathe. The dust she inhaled made her cough.

Please Lord, let it be that the girl wasn't hiding in this cold dark space for hours.

In Ella's imagination, a young woman, with a full-term baby in her belly, crouched in a dark corner. Stifling coughs and sneezes from inhaling dust. Hungry, thirsty, in desperate need to relieve her bladder. And terrified of the men who smashed things below. Goosebumps emerged on Ella's skin.

When her eyes slightly adjusted to the dark, Ella placed her hand on the wall and searched the perimeter of the room. Her knee hit an old trunk, making her gasp in pain. A protruding nail ripped her sleeve. But then, in the far corner, her leg touched something warm. When Ella kneeled, a hot liquid ran down her hand. Ella inhaled the metallic smell. Blood!

With her touch guiding her, Ella examined the blood-soaked fabric and a limp arm.

Her hands brushed against the girl's oily hair, and she slid them down to the neck and searched for pulse. Nothing. She tried again on Wendy's arm then put her ear to the girl's chest.

No heartbeat.

The girl's skin was still warm. She must have died only minutes before. Judging from a pool of fluids around her, she birthed the baby or was close. Ella's pressed on the belly, still firm and round. *If the mother is dead, the fetus can survive for thirty minutes,* the voice of her medical school professor sounded in her head. As confirmation of that lesson, a kick came through where Ella pressed. The baby inside Wendy was alive but had only minutes to live.

I will need my instruments or a sharp knife, Ella thought. Tobby was bringing her bag, but he may be too late. She had never cut out a baby from a dead woman's womb, but she had seen it done twice. The first time was when she walked in on the surgeon slicing into her mother's belly. The baby didn't live, and Ella suffered from nightmares for a long time after. The second time was when her midwifery professor cut out twins from the belly of a woman with a heart illness. The mother died in labor, but those babies lived, and Ella got to hold them and tend to them.

Forcing these memories away, Ella told herself to focus. Matilda would have sharp kitchen knives, rags, scissors, and other things she would need. The problem would be getting Wendy down. She couldn't operate in this dark, dirty attic.

She dragged the body closer to the ladder. Summoning all her strength, she attempted to lift the girl but lowered her down immediately. The feat would be impossible for her.

Afraid to lose valuable time, Ella climbed down.

I'll find everything I need for surgery first. Then I'll fetch someone to help me carry Wendy.

Her heart raced as she searched the kitchen for a sharp knife and scissors. She'd also need something to spread the incision. And blankets to keep the baby warm.

She was collecting kitchen knives when someone knocked at the door. Friend or a foe? She gripped the largest knife.

"It's open," she said, her voice pitching. "Come here quick."

Someone stepped into the house.

"Miss Parker? Is that you?" A man's voice sounded timid and polite. With her fingers still clasping a knife, she rushed into the sitting room.

A young blond man stood there, wearing a volunteer uniform, shifting from one foot to another. His face was averted from her, as he studied the withered plants. Ella's medical bag was in his arm.

"Oh, you brought my bag! I sent Tobby…"

The man startled and stepped back. His cornflower blue eyes darted between her face and the knife in her hand.

"Miss Parker…" he stuttered. "I thought you wouldn't mind."

"Mind? You are a godsend." Ella grabbed the bag from him. "I'll get the table and my instruments ready. You get a lantern and climb up to the attic. The ladder is inside the closet. You'll find a dead woman up there."

Thank the Lord. The fellow looks strong enough for the task.

"A dead woman?" His voice quivered.

"Yes. Carefully bring her body here." She pointed to the herb room. "There's a large table inside I can operate on."

The man hadn't moved. She snapped her fingers in front of his nose. "Don't just stand there! Hurry! Her baby has only minutes to live!"

Her statement produced effect on the stunned man. He stumbled toward the closet. Hoping he would gather his wits and find a lantern, Ella hurried into the herb room. After lifting the overturned table, she covered it with a tablecloth from the linen closet. Other clean linens would serve her as well. Then she opened her bag and assembled her instruments: scalpel, catling knife, retractors, needle and thread. She'd also need warm water for the baby. Once the young man would bring down Wendy, she'd ask him to heat some.

A commotion sounded from the attic. "Don't you dare drop her!" she warned as she rushed over. The man struggled down the ladder, trying to balance the body on his arm and shoulder. She held the ladder for him.

When he glanced at her, his face was paler than his shirt. "There was blood!"

"Yes. The hemorrhage is likely what killed her."

"What am I supposed to do with her?"

She led him into the herb room, where the young man lowered Wendy onto the table as if she was made of porcelain.

"She's young. About Julia's age," he muttered.

Ella pushed him out of her way. Scissors in hand, she started cutting Wendy's dress. Her pulse hammered like a ticking clock.

"What will you do?" the fellow stammered.

"Don't interrupt me with questions!" she hissed. "Warm some water and bring it here."

Done with removing the fabric of the dress and underclothes, Ella palpated the exposed abdomen. The fetus no longer kicked or stirred. She grabbed a scalpel and made a long vertical incision. Blood pooled under her fingers. Below the skin, there was hardly any fat to cut through. The girl was half-starved. Ella changed to the catling knife to slice through the muscles, praying she was fast enough. Holding retractors with one hand, she moved the bladder and intestines with another to expose the uterus. Her scalpel opened its wall, revealing a blue curled up fetus.

Her hands hurried to lift the baby and cut the umbilical cord. A small girl was limp in her arms. Ella used a cloth to clean the mucus from the nose and mouth. With Matilda's teaching on her mind, Ella blew into the infant's mouth and rubbed the chest.

Someone's heavy rasps sounded nearby, but it was not the baby. Her unlikely assistant must've returned with a bucket of water.

Ella nestled the newborn on her shoulder and rubbed the back. "Breathe, little one," she whispered.

I was too slow. Like the surgeon who was too late to save my brother.

"What if I help?" the young man asked. "I can blow air, and you rub her. Would that work better?"

"We could try. Blow only a bit of air, just enough to fill your cheeks."

She laid the newborn on the table, next to the mother. While the man breathed into the bluish mouth, Ella rubbed the tiny chest. After what seemed like a lifetime, the baby's torso rose on its own. The young man's jaw fell open. The tiny face began to turn from inky bluish to pale pink, and a feeble cry escaped the colorless lips. Ella pressed her ear to the child's heart, listening to the steady heartbeat.

"I brought the warm water, like you asked."

Ella straightened and glanced at the fellow. His face was almost as white as Wendy's, and he was supporting himself by leaning on the wall.

"Go sit on the sofa before you faint. I'm too busy to fuss over you right now." Ella gave him a stern stare.

She carried the infant to the bucket and washed off the blood and fluids. Glad for Matilda's linens, she dried and swaddled the baby.

The young man was half-lying on the sofa when Ella walked out to him and placed the infant in his lap.

"Here, hold her while I look for something to keep her warm."

She hurried to Matilda's bedroom and found a knitted blanket. When she returned, the fellow rocked the infant curled up in his coat. There was something so moving in the way he cradled the child to his chest, that Ella stood rooted on the threshold and watched.

"When my youngest sister Audrey was born, I was six," he said softly to the baby. "All the women were upstairs with my mother, while my father sat in the parlor with a couple of friends. When the midwife said that a healthy girl was born, he let me taste my first sip of wine. Papa let me see her, and she had bright blue eyes, just like you. And still does."

"Oh goodness, is she yours?" Ella said. "I didn't realize—"

"Pardon? No, no. I just remembered the day my little sister was born." The young man's cheeks gained a bit of color. "I've never seen that poor woman in my life. How did she die up there?"

Ella bit her lip. "I'm not entirely sure. She must've hidden in the attic when someone destroyed the herb shop. Perhaps..."

A guess hit her. She put down the blanket and returned to Wendy's body. The man followed, carrying the whimpering newborn in his arms.

She'll need milk soon.

Her hands raised Wendy's skirt to reveal her legs. One was severely swollen at the ankle. Ella felt the bone. "She tripped over something and broke her ankle. Most likely after it became quiet, and she was ready to climb down."

Ice went through Ella's veins as she imagined Wendy in severe pain from her broken leg, terrified that her labor would start as she lay in the dark. What an awful death, and all because someone unfairly accused Matilda of wrongdoing!

"That's absolutely horrible," the young man mumbled, averting his eyes from Wendy's body. "A pregnant woman imprisoned in the attic because of her broken leg. No one knew she needed help."

"The only one who knew she was here was the owner of this house, Matilda. But she languished in a different prison."

Ella turned back to Wendy's opened corpse and threaded the needle. "I'm going to close the incision. Would you wrap the baby in the blanket I brought?"

The infant whimpered as the fellow swaddled her.

"I haven't introduced myself. I'm James Flowers," he said as he struggled with the blanket. Ella was unsure if he was addressing her or the newborn. "Most people call me Jamie." He paused, as if expecting an answer.

The name sounded familiar, but her work required focus. The last thing she could do for Wendy was to make her body look decent before her mother saw her.

Shouts and heavy steps startled her. With one hand still inside Wendy's belly, she turned about. A constable stood behind her, staring at her with bulging eyes.

Chapter 5

"What have you done? Everyone, in here!" the tall constable yelled and two more of his colleagues stomped in, one portly and mustached, the other clean-shaven and young. Jamie stood behind them, with the baby in his arms.

"I know her!" The portly fellow studied Wendy's face. "One of Madam Moss's girls, Wendy. What a shame. She was good... I mean... young. I only know her because she'd been in trouble several times." He added the last line hastily and wiped his forehead as the other two constables stared at him.

Jamie cleared his throat. "Gentlemen, what occurred is nothing criminal. The woman died in labor, birthing the child I'm holding. The surgeon here is doing her work. Would you please tell us why you are here?"

Ella was impressed by how calm he appeared, with his feet spread wide, showing confidence he likely lacked.

"We are here to seize the possessions of Matilda Pesce, who has been imprisoned. Besides causing a death of a baby, she ran an illegal shop. There are reports that she sold poisons," the portly constable said.

Ella's head snapped toward him. "She sold medicines. And there's nothing left for you to seize, as someone ransacked the place. What I found here, besides the ruckus, was a pregnant woman who died because Matilda wasn't there to save her."

The tall constable's shoulders jumped. "She's the one the judge said to watch!" He grabbed Ella's arm.

The other constables raised their clubs as he pinned Ella's hands behind her. Ella winced at the pain.

"What are you doing?" Jamie cried. "She saved the baby. She should be thanked."

"Take him as well. He's likely her assistant," the tall constable ordered.

The young constable accepted the baby from Jamie's arms. His movements were gentle and practiced to Ella's relief.

"We are taking you two to the station for questioning about the death of this woman," the tall constable said. "All evidence points to a gruesome murder, one of the most horrible I've seen." His expression was full of righteousness and conceit. "Even if this was not a murder, this woman cannot be a surgeon. Her friend went to the gaol today, and she will join her."

No point in arguing with this dullard, Ella thought. *It would likely only worsen things. I may have better luck at the station, speaking to his superiors.*

"This is unjust." Jamie stepped in front of Ella, as if trying to shield her. "Please let Miss Parker go with the baby."

Ella shook her head. "This is useless. They will drag us by force if we don't go." Her gaze shifted to the baby crying in the young constable's arms. He was rocking her and shooshing in her ear. She decided to address him even though he hadn't spoken. "We will go to the station and answer questions. Please take care of the baby. She must be kept warm and fed soon." The constable nodded and adjusted the baby's blanket.

The portly constable secured handcuffs on Jamie's and Ella's arms and led them out of the cottage. The tall one remained in the house 'to collect evidence,' as he put it, including Ella's medical bag. The constable with the baby followed them. "My wife still nurses our son. I'll bring her to the station to tend to this baby," he said.

That was all Ella could hope for. They fought too hard to save that baby just to lose her because of poor care.

"Ella... I mean, Miss Parker." Jamie's walk was unsteady and the jugular vein on his neck pulsed hard. "Please don't be afraid. I..."

She was frustrated about the pointless arrest. In pain from the handcuffs cutting into her wrists. Grieving for Wendy. Anxious for Matilda. Most concerned for the vulnerable infant. But afraid... no.

"I take care of myself." She raised her chin. "Since you are not connected to me, they'll likely let you go. Please tell Captain Grey what happened. You'll find him with the ship or at his residence near the port."

"You are the surgeon on the *Neptune*?" Jamie jerked his head as if he solved a riddle.

"Yes. I thought you knew that since you brought me my bag."

Why did he bring me the bag and not Tobby?

Jamie straightened and puffed out his chest.

Ella rolled her eyes. *He's sure trying hard to impress me... or just trying to keep his composure. Why does he look and sound familiar?*

"Enough chitchat," the mustached constable barked.

When they reached the station after a good forty minutes of walking, Ella was led into one room and Jamie into another. The satchel with her Naval Board document was taken from her. She had no idea where they took the baby, but a lusty cry reached her ears. *That's it, baby girl, tell them you are hungry. Don't let them forget about you.*

The room, furnished with a desk and two chairs, stank of sweat and vomit. A bearded man with dull eyes entered and lowered himself into a chair across from her. Humming to himself, he sharpened a quill. Smoothed and straightened a sheet of paper. Yawned.

"Can we get started?" Ella bounced in her seat.

The man shrugged and asked for her name. Wrote it down on his paper in careful letters.

"Age?"

"Nineteen."

"Married?" He studied her face.

"No."

"Shame. A husband would keep you out of trouble. Get one soon while you are still pretty." The man winked.

Ella inhaled a deep breath to ease her roiling stomach.

"What about your father? Who is he?"

"He is long dead, so it doesn't matter."

The man clicked his tongue. "What about the fellow who was with you? Is he your brother? Or your betrothed?"

"No. He's no one I know." *Or if I do know him, I can't remember how.*

"Strange. He seems desperate to get you out. But it's bad business I'm afraid." He drummed on the table. "Very bad business, unless you confess to your crimes. That will help your case. What happened between you and Wendy Moore? She's been here a few times. We know she was a whore, working for Madam Moss. What made you kill her?"

"You are trying to intimidate me." Ella flipped her hair with bravado. "I've done nothing wrong. Wendy Moore was already dead when I found her. What I've done is called a cesarean section, a surgery to save the baby inside her. It requires cutting into the woman's womb to take the fetus out. Then I... well we, with Mr. Flowers's help, successfully resuscitated the baby."

The constable was now writing at a great speed, inkblots splashing from under his shaking quill. "But how could the infant survive if the mother was dead? You must've cut her still alive, and she died of bleeding and shock!"

"Of course not! I can tell if the patient is alive or dead. The document that was taken from me would confirm that I'm a surgeon. My qualifications were verified by the Naval Board."

The man left the room but soon returned with the document.

"This certificate belongs to Alan Parker."

"That's me."

He scratched his forehead, then cocked his head. "Young lady, are you trying to tell me that you managed to convince the Naval Board that your name is Alan Parker? That you are a man? That you have the physical and mental ability to amputate limbs and other things surgeons do?"

"Is that so hard to imagine? Ask Captain Grey. I've served on his ship for two years." Her voice lost its vigor. Another man who will not believe that she could be a surgeon. Even if he would watch her save a life, he'd say that it was her male assistant, or luck, or divine intervention. Anything but her skill.

His face turned beet red. "You must take me for a fool. It is impossible. You are either a dangerous madwoman or a liar.

And likely a murderess as well. Whatever you are, you will be imprisoned until the judge hears your case."

Ella groaned and twisted in her seat. "Bring Captain Grey here. He will confirm that I'm a surgeon."

The man stood and glared at her. "We'll talk to him when we get a chance. Many other things to work on. Meanwhile, a few days in the cell will do you good."

"If your colleagues walked in on a male surgeon working on a patient, alive or dead, they'd never accuse him of murder." Ella tucked in her upper lip. "It is in your power to throw me in jail, as you did with my friend Matilda." She raised her handcuffed hands. "But while I sit in the cell, my mind will be free to think and plan. To imagine and dream. Unfortunately for you, you can't imprison my mind. While yours, unable to comprehend that a woman can be a surgeon or whatever other profession she wants to be ... Sir, you are a prisoner of your own narrow and dim mind. And that's prison from which one cannot escape."

Now I've done it. She winced as the constable gripped her arm and pulled her to follow.

When her hands were freed and the heavy door slammed behind her, Ella took a timid step inside the cell. Straw rustled under her shoes. The odor of unwashed bodies and urine assaulted her nose. The wheezing coughs of someone severely ill mixed with loud snores. She blinked, letting her eyes adjust to darkness and rubbed her throbbing wrists.

The rattling coughs of a girl who lay on the cot next to the wall made Ella wish for her medical bag with remedies. A disheveled older woman, dressed in rags, rocked back and forth and wept. Two prisoners snored in their slumber. A slender woman sat tightly hugging her knees, her face turned to the window.

Are any of these women dangerous? What crimes sent them here?"

Ella glanced at the last occupant and gasped. "Matilda!"

"Ella! What are you doing here?" Her friend rose from a cot with no blanket. Ella rushed into her arms. Wrapped in Matilda's embrace, Ella rested her head on the midwife's shoulder.

"I was too late and found Wendy already dead. I managed to save her baby. A girl."

A moan escaped Matilda's throat. "Poor Wendy. And poor motherless infant. But why are you here?"

"The constables came to your house when I was sewing up Wendy's uterus and belly," Ella whispered into Matilda's ear. "They thought—"

"My Lord! You dissected Wendy's body?" Matilda's hand gripped Ella's elbow.

The woman who stared at the window swiveled her head.

Her finger on her lips, Ella breathed through her teeth. Even Matilda, with all her experience delivering babies, didn't accept some aspects of the surgeon's profession.

"Matilda, I wrote to you from medical school about the operation that I watched when my instructor opened the dying woman's abdomen and saved her twins."

"I remember. I couldn't sleep for two nights. And you thought that a live woman could survive such an operation."

Ella's throat parched. "That would be a nightmare of a surgery, but if it would save two lives... Anyway, I was too late to save Wendy. But the baby inside her was alive, and I got her out."

Matilda put her hand on her heart. "They'll think you are mad and send you to an asylum. Your only hope is your captain and crew get you out."

"Captain Grey will come for me. Soon, I hope." The boldness she felt in front of the warden slipped away as she studied the stone walls and the bars on the windows. And the other inmates... The woman by the window ogled her with an ugly twist on her lips and narrowed eyes. *She likely murdered someone in their sleep.*

"Matilda, did you speak to these women? Who are they?"

"They say little. The crying one is a loon. Her husband visits, but she doesn't recognize him. Those two who are snoring will likely come out tomorrow if they wake. They were dead drunk and caused some commotion. I have sympathy for the coughing one. She was a maid in a fine home, and her mistress accused her of stealing a silver ring. The girl swears it wasn't her, but... the lady insisted that she saw it in the maid's room. Now she caught that cough…"

"She sounds seriously ill. Would the guards bring a doctor or give her medicine?"

"They've done nothing for her so far."

"And who is the one by the window?"

"I can hear you two." The woman's voice was deep and throaty. "None of your business who I am."

"Her stare chills my blood," Matilda whispered.

The woman bolted off her cot and strode toward them. Ella's fists balled, ready to defend herself and her friend.

"Do you know of medicine?" The woman stood over Ella with her hands on the hips.

Resisting the urge to cower, Ella nodded.

"Then do something about that one who's sick. Her coughs grate on my nerves."

"I already told you. Nothing can be done without medicines." Matilda crossed her arms. The woman's gaze stayed on Ella.

"Matilda is right. But I could examine her to know how advanced her illness is, if she's willing."

"Do it then."

Not too happy at being ordered, Ella walked over to the coughing woman. "Hello. I'm Ella. I wish to help you with your cough. Would you let me listen to your chest?"

"Please." The girl turned her thinned face to Ella. "I'm feeling very poorly. The cough keeps me up day and night."

"And me as well," the intimidating woman hissed.

Ella loosened the girl's collar and pressed her head to the chest. The bubbling sound was unmistakable to her ear. She placed her hand on the forehead. The skin burned.

"What is your name? How old are you?" Ella asked.

"Agnes. I'm fifteen."

"You have pneumonia, Agnes."

"Can you make it better?" She doubled over from a coughing fit.

"Hmm, if you were cared for at home or in the hospital... You need medicine from the bark of the Jesuit tree for the fever, and yarrow or ginger for the cough. Then bloodletting if that fever doesn't break. Above all, rest in a warm bed. The treatment must be started urgently. You are very sick."

Agnes's eyes widened. "The guards will not send me to the hospital. I am to die."

"No. I'll talk to them."

Ella knocked on the door. "Guards!"

A rueful laugh rang behind her, likely from the woman bothered by Agnes's hacking.

"Ella, this won't do any good," Matilda murmured.

"Guards!" Ella yelled louder.

"What do you want?" the man's voice barked through the door.

"Agnes is terribly ill. She must be taken to the hospital."

"No such orders. If a doctor sends her... but he won't be coming until next month."

"I'm a doctor. She needs a warm bed and medicine to treat pneumonia. If she doesn't get that soon, she'll die."

"Then she'll die. It would be the Lord's judgement for her crime. And you, quiet down, if you know what's good for you. I better not be disturbed the rest of my shift."

Ella staggered away from the door to Agnes's cot. The young woman curled into a ball, coughing through her tears.

"No." Ella patted the girl's trembling shoulder. "Agnes, I will not let you die here. I'll find a way." Her eyes scanned the other inmates. Only three able-bodied, sane women, including herself. They would have to be enough.

"Come close, ladies. We'll have a strategy meeting," Ella called.

"A what?" Matilda echoed.

Ella waited for the two women to flank her before speaking in a hushed voice. "Agnes must be taken to the hospital. We need to hatch a plan and work together." She gazed at the frightening woman whose lips twisted into a mean grin. "What's so funny?"

"Somehow I doubt you ever planned anything other than a party, even if you know of medicine."

"Have *you*?" Ella cocked her head. "What kinds of schemes did you design?"

"You don't need to know, Duchess. That's my name for you."

"My name is Ella Parker. This is Matilda Pesce."

"Duchess and Crone."

Matilda scoffed but the woman ignored her.

"You can call me Rose. Now get to your plan."

"Well, I don't have one yet..." Ella swallowed at Rose's chuckle. "But information could help. Have you noticed how many guards there are? When do they come in?"

"They check on us every hour," Rose said. "Day and night. They don't always come inside, sometimes they just stare into the cell. If everyone's quiet, they don't give us trouble."

"What happens when someone is not quiet?"

Matilda's lips trembled. "They hate that. One time I complained about the molded bread and the guard slapped me. When the poor madwoman becomes too loud, they beat her."

"And what if we all are yelling, screaming, and throwing things? Would they bring someone in charge to hear our demands?"

"More likely they'll have us all whipped." Matilda hugged herself.

Rose raised her eyebrow. "I say we try. And we do it when they bring us breakfast. We could bang plates and throw food."

They decided on that and got on their cots to sleep.

When Ella shivered from the chill that passed through her dress, her mind showed her Jamie crouched in a cell as dark and gloomy as hers. She still could not remember how she knew him.

Chapter 6

Despite the late hour, a young servant opened the door only seconds after Jamie rang the bell.

"I'm here to see Captain Grey. It's urgent." Jamie tried to give his voice gravity.

The servant glanced at Jamie's uniform coat. "A problem with the ship?"

Jamie cleared his dry throat. Perhaps he should let the servant think that's what he came for rather than on Ella's behalf. But deception often didn't pay in the long run.

"My business is about the surgeon, Miss Ella Parker. She needs the captain's help."

The servant showed him into an antechamber.

"The master just retired but I will let him know. Would you like something to drink while you wait?"

"I would very much appreciate a glass of water." He had nothing to drink since he was so unexpectedly detained by the constables. After they established that he only arrived in Plymouth and had no connection to Ella, they eventually let him go.

The servant nodded and left. Jamie collapsed onto a chair, his body aching for sleep. Did he leave home only yesterday? Seemed more like a week ago. His mind could barely keep up with events.

When his head was about to drop onto his chest, two young women flew into the room. They looked to have dressed hastily with robes and shawls over their nightdresses. Both were quite pretty with shiny chestnut hair. The older one was about Ella's age. The other a couple of years younger and held a crystal glass of water.

Jamie rose. "Good evening, ladies. I'm Jamie Flowers, at your service." He gave a polite bow.

"I'm Bella Grey." The older girl curtsied. "This is my sister Cecilia."

Cecilia handed the glass to Jamie with her chin raised. "I don't curtsy. A proper handshake is much better way to greet people." She offered her hand to Jamie, and he shook it.

"Thank you so much for the water, ladies."

Bella clasped her hands. "Please tell us what happened to our dear friend, Ella Parker."

"She was supposed to come to talk about the trial," Cecilia added. "We wanted to go to the courthouse with her, but

Mother didn't let us. She made us visit the dance master instead." She rolled her eyes and groaned.

Jamie swallowed a sip of water to relief his thirst. "Unfortunately, Miss Parker is in serious trouble. She is being held in the town gaol. I've just managed to get out of there myself. It's quite a dreadful place, and I'm terribly anxious for her. I'm hoping your father will be able to rescue her."

"You arrived straight from there?" Bella brought her hand to her mouth. "Cecilia, why don't you bring Mr. Flowers something stronger than water. I will ask the cook to make him something to eat."

Fifteen minutes later Jamie was seated in the dining room, sipping wine. The table boasted roast and cheese, a bowl of fruit, and a dish with crumpets.

Captain Grey's daughters were now wearing plain but neat dresses and sat with their mother at the table. The smell of food made Jamie's mouth water. He made a conscious effort to use his best manners while eating and responding to the women's inquiries.

"How is it you know Miss Parker?" Mrs. Grey, a petite, fine-looking woman asked Jamie as she offered him an orange. "We are very fond of her, but she talks little of her life before arriving to Plymouth."

Jamie was about to answer, but steps sounded from beyond the door, and Captain Gray marched into the room with a grumpy expression. Even though he seemed unpleased to be disturbed, he was dressed to go out.

"What's all this?" He frowned at the late supper.

"Mr. Flowers just came from the jailhouse," Bella said.

"How many years did he spend there to warrant such a feast?" The captain raised his eyebrow.

"Only a few hours." Jamie swallowed his food and rose. "Sir, I'm here on Miss Ella Parker's behalf. She's been arrested and thrown in jail."

Captain Grey cringed. "What kind of trouble did my surgeon start now?"

"Father!" Cecilia chided. "This is serious. Ella was arrested while performing her duties."

"It's true. She saved a baby, but the constables didn't believe she was a surgeon." Jamie relayed what happened at Matilda's house. He faced the captain. "Sir, Miss Parker asked that you help her."

The women flicked anxious glances.

Captain Grey nodded. "I will go to the station and speak on Dr. Parker's behalf. This must be a misunderstanding."

Jamie jumped to his feet. "Sir, I'm coming with you."

***

"Are you ready?" Ella scanned her small crew as the eerie light of dawn illuminated the barred window. Her body pulsed with nervous energy.

"Yes, Duchess." Rose winked as she leaned on the wall, her arms and shoulders loose. Matilda paced between her cot and the door. The other women slept, including Agnes, whose body wrenched from coughing fits.

The turn of the lock made Ella stand on her tippytoes. Two guards, a balding older one and a red-cheeked younger one, carried in bowls with foul-smelling porridge.

"What have you brought us?" Ella bellowed when the men lowered the tray on the floor. "This is not suitable to eat." She picked up one of the metal bowls and thew it against the wall. Matilda and Rose did the same, while shouting and stomping their feet. The noise woke up the drunks, who yelled curses. The crazed woman gave a piercing laugh.

"What are you doing?" The older guard approached Ella. "Pipe down now or you'll be in solitary and without breakfast."

"We'll yell and scream until you take Agnes to the hospital," Ella shouted in his face. He raised his club to hit her, but she ducked.

Matilda grabbed his coat from behind, making him pivot. "Bring us decent food as well," she shrieked as the club flew by her face.

The other women continued cursing, laughing, and screaming. The noise made Ella's ears ring.

"I'll fetch the warden," the older guard said with his hands on his ears and sped away.

Rose waved her skirt as she approached the remaining guard. His face was scrunched like he was having a tough time thinking with all that noise.

"Come closer, handsome." She waved her finger at him and batted her eyelashes. When he approached, she leaned into him and caressed his neck. Shocked, Ella stopped yelling and stared. This was not part of their plan.

Rose's lips covered the guard's mouth, and her arms wrapped around him. The club dropped from his hand. He made a move to free himself from Rose's embrace and pick up the club. Like in a magician's trick, Rose's wrist flicked, and a small knife appeared in her hand from under her sleeve. Matilda froze with her hands covering her mouth. The drunks and the madwoman kept up the commotion, oblivious to the scene.

Rose pressed the razor to the guard's neck. "One wrong move, and I will slice your throat. If you want to live, you will lead me out of this place." The guard's knees shook and sweat rolled down his forehead.

Heat rushed to Ella's face. Obviously, Rose used her plan to create a distraction and to free herself, with no thought of helping Agnes or anyone else. Her eyes lingered on the club that the guard dropped. It lay at Rose's feet. Ella's body tensed as she considered her move.

With her breath stilled, she dashed to the club and raised it. "You will free all of us or I will smash your head to pieces," she screamed into the guard's ear. He bristled, trembling.

Rose's eyes blazed and lips curled. She lowered the blade from the neck to the guard's shoulder and poked him. "Let's go."

Ella stepped into their path, with the club gripped in her sweaty palm.

"You are in our way, Duchess," Rose hissed. "Move before you get hurt."

The slam of the door made Ella jump and swing round. Two guards rushed into the cell with pistols drawn. Ella's body turned rigid, and the club slipped from her grasp. Captain Grey and Jamie Flowers stepped in after the guards.

Jamie's eyes widened with horror. "Miss Parker, are you all right?"

Before Ella could respond, Rose launched on her like a tigress. Ella's back hit the straw floor. Rose's body was on top of her, knees pushing into Ella's belly. Her lungs couldn't inhale from Rose's weight on them. A pistol shot boomed over their heads.

Cold steel touched Ella's neck. "One move and I kill her," Rose bellowed.

Ella's eyes squeezed shut as the blade pushed into her skin. Blood froze in her veins. Every muscle in her body tensed.

"Please, don't hurt her." Jamie's voice rang. "What is it you want? Perhaps Captain Grey and I can help."

Rose's blade moved slightly, and her knees slid off Ella. Panting, Ella sat up.

"A captain of the Royal Navy?" Rose's head turned to Captain Grey. "Sir, I must speak to you alone."

At that moment, Ella sprang on Rose. The sharp blade sliced Ella's arm, but Rose lost her grip on the knife. It fell a few inches from them. Jamie rushed to pick it up.

"Everyone freeze and be quiet!" A large man stepped into the cell. His eyes scanned the room.

Ella straightened. A small stream of blood trickled down her arm. Jamie rushed to her side, his hand putting pressure on the cut. Rose was held by a guard, but her eyes were locked on Captain Grey. Matilda was leaning on the wall, holding her chest. Other women seemed to have exhausted from their shouting and quieted down. Only Agnes continued coughing and rasping.

"All right, I heard you. This one will be taken to the hospital." The man, likely the jail warden, pointed at Agnes. "These two," he said, nodding at the drunk women, "are free to go. Their husbands are here. Ella Parker is free as well."

"Captain Grey argued all night with the chief inspector. Only when another surgeon confirmed that the operation you performed was to save the baby, did he agree to let you go," Jamie whispered to Ella as he tied his handkerchief around her arm.

The room was spinning in front of Ella's eyes. She leaned on Jamie as she stood up.

"Nothing about me?" Rose's nostrils flared. Then her anger seemed to wane as she stared at the captain. "Captain Grey, please. I have a letter you must see."

"Well, give it here," the captain said.

"It's in my petticoats." Rose's cheeks pinked a shade, and she gave a side-glance to the large guard that held her.

"It's her trick," the guard warned. "I bet she's hiding another weapon there."

"No. Hold my hands if you wish," Rose grunted and gazed at Ella. "Duchess... I mean Ella... would you take the letter from my underskirts?" Her eyes pleaded.

"Don't go near her!" Matilda and Jamie exclaimed at the same time.

"And don't ask me. I'm not a fool," Matilda added.

A wave of anger chased away Ella's dizzy spell for a moment. "You are asking me to help you after you cut me? The guards can rummage in your underwear."

A guttural roar escaped Rose's throat. "I hate you! Pray we never cross paths again because I will make you pay for this, Duchess." Her head swiveled to Captain Grey. "Take it yourself, Captain. You'll know what to do with the message."

"A delicate mission, young lady. But if your message is as important as you hint, I must accept it." Captain Gray smirked and bent down before Rose.

"Come, Miss Ella. You are free. And you look like you need fresh air." Jamie's arm was around Ella's shoulders.

Black dots were dancing before her eyes, but she gathered her strength and walked to Matilda.

"I will not leave you here," she vowed to her friend as they embraced. "My friends will hire a lawyer."

Matilda sighed. "Get out of here, Ella. Lad." She gestured to Jamie. "Take her outside before she swoons."

With Jamie's shoulder under her arm, he was leading out of the cell. Her legs dragged. The room spun faster.

"I'm afraid this letter is of significant importance. I must take it to the port admiral immediately." Captain Grey's voice sounded further and further away. "Mr. Flowers, please take Dr. Parker to my home. My wife and daughters will...."

Ella didn't hear the end of the phrase as the world turned black.

Chapter 7

“**M**r. Flowers, your pacing is going to tear up my favorite rug.” The captain's wife, Mrs. Grey, raised an eyebrow. “Please, have a seat on the sofa.”

“I'm sorry, ma'am.” He sank into the soft cushions. Mrs. Grey proved to be a thoughtful hostess. After ushering Ella upstairs and calling for her maids to prepare a bath and a bed for her, she had a valet take Jamie to the guest room and offer him all he needed to wash up and shave. The servant then brought him fresh clothing that had the scent of jasmine soap instead of sweat and dirt. After being shown to the parlor, he was offered food several times, but his stomach churned as he waited to hear of Ella's condition.

“Is Miss Parker any better? Perhaps I should fetch a physician.”

“There's no need.” Mrs. Grey studied him. “I've cleaned her cut. It's merely a scratch and does not require stitches. As for a brief weakness she experienced, it was likely brought on by hunger. Now that she had eaten a bit, she's feeling much better. Telling my daughters quite a story of her imprisonment while my servants prepare a breakfast for all of us."

Jamie expelled a long breath. "Thank you for taking good care of her."

Mrs. Grey sat down next to him. "You seem greatly concerned for Miss Parker. How do you know her? She wasn't sure if you were acquainted before yesterday."

His head dropped. "If she forgot… It doesn't matter."

What a fool I was to think she would remember me!

"Perhaps you have something to remind her. A letter or a memento of some sort?"

"The shell." Jamie's heart sped up.

"How interesting. Do you have it with you?"

Jamie's hand went to the breeches he wore. "It's with the clothes your servant took to clean. Oh, I hope it is not lost."

"I'll go check." Mrs. Grey rose.

When she left the room with an amused smile, Jamie summoned all his will to prevent himself from pacing again. Minutes stretched like hours. His eyelids grew heavier, and his head leaned on a decorated pillow.

A girlish squeal pierced his ears and jarred him awake.

"Miss Ella, don't run down the stairs. You aren't fully recovered," Mrs. Grey warned.

Ella must've ignored the advice because a moment later she burst into the room with Bella, Cecilia, and Mrs. Grey on her heels. He rose to greet the women.

"Jamie! Why didn't you say it's you?" Ella looked like she had to restrain herself from jumping for joy. Her cheeks were still pale, but her eyes sparkled, matching a deep green dress she was now wearing.

"She remembers all right." Mrs. Grey chuckled.

"I... I tried to tell you," Jamie stammered.

Her palms touched his shoulders, and, for a moment, he thought she might embrace him. His breath stilled. But then her hands fell to her sides, and she stepped back.

"You can't blame me for not recognizing you," she said after studying him. "You grew tall and thick in shoulders. No longer the frail boy I remember."

Heat rushed to Jamie's cheeks. After his family moved from London to Dorset, he stopped catching lung illnesses. Swimming and fencing made him stronger, even though his father insisted on frequent breaks. But Dr. Miller said that while fresh air and exercise may prolong his life, they will not cure him.

Bella rose to her tippytoes. "This is sweet. You must tell us how you know each other."

"Over breakfast, please." Mrs. Grey ushered everyone to the dining room.

When everyone had a square meal of eggs, bacon, and strong coffee, Bella asked again if Ella would tell the story of how they met. Jamie let Ella speak first, as he was unsure how much she wanted to reveal.

"When I was thirteen and lived in Newcastle, my parents planned a holiday to the seaside," Ella began.

"Newcastle?" Jamie exclaimed. "I thought you were from London."

Ella frowned and gave him a quick shake of her head.

Each time we returned to London, I searched for her. No wonder I could not find her.

"We were all prepared to travel, and then my mother ... became indisposed." Ella's lips turned down, and she blinked rapidly.

Jamie stifled a sigh. Norma, Ella's maid, told him that Ella's mother suffered a miscarriage. It made him a little sad that Ella couldn't talk about it even with her friends.

Ella sipped from her cup. "My maid convinced my mother that she could take me on the holiday and be my chaperone. She wasn't exactly suitable for the job, because once we reached Seatown, I did as I pleased. One morning, I ventured to the beach to gather shells. There I met Jamie, who was holding this beautiful shell." She held up his find for all to admire.

"Right." Jamie smiled. "I collected shells to amuse my youngest sister."

"How thoughtful!" Bella beamed. "How many sisters do you have?"

"I have three sisters, and we are close. Caroline is two years older than me, while Julia and Audrey are younger."

"That's what I remembered the most about you, how nicely you played with your sisters. Jamie introduced me to them, and we had a wonderful time." Ella's voice bubbled. "I didn't come home till well into the evening. Norma didn't chide me, only asked if I'd had fun. I told her I had the best day of my life."

Jamie's throat thickened. That evening, he so wanted Ella to like him and his family. Her statement warmed his chest.

"What happened next? Did you come back next day?" Cecilia asked.

"No." Ella's smile waned. "I was looking forward to playing with my new friends, but … my parents arrived. My mother grew anxious to see me. Upon learning of my behavior during the holiday, my father decided to take us home immediately. He was a hard man."

With the temper of a raging bull. Jamie remembered how the tall man slapped Ella.

"We left before dawn. I didn't get a chance to say goodbye to my new friends," Ella finished.

There was significantly more than Ella told, but he understood why she didn't want to share those details.

Mrs. Grey's smile brightened her eyes. "How lovely that you are reunited."

"Yes, it is a marvelous surprise. There's so much to catch up on." Ella bounced in her seat. "How is your mother, Jamie?"

Ma's hair grayed, and her face thinned after that summer, but she wouldn't like him to speak of such things. "She's doing well, keeping a busy schedule, ensuring my sisters receive proper education and appear in society."

"As a mother of daughters, I quite understand." Mrs. Grey beamed at Bella and Cecilia.

"What about your father?" There was a mournful note in Ella's voice, and her smile vanished.

Why is she bracing herself like I'm about to deliver some sad news? Jamie wondered. Then his stomach dropped. *When she found me crying after the doctor's visit, I let her believe that it was my father who saw Dr. Miller and received a terrible diagnosis. I didn't want to tell her that I'm deadly ill. I hope I will never have to tell her.*

"My father is well. He continues to extract teeth. His practice is immensely popular."

Ella gasped and clapped her hands. "How incredible. He's such a warm and kind man. I'm so glad he regained his health."

"Your father was deadly ill but recovered?" Mrs. Grey's eyes widened. "It's so good to hear such stories. And I'm glad Ella learned that he lived. Her cheeks are rosy again. No sign of earlier faintness."

Staring into Ella's twinkling eyes, Jamie swallowed. *Let her keep smiling, thinking my story is a happy one. I want to see that smile as long as possible.*

"Jamie's family is wonderful. They hardly knew me, but they made me feel so welcome," Ella said. "Are your parents and sisters here with you? Or are they home in London?"

"They are in Dorset. After consulting a physician, my family relocated to Seatown permanently. The house you visited had been our home ever since."

"I'm glad you took this advice. Your father must have benefitted from the sea air. And what brought you to Plymouth?"

Jamie filled his lungs to answer, but Captain Grey entered the room. "Good morning, everyone. Although it hardly feels like morning." His sea green eyes scanned the room, pausing on Ella. "You are looking much better."

"Thank you." Ella gave a weak smile. "I was faint from hunger, but I'm well now, thanks to your family's hospitality."

"From hunger? I better eat before I am afflicted with the same." The captain sat down at the table next to his wife. "I see Mr. Flowers is still visiting us." His voice revealed a slight annoyance.

"Mr. Flowers was telling us what brought him to Plymouth," Mrs. Grey said, filling a plate for her husband. Ella sipped from her cup.

Jamie rose. "Sir, the navy recruiter, Mr. Webster, told me you have a volunteer position I can fill. I've purchased all the needed supplies and uniform, and I am ready to sail with you."

The captain frowned and tapped his fingers on the table. As he opened his mouth to speak, Ella lowered her cup with a thud. Coffee spilled on the white cloth, but she didn't seem to notice.

"You will enlist? On the *Neptune*?"

Jamie rubbed his hands together, aware of the stares on him. "Yes. The recruiters at Seatown told me of the vacancy."

"I now recall that I received a note from Webster. Unfortunately, that vacancy has been filled." The captain cringed and gave a side-glance to his wife. "Captain Leach sent me his son. I couldn't say no."

"Well, perhaps another position?" Mrs. Grey added another helping of food to her husband's plate and grinned at Jamie. "Mr. Flowers helped in rescuing Dr. Parker."

"No!" Ella's voice dipped. Her fingers wrinkled her napkin.

Everyone stared at her, but she kept her gaze locked on Jamie, cutting through him. Her cheeks turned scarlet red. "You have no idea what battles or ship illnesses are like. Your family loves you. I will not allow you to lose your life in this bloody war that took many of my friends."

Words came up to his throat but wouldn't form on his tongue. "But you are on the warship..." He finally stammered.

"I boarded the *Neptune* because I couldn't practice my calling anywhere else. I stayed to preserve lives. Hardly any lives, compared to how many I couldn't save. You have no reason to be on a warship. And since, thankfully, the posting had been filled, you shall return to Seatown. Please give my love to your family."

Ella's words sank in like a cannonball into the water. He sat down and waited for his pounding heart to slow.

"My mind is made up. I will take your words as a sign that you care about my fate, and I will treasure them. But I see it would be best that we serve on different ships."

"What?" Ella's head jerked as if she's been slapped. "That's an even worse idea. Some ships don't even have a surgeon."

"Perhaps I better leave." Jamie stood and bowed to the captain, then his wife and daughters. "Miss Parker, I'm so fortunate to see you again."

Her head stayed down.

"Ella." Mrs. Grey touched her shoulder. "Won't you say goodbye to Mr. Flowers?"

Jamie held his breath, waiting for her to raise her face to him. If this was the last time he saw her, he wanted to fix her expression in his mind.

Ella kept her eyes lowered. "Mrs. Grey, thank you for your hospitality. I must take care of a few things today, starting with visiting the station to retrieve my medical bag and documents."

Mrs. Grey's brow knitted. "You shouldn't go there alone. Think of what happened last night. Perhaps Mr. Flowers could come with you?"

"It would be a pleasure." Jamie bowed.

Ella rose. "I don't need—"

"Yes, you do, my dear." The hostess sighed. "You know how I worry. I would feel much better knowing Mr. Flowers is with you."

She gave Jamie a wink.

Chapter 8

After walking through several winding streets, Jamie was staring at a familiar building. Not a place he wished to visit again. The narrow windows of the station reminded him of that revolting room where he spent hours answering ridiculous questions.

His disgust must've shown on his face, because Ella said, "You don't need to go in. I'm only going to retrieve my belongings."

"Oh no, I'm coming with you."

She waved him off. "Wait here. If I'm not back in an hour, run to bring Captain Grey. I think that's the wisest approach."

He showed her his pocket watch. "I will be counting minutes."

When she disappeared inside, he paced the yard. His eyes glanced at the watch every few seconds. Images of Ella flickered in his mind. Ella saving the baby. Later, her body going limp in his arms as he led her out of prison. Her burning eyes when she learned that he was enlisting for the navy.

His back was to the building when an infant's cry reached his ears. He turned to see the most endearing image of Ella yet. She awkwardly balanced Wendy's baby in one arm, while holding her medical bag in the other. She was obviously uncomfortable, holding two objects dear to her at the same time. Yet he remained rooted in place, watching her.

"Well, don't just stand there. Help me."

He hastened to her and reached for her bag. She pulled it away. "No, silly. Take the baby. I know you want to hold her again."

The precious bundle nestled into the crook of his arm. "She feels a bit heavier already."

"The constable's wife took diligent care of her. We better go. The baby should not be out in this wind for too long."

He removed his coat and wrapped the baby in it. She stopped crying and yawned.

"Did the constables let you keep her?"

"They were about to carry her to the orphanage, but I convinced them to let me take her."

"You will raise her?" Warmth spread in his chest. "That would be wonderful."

Her head shook vigorously. "The ship is no place for a baby. My friends may be willing to look after her, but I think I know who will care for this baby the most."

***

The weight of the medical bag in her hand gave Ella confidence, and she strode faster. Jamie followed with his gaze glued on his feet, as if afraid to stumble and drop the baby. As they walked, the infant was falling asleep in Jamie's arms. Ella couldn't help but see something endearing in how Jamie hummed a song into the baby's ear.

He was a sweet boy and grew to be a sensitive young man. Life on the ship takes resilience he likely lacks.

Streets were busy with working men and women going about their business. The houses in this neighborhood were shabby and unkept. Ella stopped by a home with broken windows and a dilapidated roof. Five children of various ages sat by the door.

"Is your mother home?" Ella asked.

"Yes, she's inside," the oldest child, a girl of thirteen in a soiled dress, replied.

Ella knocked. A woman in a frock with rough patches opened the door and stared. "What do you want?"

"Good afternoon Mrs. Moore." Ella kept her face composed despite the unfriendly greeting. "May we come in?"

"What's your business? If you are here to collect my husband's debts, I have no money."

Ella filled her lungs. "I have some sad news I must give you. Better we come in and sit down to talk."

The woman stepped aside. They entered a poorly lit room that held a table, several chairs, and a couple of children's beds. One child, pale and extremely thin, slept there.

Mrs. Moore's gaze stayed on Jamie and the baby for a moment, then lingered on Ella's dress. "I'm sorry, I have nothing to offer you to drink, madam. Fine ladies like you don't visit this house. Please sit but be careful. The chairs could break. What is it you came to tell me?"

Jamie stayed on his feet as he rocked the infant to sleep. Ella perched onto a rickety chair. "Mrs. Moore, the baby we brought is Wendy's. Your granddaughter. I'm afraid..."

The woman turned her back on Ella. "No. Tell Wendy she must take care of her child. I have enough mouths to feed."

Ella stood and placed her hand on the woman's back. "I wish I could tell Wendy that, but... Your daughter is dead. Perished in childbirth." Recalling the moment she discovered Wendy's body in the attic, with the baby still moving inside, Ella chose to spare her mother the gruesome specifics.

Mrs. Moore's spine stiffened. Then tremors and wails shook her body.

"I didn't want to throw her out. But my husband was due to return. He's the bosun on the *Neptune*. If he saw Wendy with her belly, he'd beat her and me. Take a cat o'nine tails to us like he does to punished seamen."

Ella's chest constricted. "Mr. Moore I knew was not like that."

The baby in Jamie's arms whimpered through sleep. Mrs. Moore turned and stared at the infant's face.

"She has something of little Wendy in her." Her chest caved in. "My husband won't let me keep her. We can barely feed our own." She closed her face with her hands.

Jamie blinked and swallowed.

When the woman's weeping quieted, Ella squeezed her hand. She had been a messenger of terrible news many times, but the pain in her chest rattled her.

"Mrs. Moore, I'm afraid we will never know what your husband's reaction would've been. He was mortally wounded."

Jamie gasped as if punched.

A lump formed in Ella's throat, but she continued. "I cared for him for three days as he fought for his life, but ultimately, he succumbed to his injuries and was buried at sea. Before he died, he told me he dearly loved you and all his children. I don't remember all the names, but he mentioned Thomas, John, Susan, and Wendy. He spoke of Wendy the most. She was his favorite."

The woman's knees hit the floor. She crouched into a fetal position and howled like a wounded animal. The child who was sleeping opened his eyes and started weeping.

Jamie leaned on the wall. Afraid he may drop the baby, Ella took her.

"Children, in here," Mrs. Moore cried.

With wide eyes and trembling chins, the children rushed into the room from the outside and other places in the house. Two girls kneeled with their mother, hugging her with their little arms, while others stood shifting their feet. The baby Ella held gave a piercing cry.

"Children." Their mother's voice quivered. "Your father and your sister Wendy are dead." As the children's eyes filled with tears, she added quietly. "We won't be separated from them long. Hunger is sure to kill us soon."

"No!" Jamie and Ella said at once. Ella's insides burned as she stared at the children's pale faces.

"Mrs. Moore, your family will not starve." Ella gave her a hand to stand. "As a widow, you are to receive your husband's pension. Here. This is the first payment." She unhooked a money purse from her belt and laid it in the widow's hands. The money was Ella's, but Mrs. Moore didn't need to know.

The widow loosened the strings and peered inside. A gasp escaped her throat. "It can't be that much. I know how much other widows received. There must be a mistake."

"No mistake. When you receive documents of your husband's death, you will collect a monthly payment. But this should be enough to sustain you, your children, and your newborn granddaughter for a while. I know a good wet-nurse for the baby."

Mrs. Moore's eyes widened. "My granddaughter. Let me hold her."

Ella placed the crying infant in her hands. Mrs. Moore rocked and shooshed her. Her expression warmed as she stared into the baby's eyes. Several of the children wiped their tears and tiptoed closer, craning their necks to see the infant.

"I will hire a wet-nurse and raise my grandchild," Mrs. Moore said with her eyes closed. "My husband would want me to. He loved our Wendy. Her daughter should be named after her."

When the children gathered around to hold their niece, Ella grabbed Jamie by the elbow and led him outside. For a few minutes, they walked in silence. The face of Mr. Moore, contorted with pain after a horrible wound, was on her mind. What she told the widow was true—he had spoken of her and all the children with great love.

"Jamie, I wanted you to see that woman's pain." Her hand rubbed at her throat. "At least she has a new granddaughter as a comfort. Most families receive a piece of clothing or a lock of hair as a last memento of their husband or son. I take on the solemn job of delivering the news when I can. It's a penance of sorts. For not saving the life of their loved one."

Jamie's lips shook, and he paled. "You have nothing to blame yourself for. You are so brave and kind, caring for the wounded."

Her hands tightened into fists. "It's not only the battles that kill. When we were in West Indies, we lost a quarter of our men to yellow fever. Young, strong men died within hours. And you want to enlist. Do you want your mother to collapse to the floor and weep like Mrs. Moore? Your father to become ill again?

Your sisters fall into melancholy? Because they all love you so much, their grief will be awful."

Jamie fidgeted and touched his face.

"But you choose to go to sea."

"The Neptune is the only place where I belong. My parents are dead—"

"I'm sorry, I didn't know." He gave her a pained look. "You are so young to be alone."

"I'm not alone. My mentor, Dr. Pesce, gave me a chance to learn medicine at a prestigious university and then hired me as his assistant. After he died, I became the ship's surgeon. The crew is my family. But you are different. You have loving parents and sisters."

Ella held her breath and waited for him to say that he would go back to his family. She would miss his blue eyes, his lovely smile. He grew into such a handsome young man. But sending him away was best for everyone.

He averted his gaze. "Ella, it cannot be helped. I must enlist. Since the *Neptune's* vacancy is filled, I will find a different ship."

"You still mean to go?" Her head jerked back. "After what I told you? Well, thank Heavens it won't be my job to sew the bag for your corpse or deliver your last letter to your family. Goodbye, Jamie Flowers."

Clutching her bag, she sped away. When steps echoed behind her, she ducked behind a building. After catching her breath, she returned to the street. Jamie was gone.

Chapter 9

Mr. Flowers,

Tomorrow, at eight in the morning, report to the Neptune. Bring your sea chest.

Captain Grey

Jamie read the note again. A ship boy, not Tobby but a different one, older and more reserved, delivered the note last evening. Given up on finding a posting on any ship, Jamie was packing his things to return home the next morning. The captain's note restored his spirits.

Except, how would Ella feel? She made it clear she didn't want to sail with me. And why does Captain Grey want to see me if the position is filled?

A glance at his pocket watch reminded Jamie he had to hurry. He assumed that being late would displease the captain. His chest was packed and tied with a rope to keep the lid from opening, and he was wearing the uniform blue frock coat with white button collar patch, matching breeches, and a crisp white shirt he paid the maid to iron last night. His boots were clean to the shine. He checked his appearance in the glass one last time before leaving.

Ma would approve of how I look.

Pain punched him in the stomach at that thought. He was taking another step in his plan to find adventure and do something meaningful before he died. It also meant his family would never see him again. Mrs. Moore's howls echoed in his ears. He swallowed and forced the memory out of his head.

The Plymouth port overwhelmed his senses. Seamen, officers, peddlers, and beggars surrounded him as he searched for the way to the ship. Peddlers yelled as they hawked their wares. A bearded man in black clothes, with long side-locks falling from under his hat, offered to sell him slop, which turned out to be second-hand clothes. When he got away from the seller, a woman his mother's age tried to persuade him to have a little fun with her before the voyage. He pushed his way from the pesterers to the pier. The view of the ships swaying on the bobbing waves took his breath away. The noise of the harbor dissipated to his mind, and all he could hear were the swash of the surf, the whistle of the wind, and the jabbering of the gulls.

When speaking to a boy who was selling oranges, Jamie learned where to hire a boat to take him to the ship. Fortunately, the boater was rowing toward the pier, and Jamie jumped in with no delay.

"I just brought another fellow to the *Neptune*, wearing the same uniform," the elderly boater said as he oared. "I'm surprised Captain Grey wants two volunteers. Rumors say he's not keen on having any."

"I heard he believes in giving people chances." Jamie gave a hopeful gaze to the small but graceful ship before him.

"That could be. Anyway, the other fellow thought I was too slow and cursed me most unkindly. Said I made him late and didn't pay me."

"I'm sorry to hear that. Perhaps he was anxious to make a good impression on the captain and forgot." Jamie loosened the strings of his money bag and paid for two fares.

At the deck, a weathered-looking officer with a scar on his cheek introduced himself as First Lieutenant Wyse and showed Jamie the way to Captain Grey's cabin. When Jamie entered, the captain sat at his desk, covered with papers. A young man, about Jamie's age, black-haired and swarthy, gestured with animation as he spoke.

The young officer tossed his head back as he answered the captain's question. "Yes, sir. I spent five years under my father's command. Been in many fierce battles."

As the young man boasted of his career and his skill at navigation, Jamie studied the cabin. It was of a comfortable size and held nothing showy. A neatly made bed, a bookcase with navigation manuals, charts hanging on the bulkheads. The only decorative item was the large portrait of Mrs. Grey and the two little girls, much younger than the Miss Bella and Miss Cecilia he met. Mrs. Grey's face was also that of a younger woman, but the expression was just as motherly. He suspected it was thanks to her he received summons to the *Neptune.*

"As you see, my father gave me no slack," the young man finished his speech that sounded rehearsed to Jamie's ear.

"Captain Leach giving someone slack... I cannot imagine that." Captain Grey laughed and tilted his head. "You must resemble your mother, whom I never had the pleasure of meeting, but your voice, your manner... So much like young Leach, when I met him in the midshipmen berth. Ferociously brave man. It was an honor serving with him. I expect great things from you, lad."

The young man gave a curt nod. "I won't disappoint you, sir."

"I expect not." His gaze shifted to Jamie; the captain's lips pursed, as if he was seeing someone who *would* disappoint him. "Mr. Flowers. As you know the volunteer position had been filled. By Mr. Conor Leach, who has already spent five years at sea." He gestured to the young man who sneered. "But my wife proposed an interesting idea. I can hire you as a personal servant to take care of my clothes and my personal meals. What do you say, Mr. Flowers? Are you interested in being my servant? Or is that something... beneath you."

Conor Leach snorted.

Thoughts buzzed in Jamie's head. *Ella would be vexed to learn I enlisted despite her warning.*

"I would never think of honest work beneath me. But I have some reservations."

"What are they?" The captain's eyes pierced him.

Jamie rubbed his jaw. He didn't want to bring up Ella in front of Conor, whose smugness was written all over his tanned face. "I wanted to have a chance to do something heroic. Participate in battles and missions."

"You will fight. When battle occurs, every man gives his all. On this sailing, we'll be in French waters, and I hope to capture an enemy ship. Does that mitigate your concerns?"

Jamie stopped his hands from wrangling. "Can I have time to think?"

The captain glanced at his pocket watch. "Five minutes. I must finish preparations for sailing." His head snapped toward Conor. "Mr. Leach, please go find Mr. Wyse. He'll have you start on your duties."

When Conor left, Captain Grey rose and crossed his arms. "A few days ago, you were much more eager to go to sea. Is it the position? Or is it Miss Parker?"

Jamie's shoulders dropped. "She doesn't want to see me on the *Neptune*."

The captain cleared his throat. "Her uncharacteristic conduct convinced my wife you should sail with us. She's fond of Miss Parker. She also thinks that I should have a manservant that understands a gentleman's needs. Judging by your manners, by how you dress..." the captain scanned Jamie's clothes, "you have knowledge of those things."

I've had servants care for me all my life. I should know what they do, Jamie thought, fidgeting. *And the captain promised that I would fight in battles. This is what I planned.*

"You can share the sleeping space in the cockpit with Mr. Leach. I expect you will become friends. He could help you get your footing on the ship."

Remembering the expression on Conor's face, Jamie doubted that.

"Sir, but what about Miss Parker?"

The captain raised his head. "This is my ship, and I hire the crew. My surgeon is busy examining new recruits and treating those who caught diseases at the port. If you keep away from the sickbay, she won't know you are here until we are far at sea. After some brooding, she'll come around." He scratched his neck. "Never thought I'll be giving advice in such matters."

"But since I'm a new recruit, shouldn't she examine me?"

If Ella listens to my heartbeat, she'll know that I'm deadly ill. Even if she lets me stay, things will never be the same between us.

The captain waved his hand dismissively. "You look healthy enough. I permit you to skip the exam. Now, I'd like some coffee. Bring it to the quarterdeck."

***

Clutching his abdomen, Jamie leaned on the bulkhead. The stuffy air of the orlop was making his seasickness worse. The *Neptune* was out in the open sea, and each pitch and roll made his stomach roil. After a day of fetching various things for the captain, brushing his uniform, and sharpening his quills, Jamie's body craved rest. His head as well, as it was muddled with all the ship's various berths and storages that he was shown today.

He was ready to collapse into a cot and sleep off his weariness and nausea. But there was no cot here. A hammock hung between two beams. He threw off his boots and awkwardly climbed in.

When his eyelids drooped and his muscles relaxed, a lantern shone in his face. It illuminated Conor, whose lips were curled.

"That hammock is mine. You swing your own hammock."

Half-asleep, Jamie clambered out of the hammock. The half-digested supper of salted pork rose up his throat. He already vomited twice today and didn't wish for another meal to go to waste. With heavy breaths, he forced his sickness down.

"I don't know how. Would you please help me?"

Conor huffed with annoyance. "Don't you know anything? Why are you here on this ship?"

"I admit my ignorance. Would you be kind enough to instruct me?"

Conor stretched on the hammock and rested his arms behind his head.

"Did you shine the captain's boots today? Shine mine."

Jamie gave him a long look. The rocking of the ship grew worse, and he was afraid to get sick right in front of his arrogant companion.

"It's a simple kindness to show me what to do."

Conor gave a mean grin. "Shine my boots. Or sleep without a hammock."

Another wave of nausea clasped his stomach. Cringing, he doubled over. "Please. I don't feel well. Let me lie down for a bit."

"If you are about to retch, go up to the deck. It stinks here already." Conor grimaced and wrinkled his nose.

"What do you do to keep seasickness down?" Jamie asked with envy, seeing that Conor's face displayed none of the discomfort he was feeling.

Conor frowned, as if remembering. "I was never seasick in my life. Perhaps I have sea water in my veins instead of blood."

What a boaster.

The ship tossed again. Acid forced its way up Jamie's throat. Breathing hard, he stumbled to the dark stairway.

The deck shook under his feet as though he stood on the back of an angry whale. Near him, men moved about unfazed by lobs and dips. Jamie bent over the railing, holding on with his fists as he emptied his stomach. Relieved, he filled his lungs with salty air. His hands relaxed his hold on the railing. As he stood to catch his breath, a giant wave tossed him backwards. His head hit the deck hard. The stars in the sky mixed with more stars dancing in front of his eyes, and everything went black.

***

A cold cloth dripped into his hair when he opened his eyes. He was lying on a cot, with his throbbing head resting on a pillow. Smells of chamomile and ginger mixed with less pleasant ones of vinegar, blood, and vomit.

This must be the sickroom, or whatever it's called on the ship. Ella works here.

As a confirmation, her melodic voice came from a few feet away. He raised his head toward it, but a thump of pain forced him back down.

"This is ointment made from quicksilver, Mr. Morgan. You are to apply it daily. The syphilis is now advanced."

Heat spread on Jamie's neck, but the young woman's voice was as calm as his father's when he told a patient that he must extract the rotten tooth.

"The ointment should help, but its effects are unpleasant. Hair loss, vomiting. Your teeth may become loose. I still urge you to use it."

Her patient's voice sounded cheerful despite Ella's prognosis. "I heard of another cure. Come closer, pretty lass."

Hearing the man address Ella with such familiarity, Jamie's gut burned. He braced himself to get up.

"Knowing your tricks, Mr. Morgan, I better keep my distance. What exactly is the treatment you propose?"

The man chuckled. "An old friend told me of a cure that never fails. He used it and said it worked like a charm. Would you like to hear it?"

"I'm all ears."

"He told me that if I sleep with a virgin, I will be well again. Have you seen any virgin lasses about?"

Jamie removed the cloth from his head and pushed through pain to sit up. Nausea came up his throat again. Ella's posture was stiff as she stood next to the vulgar seaman. Jamie's eyes widened as he stared at her clothing: she wore trousers that revealed her shapely ankles. He forced himself to stop ogling.

"Sir, apologize to the lady. This is no way to speak to her. If you don't, I will defend her honor."

"Who is this?" A large man came into Jamie's view. A patch over one eye gave him a fierce impression. "My fists are always ready for a fight, so don't tempt me, boy."

Grabbing the bulkhead, Jamie stood on his shaky legs. "Sir, I repeat. Apologize to Miss Parker who treated you so kindly."

"Mr. Flowers, lay back down." Ella's tone could've frozen the vial with medicine she was holding. "I don't need protection."

"Ah, that's Grey's new pet. The lower deck was buzzing about a good-for-nothing lad the captain brought on as his servant. They said he was retching overboard and then fell and hit his head." Morgan covered his mouth with his hand as he laughed.

A splitting headache and nausea swept Jamie, but he kept his gaze on Morgan. "I don't see what you find humorous in that, but I have no objection to your amusement on my account. I know I have much to learn before I master my duties. But I insist you show Miss Parker the respect she deserves."

Morgan turned to Ella. "Did I hurt your feelings, lass? You know I was only joking."

"I know, Morgan." Ella handed him the vial. "But stop taunting Mr. Flowers."

"See lad, Doctor Ella is not mad at me. We are old friends." Morgan winked. His grin made him appear much less intimidating.

"And as a friend and a doctor, I'm asking you to get some rest and let Mr. Flowers do the same."

When Morgan left, Ella crossed her arms. "Lie down. You have no business being on your feet. Or on this ship at all."

He collapsed on the cot. Her hand pressed the bump on his head. "Do you feel nauseated?" When Jamie nodded, she prepared a bowl by the cot and wet another cloth to hold to his head. "Vomiting is common with mild head injuries."

"I've been seasick all day. I'll hardly feel the difference."

"Seasick? Why didn't you see me?" She huffed and her eyes blazed. "Of course you wouldn't see me. You and Captain Grey made some deal behind my back. Did he let you skip the medical examination?"

"Um... I am sorry," he muttered as he couldn't think what else to say.

Her hands grabbed the bowl just in time as sickness poured out of his mouth. When the bout of vomiting finished, she washed his face. "You could've broken your skull. You could've fallen overboard and drowned. Why didn't you ask someone come up with you?" Her nostrils fumed as she spoke. "Unlike me, you *do* need someone to help you."

Jamie winced. Her pitched voice rang in his ears. "Conor Leach is not exactly a friendly fellow. He made me go up to the deck when I was unwell."

"Do you sleep in the cockpit?"

He rubbed his aching head. "Yes, I think that's what the place is called. It's below other decks. Only Conor Leach and I sleep down there. Anyway, he's not so nice."

His lids were so heavy, he could not keep his eyes open.

Ella's voice asked him something, but he could no longer follow. A warm blanket enveloped him, and the world drifted away.

Chapter 10

As Ella, carrying a lantern, descended to the orlop, she uttered curses under her breath that would impress her crew. For two years she toiled to receive the respect for her position on the ship. She was the surgeon, responsible for the health of the men. By enforcing some rules and common sense, she prevented the spread of diseases and decreased injuries. Yet the captain found amusement in bringing Jamie onboard despite her objections and allowed him to skip the medical exam. Utter disregard for the policies she worked to upkeep!

She couldn't barge into the captain's cabin and give him a piece of her mind. She couldn't shake Jamie like she wanted to because he was her patient. Her stomach hardened as she thought about his injury. In the sickbay, she had treated men with much worse head wounds, even done successful trepanning. But Jamie's relatively minor hurt made her blood boil. And there was one man who could receive her wrath.

The cockpit, despite its position below the water line, was a privileged place to sleep. The air was heavy, and rats scurried from footsteps, but the midshipmen and volunteers assigned there were away from the bodies and voices of hundreds of men sleeping in the forecastle. Since Conor Leach shared the sleeping space with Jamie, Ella thought to make a couple things clear to the new volunteer. She well remembered his disdain at the medical exam. He kept his mouth shut, but his expression made it clear that he doubted her qualifications as a surgeon.

Ella took in Conor's relaxed shape as he slumbered in the hammock. The second hammock was folded neatly on the deck. Jamie likely didn't know how to swing it. And Conor didn't help him.

With her teeth clenched, she shined the lantern on Conor's face. When the young man's eyelids fluttered, she put her hand on her hip. "Jamie Flowers is in the sickbay. He hit his head and lost consciousness."

Conor snorted.

Ella's hand itched to slap him on his sneering lips. "Don't you want to ask if he'll be all right?"

"He's a clumsy good-for-naught. Why did you wake me?"

"You knew he was seasick. Why did you make him go up alone?"

"What do I care if he fell?"

Ella gave his hammock a vigorous shake. "It's only him and you who sleep in this cockpit. Yes, he's inept, but he's here. Can't you be his friend? You are new here as well."

Conor rubbed his forehead with his fist. "I don't need a friend. Least of all a pathetic ninny like him."

"Don't call him that!" Ella stomped her foot. "You would be lucky to have a friend in him. He's thoughtful and kind."

Conor cracked a laugh and sat up. "You fancy him, lass. It must be bad if you had to wake me at night. Do you want me to relieve your thirst since Jamie is too sick to do it?"

Ella glared at him. "I'm Dr. Parker to you. None of this is a laughing matter. Have you ever been ill or injured, and no one cared for you?"

The grin disappeared from his lips. He winced and blinked rapidly.

"Caring for each other's hurts is what makes us human. When an animal breaks its paw in the wild, it dies. Other animals do not bring it food or protect it from predators until it heals. But people do. It's basic human decency to care for your fellow shipmate."

Exhaling with a hiss, he averted his gaze. "What do you want from me? I need my sleep. And if you are so worried about Jamie, should you not be with him, caring for his scratches?"

Ella grabbed the lantern and turned. Anger burned through her blood. "You will be kind to Jamie. At least help him hang his hammock. I doubt he knows how."

As she stormed out, a whisper reached her. "I don't know how to."

How to be kind or how to hang a hammock? she wondered.

***

When Jamie opened his eyes, a young man carried in a tray. He was spectacled and wore a serious expression.

"Oh good, you are awake. Dr. Parker said to feed you breakfast. I'm Tyler Monk, her assistant."

The smell of porridge made Jamie's stomach queasy. "Thank you, but I don't think I can eat."

"Try. You need food to get better."

Seeing that Tyler dipped the spoon into the thin porridge to feed him like a child, Jamie pushed himself into a sitting position. Pain squeezed his temples, but he was able to stay upright. He reached for the tray.

Tyler raised an eyebrow and positioned the tray on Jamie's lap. "Dr. Parker added some ginger in the tea to help with nausea."

Jamie sipped, letting the sharp flavor keep the sickness at bay. "Where's she now?"

"She has various responsibilities." Tyler shrugged. "Could be teaching the ship boys, could be checking on the food and water supplies, could be reading medical journals in her cabin. She said she'll likely be busy all day. I'm to keep an eye on you and call her if another patient comes in."

The watery porridge tasted bland, but to Jamie's relief the nausea eased. After several spoonfuls, he slid back on the pillow. "I think I'm feeling better. Thank you."

Tyler touched the bump on Jamie's head. "I'll tell Dr. Parker you are progressing. She'll want to examine you."

And that's when she'll learn about my heart. The queasiness returned.

***

"For never was a story of more woe than this of Juliet and her Romeo." After a dramatic pause, Ella raised her eyes from the book. Tobby clapped his hands vigorously. The other ship boys were shifting in their seats and yawning. The afternoon sun warmed the deck and made everyone sleepy. Or Shakespeare's tragedy failed to impress them.

"Can we go now?" Digby asked. At sixteen, he was the oldest in her class. "We have work to do."

"Don't you feel like discussing the play?"

Digby rose. "It's a stupid play. They all acted like fools, especially Romeo. Why did we have to listen to it?"

Ella closed the book with a thud. "Don't you think there's a lesson in it?"

The tall boy rolled his eyes. "If love makes you want to gulp poison than it's stupid."

"I would prefer a different tone, but I agree with you."

Digby frowned and scratched his cheek. "You do?"

"Yes. The play demonstrates that love leads to reckless decisions and brings terrible woes." Her friend Marietta would disagree and say that love was worth the risks and obstacles. But since the body count in this play was as high as after a ship battle, Ella was sure she was right. If Juliet never fell in love with Romeo, both would be alive and well.

I will never let myself fall in love again. I have my work, my crew, and my friends. I don't need love to make me happy.

Jamie's blanched face came to her mind. A trickle of blood from his head affected her worse than the gruesome wounds she tended to after battles.

At the bell's chime, the boys scattered away to perform their various jobs. Only Tobby remained.

"I liked the play, Dr. Ella." Tobby's eyes glistened. "I like how you read it."

"Thank you, Tobby. I'm glad you enjoyed it." She smiled at the twelve-year-old who seemed just a little taller and older every time she saw him. "I hope someday you'll see it performed on stage."

"Have you seen it? What's it like?"

"Oh, it was grand. All the characters had beautiful costumes. Juliet stood on a balcony built just for her. She was marvelous."

"And Romeo?"

Ella cringed. "He was puffed up and conceited. Also botched his lines. I swear I would've been better."

Tobby's eyes widened. "You are an actress?"

"Not a professional one." Ella grinned. "But I staged plays with my mother. And once on a holiday at the seaside. I thought it would be fun to play a boy's role. And Jamie didn't mind, since he didn't like learning his lines." She said this more to herself, reliving the memory of rehearsing the play with Jamie and his sisters.

Tobby grinned. "Are you speaking of Jamie Flowers, who's here on the ship?"

"You know him?"

"Yes. I let him bring your medical bag, remember? He said he's your friend."

"He is. Like I said, we were once in a play together. When we were children."

"Then how is he here?" Tobby bent his head.

She was about to tell Tobby that it was a wild coincidence that Jamie was recruited for the *Neptune,* and then the captain hired him as his servant. But as she formed the words in her mouth, they refused to spill. The story felt... like it was missing a piece.

Why would the recruiters want him if he had no naval experience? Why did Captain Grey hire him as a servant?

"Tell me again how you met Jamie."

Tobby shifted on his knees. "I came to the Cooked Goose and asked Miss Jenny about your medical bag. Jamie was there, eating a large plate of meat and drinking a beer. He called me over."

Ella raised an eyebrow. "Why?"

"We made a deal that he would bring you the bag, and I would finish his dinner. He even gave me a coin to order more. We shook hands as friends and future shipmates."

"Awfully good deal for you, Tobby." Ella pursed her lips in thought. "What was in it for him?"

Tobby scratched his cheek. "He wanted to see you."

Her nose wrinkled as if she could smell deception. "So much that he fed you and fetched the bag for me. Why would he do that?"

Tobby's eyes grew wide. "Love. Like in *Romeo and Juliet*."

"Oh no." Ella sprang to her feet. "I barely gave him a thought in six years."

"He might've still thought of you. And one day... he decided to find you."

Even though she was long used to the ship motions, suddenly the swaying made Ella dizzy. She grabbed the mast. "No. I swore off love. Robert Weston's rejection was an inoculation everyone should receive."

"What's inculeshin? Did I get one?" Tobby's brow knitted.

A giggle tickled Ella's throat. "You did for smallpox. But there should be one against love, so people don't act foolishly and always use their best judgement. If Juliet had such an inoculation, she'd never fall in love with a man forbidden to her, never drink the potion, and never stab herself."

"But what if Romeo still loved her? What would he do?"

He'd leave his family, enlist on a warship as a captain's servant, and hit his head badly. How did I not see it immediately? I likely encouraged him.

Heat rose to her cheeks. "Tobby, the play is not real life." When the boy frowned, she patted his back. "You'll understand someday. Now run along."

The boy didn't run along. He limped, worse than before. Watching him hobble, Ella wondered if he hid his pain from her.

We all hide our pain, even from the people we love. Why do we do that?

***

After finishing his dinner, Jamie laid back on the cot. His head throbbed but less so than before. Tyler told him that by evening he may be well enough to leave the sickbay. That would be Ella's decision, but Jamie hadn't seen her all day.

She must be angry at my deception and keeping her distance.

His eyelids were drooping, when someone's loud footsteps pounded through the berth.

"What do you need, Tobby?" Tyler asked. "Belly hurting again?"

"I've been well for two years now, Mr. Monk, and you still remember. Can I see Mr. Flowers?"

"Why? Does the captain want him?"

"No. I thought I could visit him. As a friend."

Not hearing Tyler's answer, Jamie rose on his elbows. "Good day, Tobby. It's awfully kind of you to visit."

Tyler brought a chair and placed it by the cot. "Don't chat too long. Mr. Flowers is supposed to be resting."

When Tyler walked away, Tobby hobbled over and plopped on the chair. He glanced around and grimaced. "I used to come here often. My belly would hurt. The old doctor gave me enemas, but they didn't help. Then Dr. Ella made me a remedy to drink. It tasted awful, but soon my belly stopped hurting. The doctor told me I had worms living inside my guts." The boy rubbed his abdomen and winced.

Jamie wanted to cringe but kept his face even. The complaints his father listened to often sounded repulsive, but his father always kept his expression kindly and listened with attention.

"I'm glad you are better now. What about your leg? Does it hurt?"

"A bit." Tobby sighed. "I was wounded with shrapnel. Dr. Ella worked hard to make it better, but it never fully healed. I don't complain about it anymore. Dr. Ella will feel bad that she can't fix it. Better to say nothing, right?"

How I understand you, friend, Jamie thought.

"Have you seen Dr. Ella today?" he asked the boy.

"Yes. She read *Romeo and Juliet* to the ship boys. Then she and I talked, and she became vexed. It was about you."

Jamie swallowed. "What did she say?"

Tobby frowned and stared up, as if trying to remember. "She mentioned Robert Weston, who used to be her betrothed."

"I didn't know…" Jamie blinked. "But she's not betrothed anymore?"

"Right. I remember the men talking about that and Ella crying. The old doctor died about that time, so she was all sad. She even left the ship for a while, and I went to find her."

Jamie smiled. "You sound like a great friend. What else did Dr. Ella say?"

"She said this word… inculeshin? It has something to do with smallpox."

Jamie's brow pinched. "Inoculation? But why?"

"She said she had that against love. And everyone should." Tobby rubbed his forehead. "Does that make sense?"

Jamie's belly knotted. *If it existed, I'd give it to my parents and sisters, so they don't grieve for me. Without one available, I did the second-best thing.*

Tobby's eyes narrowed. "Do you love Dr. Ella?"

Taken aback by such a direct question, Jamie blinked. "Um... Well..."

"It's an easy question." Tobby gave him an accusing stare. "I know I love her. How could I not? She cared for me when I was sick. She reads me her books. I love her very much. And since I have no family, she is my only love."

Jamie's heart melted. Once again, he was reminded how fortunate he was to grow up in a loving home. He patted Tobby's shoulder.

"You are right. I do love Miss Ella because she's the most extraordinary woman I've met. And though I have a relatively large family, you can be my little brother."

Tobby touched his chest. "That felt good right here. Like honeyed tea that warms you inside. Why does Dr. Ella not like that?"

"Because it does not always feel so good." Ella walked in with heaviness in her step. "Realizing that you've been fooled, or taken advantage of, or betrayed, makes one see love in a different light." She stared at the boy and exhaled. "That doesn't concern you, Tobby. I know you are a loyal friend. If only people would stay kind and true like you."

Tobby beamed. "I'm not the only one. Mr. Flowers is kind and true. He said he loves you."

Heat rose to Jamie's cheeks, while Ella's turned scarlet. She crossed her arms and averted her eyes. "He cannot love me. He doesn't know me. Six years ago, he met a girl who enjoyed pretending to be someone else. That girl lied often and thought only of herself. Luckily, she grew up and learned to care for others and to speak the truth, but that took some harsh lessons. And one of them was to swear off romance and focus on her calling." She pushed her shoulders back. "And that reminds me. It's time to examine my patient. Tobby, please give us some privacy."

"Aye, aye, Dr. Ella." Tobby jumped off his chair and nodded to Jamie. "Feel better, brother." He hobbled away.

Ella raised an eyebrow at Jamie. "Brother?"

"He has no family. I thought it would make him feel better if I called him that." His lips seemed to dry from her stare.

"I'm sure you meant well. Tobby is a sweet boy and loves people who are kind to him." She sighed and then peered at him. "But I doubt this ship life is for you. Whether you seek adventure, or love, or both, this fantasy won't last. The hard toil will drive it out of you, if you are lucky enough to survive. And meanwhile, Tobby will get used to thinking that he has a brother. What will you tell him when you decide to leave?"

Jamie winced as his head ached again. *I hadn't thought of that. The lonely boy would get attached. And then grieve for my death.*

Ella's expression grew more frustrated. She turned to Tyler who was sitting on an empty cot and reading a heavy book. "Tyler, are you studying?"

Tyler raised his head. "Yes, reading about head injuries."

"Perfect. Please give our patient a full exam and tell me if he can be discharged." She stepped away to let Tyler sit by Jamie's side.

In his childhood, Jamie had more medical exams than he could count. Tyler was as thorough as any physician he encountered and gentler than most. He assessed the swelling and poked in other places on his head. He checked his eyes by holding up his fingers and asking Jamie how many he saw. He had him open his mouth and peeked down the throat. Finally, he counted Jamie's pulse on the wrist.

After all that, Tyler turned to Ella. "I believe he's well enough to be discharged."

"You didn't check his heart and lungs."

"Oh right, sorry."

Jamie held his breath. Every muscle in his body tightened as Tyler put his ear onto his chest. *Now he would hear the defect and tell Ella.*

"Sounds fine to me." Tyler straightened. "I say he recovered enough from his injury to return to his duties."

Jamie exhaled with relief. *He must be unfamiliar with heart murmurs.*

"Very good." Ella's voice sounded bright. "Mr. Flowers, you are discharged. I'm sure the captain will be glad to have his servant back. Please try not to hurt yourself again."

"Don't you want to examine him?" Tyler asked. "In case I missed something?"

Jamie, who was rising from the cot, froze.

"No." Ella's curls shook. "I've trained you well and trust your judgement. Now, I need a hand in organizing the dispensary."

As they turned to open the drawers, Jamie took the hint. He pushed his way through the crowded deck and descended the dark stairs, his breaths growing heavy. The sickbay was a holiday compared to sharing the cockpit with Conor. He braced for the young man's unpleasantness. Surely Conor would taunt him about hitting his head.

To his relief, the cockpit was empty. He glanced about the small space and stepped back in surprise. There were two hammocks strung between the beams. His pillow and blanket lay neatly on one of them. Perhaps there was more to Conor than his demeanor revealed.

Chapter 11

"Your sobbing woke me up again, you ninny. All week I hear your snivels."

Conor's voice cut through Jamie's dream, and he blinked his eyes open. Salty tears burned his mouth and throat.

Not again.

The ring of the bell and the sway of the ship brought him back to his hammock in the orlop. It's been a week since they left Plymouth. An extraordinarily long week, full of reprimands from the captain, laughs from his shipmates, and taunts from Conor. Whenever he spotted Ella on deck, she turned her back and walked away, except one time when she asked if his head had healed. At least his sea sickness was gone.

"What are you crying about, sissy? Your head hurts?"

"No, it's healed, thanks for asking. Just a dream."

"A nightmare?" Conor sat up on his hammock and lit a lantern on the small table. In the dim light Jamie could see Conor's sneer. "Since you woke me up with your whimpers, you could as well tell me. What scares you, Flowers?"

Jamie rubbed his forehead. "Snakes." He stopped, seeing Conor's widening grin. "Why is that funny? One time, when I went swimming, a boy I considered my friend hid an adder in my clothes. I was lucky I wasn't bitten. Ever since, I'm horribly afraid of snakes."

"Were you dreaming about them? Their cold scales slithering up your legs." Conor hooted at Jamie's cringe.

"No. At least not tonight. I was dreaming about my mother and sisters. Home."

Conor's lips twisted like he bit into something bitter. "Why did that make you cry?"

"I miss them. We were close. Don't you have anyone you miss?"

"No." Conor's voice rose. "No one."

"Not your father, the valiant captain?"

Conor's nostrils flared. "Especially not him."

"I simply asked..."

"Don't ask." Conor bent over his chest to find his clothing.

Jamie was surprised to see him get dressed at this hour. Only two bells rang minutes ago.

Conor threw on his uniform coat. "I don't need anyone. And while you cried into your pillow last evening, I won a purse full of coins in cards."

"Congratulations." Jamie shrugged.

The young officer turned and narrowed his eyes. "Do you play cards?"

"With my sisters." Jamie cracked a smile remembering the long winter evenings when they played by the fireplace. "There was a game we played. I can show you if you like. It's an enjoyable way to pass the time."

A loud groan escaped Conor's throat. "I mean for money. You have plenty of it, don't you? I can tell by the way you dress."

"I don't gamble. Father warned me against it. Said that luck is fickle and can change at any moment. But as a game between friends..."

Conor groaned. "I'm not your friend."

"You hung the hammock for me while I was at the sickbay."

"Don't make me regret it." Conor sat down at the desk. "I have better things to do with my time. I must prepare my navigation notes for a lesson with Mr. Wyse."

"That must be interesting." Jamie gave a pensive smile. "I always wanted to learn navigation. Could you show me what you are studying?"

"Don't you need to be in the galley, making breakfast for the captain? Or cleaning his uniform?"

Jamie checked his pocket watch. "Blast it! I didn't realize it's after five already."

"Didn't you hear the bell? It rang twice."

"I thought that meant two in the morning." He climbed down from his hammock.

Conor shook his head. "I'm shocked there was anything in your head to break, Flowers. You still don't know what the bells mean."

Jamie bit his lip and hurried to dress. Minutes later he was at the galley, preparing a breakfast of bread and jam for the captain under the disapproving gaze of Mr. Black.

The jar slipped out of Jamie's hands. Upon hitting the deck, it exploded like a grenade. Glass and raspberry jam spilled all around the galley.

"Blast it."

"Captain Grey's favorite jam." Mr. Black crossed his arms. "You should be flogged. In all the years I've served the captain, I've never broke a thing of his."

"I... I will clean it up." Jamie grabbed a mop and a bucket.

"Have you ever held a mop, lad?" Mr. Black bared his teeth as he watched Jamie wrestle with the spill. "Can't see why the captain brought a good-for-nothing landlubber as a servant. I made his meals for years without a folly like that."

As he mopped, Jamie remembered their housekeeper, Mrs. Armstrong, cleaning the floors. He never appreciated her more.

When he finished, Jamie searched through the shelves. "Is there more jam?"

Mr. Black shrugged. "Don't know. Not my business anymore."

Since he couldn't find more jam, Jamie hastened to the cockpit. Thankfully, Conor was gone. At the bottom of his sea chest, Jamie found a jar of currant jam, carefully wrapped in paper by Caroline. Another small jar was next to it, with a label in Caroline's careful handwriting. Cinnamon. He opened the jar and brought it to his nose. It smelled of home.

No. This is my new home. I will make the best of it. He carried the jars to the galley. Mr. Black was gone. Without his chiding, Jamie composed himself and made the captain's breakfast without more mishaps.

When Captain Grey inspected the tray Jamie brought to his cabin, his lips curled.

"What spell turned my raspberry jam into currant, Mr. Flowers?"

"I'm sorry, sir. I broke the jar." Jamie hung his head. "I couldn't find more, so I used the jam my sister Caroline packed for me."

"Hmm..." As the captain sampled the jam, Jamie sucked in his breath.

The captain chewed slowly. "Not bad. Please be more careful next time."

Jamie exhaled. "Yes, sir. I mean aye, aye, sir."

The captain sipped from the steaming cup. "What is that in my coffee?"

"I mixed cinnamon into it. Caroline always made it for me like that." Jamie's neck tightened.

"Hmm... Good. Can I hire your sister for the next voyage?" Captain's lips cracked a smile.

"She'd likely do better than me." Jamie's arms hung at his sides. "I realize I don't have useful skills. I spent my boyhood reading and being idle."

Captain Grey cocked his head. "How fortunate for you. Most of us didn't have it so easy. I was twelve when I went to sea."

"I know I had a privileged life." Jamie bit his lip. "But now I regret that I am so incompetent and clumsy."

"Well, Mr. Flowers..." The captain's sea green eyes were fixed on Jamie's face. "You can change that. A ship is a great place to learn skills and grow as a man. Or as a woman, I should say. Do you know why I hired Miss Parker?"

"Because she's a great surgeon. She's strong, valiant, and caring for others. And seems to be well-adapted to ship life."

"When I first met her, she was hardly any of those things. She was inexperienced as a surgeon. The men didn't trust or like her. And she certainly wasn't adapted to ship life." He chuckled with an expression of a father laughing at his child's innocent mishap. "Despite all that, I gave her an opportunity, and she exceeded all my expectations. You have the same chance to improve and grow. Since I don't demand much of you, there should be hours in your day to learn new skills."

Jamie's insides knotted. He knew he was inept and unaccustomed to hard labor.

I wanted to make friends and do something good with my life. I must make the best of the opportunity Captain Grey gave me. And I pray that my heart won't fail at the worst moment.

He came out to the deck and surveyed the jobs seamen were performing. There were topmen high up on the mast, raising sails. While he wished to admire the view from such height, he was not going to attempt climbing up there just yet. First Lieutenant Wyse's thundering voice drilled men through exercises with the guns. His curses made Jamie blush, and he decided to stay away for now.

A group of men were swabbing the deck. That seemed like a proper job with which to start. Jamie approached them slowly, thinking how he might convince them to join in their work.

"What do you want, captain's pet?" one of the sailors said. He had an earring on one ear and tattoos running down his muscular arms.

Jamie fingered the buttons of his coat. His hands sweated. "I want to be of service. It would be my honor to learn from you. Please give me a chance to share in your labor."

A boom of laughter made him step back. He squirmed as his ears and neck became impossibly hot. Forcing down an urge to flee, he planted his feet in a wide stance. "You may think I'm not good at anything. And you are right. But a man cannot learn if he doesn't try."

The sailor who called him "captain's pet" tilted his head. "You are good at talking. Sound like some sea lawyer with fancy words and all. But if you want to work, stop gabbing and swab." He tossed Jamie a mop.

***

After a long day helping with various jobs as well as running errands for the captain, Jamie's muscles cramped. His last job was standing watch till midnight. When eight bells clanged, signaling the time to get below to sleep, he realized that he snoozed while leaning on the foremast. He wondered if Conor was already sleeping or playing cards again.

When he entered the cockpit, carrying a lantern, the foul odor of spirits, half-digested food and stomach acid made him gag. He almost slipped in the dark and grabbed the bulkhead for support. He shined the lantern toward Conor, who lay on his hammock still in his boots, snoring. His face and blanket were soiled with vomit.

Serves you right, Jamie thought, recalling the way Conor laughed at his seasickness and made him go to the deck. *Except, he's too drunk to clean his mess.* He tried to shake Conor awake, but the fellow's eyes stayed shut.

For the tenth time that day, Jamie picked up the mop. After the day of work, his hands were covered with blisters that ached as he gripped the wooden handle. His muscles screamed with pain.

A cough made Jamie pause his work and glance at Conor. The young man's breathing had a high-pitched grating sound. Jamie approached him, wondering if he should help him sit up or lay on his side. Before Jamie could move him, vomit poured from Conor's mouth. Jamie jumped back to avoid being sprayed. After an abundant retch, Conor coughed. The flow from his mouth stopped.

Let's hope that's over, Jamie thought. *There can't be much more left in him.*

Conor's breaths struggled, and a rattling sound came from his throat.

Oh God, he's choking. Jamie's heart skipped a beat. The sinking feeling inside his chest angered him. *You were fine all through the grueling day of work, and you are fluttering now?* he demanded of his racing heart. Yet his mind raced even faster.

With a struggle, he turned Conor to his side and hit him on the back. The stridor in Conor's windpipe became louder. Cringing from disgust, Jamie thrust his hand into Conor's mouth to the back of his throat. His fingers found something lodged in there. Hitting Conor on his back with the other hand, he pulled out a chunk of vomit. Conor breathed, and Jamie found himself gasping for air.

Jamie waited for Conor to wake, but the young man snored, oblivious to danger he slept through. Exhausted by the long day, Jamie washed his hands and face, snuffled out the lantern and threw himself on the hammock.

Hours later, he woke up to Conor's gasp. "My head... Bloody hell... What happened?"

Jamie soaked a cloth and offered it to Conor to wash himself from the vomit and sweat. After Conor cleaned his face, Jamie gave him his flask. "Drink. This is water."

Conor sat up to drink. When Jamie relighted the lantern, he saw that the fellow's face was ghostly white. He spread a blanket over Conor's shoulders. "How poorly are you feeling? Should I fetch Dr. Parker?"

"I don't need her to see this." Conor winced and shook his head.

Jamie picked up the mop to finish cleaning the mess. "How did you get that sodded?"

"I... what was I doing?" Conor rubbed his forehead with a fist. "I played cards with a few fellows. Oh..."

He reached for the money purse attached to his belt. When he peered inside, he gasped. "You didn't take anything?"

Jamie scoffed. "What kind of a question is that?"

"How did I lose this much? ...Oh, right. My last wager." He dropped his head into his hands. "What was I thinking?"

"You weren't thinking. You were drinking. So much that you were sick all over yourself and this place."

Conor blinked a few times. "You cleaned up after me?"

Jamie shrugged and put down the mop. "Not something I want to do again. More than that, I pulled out a piece of vomit you were choking on."

Conor shivered and pulled the blanket tighter around his shoulders.

"I don't know what to say."

"'Thank you' is a good start." Jamie straightened his sore back. "An apology would also do."

Conor lowered his head and stayed silent. When Jamie turned away and shook his head in disappointment, Conor gripped the hammock and stood. Drops shimmered on his cheek and ran down.

Tears? No, it must be sweat. He laughed at me for crying in my sleep.

"Jamie, I truly am sorry." His voice was hoarse and barely louder than a whisper. "I thought the best way to start here was to show strength. Instead, I've made a fool of myself. Hardly anyone would help me after the way I've treated you."

Jamie's upper body relaxed as he drew closer to Conor. "You couldn't breathe. Anyone in my place would…"

Conor shook his head vigorously, then cringed and rubbed his temples. "Not anyone. The people I knew wouldn't care."

"I hope I never meet such people. You are not like them. I know this because you slung the hammock for me." Jamie thrusted his hand to Conor. "I accept your apology."

Conor smiled. Not a smirk—a genuine smile. He shook Jamie's hand. "Thank you."

Jamie did his best not to cringe from Conor's reek, but Conor must've noticed his wrinkled nose.

"Let me wash some more and change into fresh clothes."

As Conor rummaged through his sea chest, two bells rang at that moment.

Jamie hastily dressed, as it was time to make breakfast for the captain.

Conor, wearing a fresh shirt and breeches, rubbed his head as he sat at the desk. "I must finish my navigation homework. Except it's hard to think when a drum is pounding inside my head."

Jamie placed a flask on the desk. "Drink more water. I'll bring you coffee when I get a chance."

He hurried up the stairs to the galley. After breakfast was served, the cabin tidied, and the captain's uniform cleaned, Jamie returned to the cockpit with a cup of coffee for Conor.

He found his new friend with navigation books spread over the desk. Despite the headache Conor complained about, he was writing vigorously in his journal.

"Thank you. Have you read any of these books?" Conor asked as he accepted the coffee.

"I glanced through them when I thought I would be a volunteer." Jamie shifted his feet. "I didn't understand much. Especially the mathematics."

"Do you want to study with me?"

Jamie grinned. "I would love to."

"Good." Conor handed one of the books to Jamie. "Start with Robertson's *Elements of Navigation*. And read it carefully. When I become the captain, I'll make you my lieutenant." He winked at Jamie.

"Aye, aye, sir." Chuckling, he brought his fist to his forehead.

I don't have enough time for a career of any kind. But if I could, I'd choose a naval career.

"I'm serious. You can do better than being a servant. Captain Grey said he'll give me an opportunity to prove myself. A mission of some sort. If I can, I will take you with me."

Excitement and premonition tingled through Jamie's nerves.

This was my plan. To do something dangerous and heroic. To save lives... while paying with my own.

"You have a deal," he replied to Conor.

Chapter 12

"I can't take any more mathematics." Jamie threw the navigation book onto his hammock. "My eyes and head hurt."

Conor stood and stretched. "You are right. We've studied enough. Let's nap before the watch. Or do you need to attend to the captain?"

"No, when I told him we are studying trigonometry together, he seemed pleased and said he won't need me for the rest of the evening. But I have something else in mind. I want to practice climbing aloft and watch the sunset from the fighting top."

Conor sighed. "Fine, I'm coming, too. Can't let you fall and smash your head."

"A month ago, you didn't care."

"I guess I got used to you." Conor rolled his eyes. "Even when your sniffles wake me at night."

Jamie bit his lip. "I can't help what I'm doing in my sleep." He kept dreaming about his parents and sisters mourning him.

"I'm not going to tease you about that. But if you get scared as you climb, I *will* laugh at you."

When they ascended to the deck, the gentle breeze swept through their clothes. The sun only started to set over the horizon, reflecting in the bubbling waves. Rose clouds made the seascape perfect for an artist's brush.

Smitten by the view, Jamie walked towards the mizzenmast. His eyes studied the ratlines, the thicker shrouds he could hold onto as he climbed, and the platform above him.

This should be easy.

As he ascended, he found himself smiling. His hands, covered in calluses from arduous work, gripped the shrouds with confidence. The deck was smaller and smaller below him. Conor was below him as well, climbing at a slow pace.

He must've done it before. Why is he so slow?

"Are *you* afraid of heights, Conor?"

If Conor replied, his voice was lost in the gust of wind. The world careened to the left. Jamie grabbed on to the shrouds with all his might. When the ship righted itself, Jamie's eyes went to Conor to ensure he was still below him. Conor was there, his arms and legs gripping the ratlines like a giant spider.

Jamie's heart sped up, constricting his breath. His shirt stuck to his sweaty back.

What was I thinking, climbing to such a height? My heart can give up. And falling off the mast is not exactly a heroic death.

With his teeth clenched, he kept climbing. The lubber's hole loomed above him. About to climb through it, he hesitated, wondering if Conor would mock him for using it. It was called a lubber's hole for a reason.

He called out to Conor. "How do I get up there without the lubber's hole?"

Again, Conor didn't answer.

Jamie sighed to slow his pulse and think. The only way he could see was to use the shrouds below and then above the platform. He sucked in his breath and maneuvered himself onto the shrouds, hanging backwards, a good hundred feet above the deck. When he planted his feet on the platform and waited for his heart to slow, Conor squeezed himself through the hole.

He was about to comment on Conor's method of ascending to the fighting top when a voice startled him. "This is my place at sunset. No one else allowed."

Glad that his hands still gripped the shrouds, preventing him from falling from surprise, he turned to Ella. She was seated with her back leaning on the mast, a book in her lap. Once again, she was wearing trousers. With her hair wild in the wind, she reminded him of female pirates Caroline told him about. He greeted her, but she groaned and kept her eyes on the book.

After a few protracted moments of reading, she closed her book with a thud.

"Gentlemen, you are imposing on my reading time."

Even though Ella furrowed her brow, Jamie couldn't stop grinning at her.

She shook her head and glanced from him to Conor. "I hear you two are inseparable these days."

"We are." Jamie's voice rose with excitement. He was so relieved to have made it to the top. Finding Ella there made the triumph even sweeter. "Conor can be a nice company and a good teacher of navigation matters." He winked at his friend.

Conor did not smile or wink. His posture was rigid and his face white.

Ella inclined her head. "Since you are here, admire the sunset with me."

The scarlet sky reflected in the sea like strokes of paint. Waves gently lapped against the ship's hull, twinkling like diamonds scattered across the water. The view left Jamie breathless.

"Sunsets remind me of my dear friend and mentor, Dr. Pesce." Ella said. "He loved to watch them. His body is somewhere at the bottom of the sea, but I feel his spirit when I gaze at the waves and the clouds."

If all goes to my plan, I will be buried at sea as well. Perhaps Ella and Conor might climb here to remember me.

His eyes brimmed with tears, and he held his breath to prevent them from falling. He felt Conor's eyes on him, but this time Conor hung his head and said nothing.

Ella stood. With one hand on the shrouds, she approached him and touched his elbow. "Oh, Jamie. You have a compassionate heart."

With her hair tickling his neck, he held back his arms from wrapping them around her. But he sensed such a tender gesture, especially in front of Conor, would upset her.

"Doctor Ella, are you up there?" Someone's tense voice came from below. "Mr. Olson injured his arm."

Ella's shoulders jumped. "I'll be right down."

She turned on her heels, and with the gracefulness of a lynx, leaped onto the shroud. Jamie watched with his jaw hanging how the young woman slid her slender body down to the deck.

"Can you do that?" Jamie glanced at Conor.

"I am... a bit out of practice." Conor scratched his neck. "Better we descend like we got up here. And don't you want to stay here some more?"

"I want to slide down like she did," Jamie said, slightly lightheaded from watching Ella's stunt. His pulse was rising, but instead of concern, he craved to throw caution into the wind and glide down that rope. Caroline said that everyone dies, but not everyone gets to live. When the rope ripped the callouses on his hand to blood, and the deck flew to meet him, he knew that at least that day, he lived.

***

Mr. Black chewed the piece of sailor duff Jamie cut off for him from the corner and licked his fingers.

"That tastes like... something fine enough to serve to the captain and his officers."

Jamie grinned. He's been trying to get the dessert right for a couple of days. It was a simple recipe of flour, molasses, sugar, and boiled water, but finally the texture was moist and appetizing. The captain usually dined alone, but today he asked to prepare dinner and then coffee for four.

"I'll serve it to them with their coffee. Thank you, Mr. Black, for instructing me."

"Never mind, lad. I hear you are trying hard to learn various jobs. We'll make a seaman out of you after all." Mr. Black gave him a pat on the back.

The first friendly gesture from the old steward warmed Jamie's weary body. He stretched his arms and shoulders, sore after working the pump. A month ago, he lasted fifteen minutes at the job, but today he labored a full shift, same as others. And what was even more odd, his heart didn't bother him for days.

He beamed at Mr. Black. "I want to be useful."

"Then you better bring the officers their coffee." Mr. Black's tone made it clear that neither of them had time to chat.

Jamie chose a white china platter from the captain's set for the duff, poured the cups of strong coffee, and carried the tray to the wardroom.

When he entered, Captain Grey, Lieutenant Wyse, Conor, and Ella were finishing their dinner. The men were done eating and speaking of battle tactics. Ella's plate was still half-full as she cut her mutton into tiny pieces. Dressed in male clothes again, she was wearing an elegant onyx coat. Her eyes were half-closed, as if from weariness or boredom, but her face brightened as she noticed the duff.

"That looks scrumptious. Did you make it, Ja... Mr. Flowers?"

"Yes, I did. I hope it pleases you."

Jamie served the captain first, and then Mr. Wyse. Neither sampled the dessert, still consumed by the conversation. He gave a decent portion to Conor, who stuffed his mouth and kept on talking. Then he beamed at Ella as he offered her a piece.

"Please tell me if it's adequate, Miss Parker."

She raised her eyebrow. "Why should I be the judge?"

"Everyone else seems too occupied with their conversation to notice my effort."

"All right." She lifted her fork to her mouth and chewed slowly, with her coral lips sealed. Just as she opened her mouth to give the verdict, a knock on the door made everyone silent.

"Captain Grey, sir!" came the voice. "We spotted a ship at three points of the larboard. A French corvette by the looks of it."

The men jumped to their feet. Ella pushed her plate away and groaned.

"Take Mr. Leach with you to command the guns." Captain Grey said to Lieutenant Wyse. Then his gaze shifted to Jamie. "Mr. Flowers, help me with my uniform. Then... find something useful to do."

Jamie's pulsing nerves chased away weariness. He'd describe this sensation as elating, but his heart thumped, and he resisted pressing his hand to his chest.

"He could help me in the orlop with the wounded," Ella said. Forced casualness seeped through her voice.

"Flowers is not a coward to hide from the battle." Conor's eyes shone as he turned to Captain Grey. "Could he join me, sir?"

The captain gave an impatient wave. "Yes, that would be fine. Now, everyone to their stations."

Jamie's hands sweated as he assisted the captain with his uniform. As he tied the captain's sword to the belt, he fumbled. "I'm sorry, sir. There."

Captain Grey glanced down at his clothes and fixed his triangular hat. "Are you nervous, Mr. Flowers?"

Jamie rocked in place. He was unsure of the captain's response if he admitted his anxiety, but he preferred not to lie. Besides, he suspected the captain noticed his shaking hands.

"Yes, sir. I guess I cannot help it. But I want to fight."

The captain cracked a smile. "Everyone is nervous before their first battle. You'll do fine. Just don't stand behind the gun when it's about to fire or it will roll back and crush you."

Jamie knew that. He had participated in gun exercises with the men.

There seemed to be myriad ways to die on this ship. Yet there were days like when he went aloft for the first time. The days that were worth more than an uneventful year.

"Sir! The ship has shown its colors. It's French!" Conor's voice rang from the door.

"Run out the guns!" Captain Grey commanded. The captain grabbed his telescope from the desk and hastened to the door. Jamie sped after him. When he ran out of the cabin, Conor grabbed his arm and led him to the gun deck.

***

Ella could gauge the intensifying battle by the steady stream of injured men being brought to her. The latest group were wounded by debris as cannons hit the railings and masts. When she finished suturing and bandaging one wound, there would be another to attend to. She hated to admit to it, but she was glad to be busy. During lulls, her mind would show Jamie getting maimed in various ways.

Confound that man, Conor Leach! Had to take Jamie with him to the gun deck. Jamie could've been safe here. Well, relatively safe.

Her chest tightened when Tyler and Sully carried in a new patient on the stretcher. The face was covered with blood. But the straw blond hair... *Jamie!* As her assistants transferred him onto the operating table, she grabbed a cloth to wipe off the blood and see where it was coming from. When she found the cut on the forehead, she pressed to stop the hemorrhage.

"Jamie, you will be all right," she whispered. Tyler, who was threading a needle, furrowed his brow.

When the bleeding ebbed, she cleaned the patient's face. Her lungs deflated with a hiss. Not Jamie. Besides the similar shade of hair, there was little resemblance. The man's arms and shoulders were wider than Jamie's. His clothing was a simple shirt and breeches, discolored and patched. She couldn't believe her mind played such a trick on her.

I cannot let myself get distracted. My work is too important.

Tyler brought the lantern closer. "Would you let me suture?"

Does he think me incapable because of a slip of my tongue? Two years of proving my skill to these men, and now they doubt me.

She straightened her spine. "I am perfectly able to care for this patient."

Tyler blinked. "I know you are able. I just wanted to try."

Heat rushed to Ella's face. She gasped the heavy air permeated with the metallic scent of blood. "Yes. Go ahead, Tyler. You can do this one."

While her assistant closed the wound with confident move-ments, she stepped away and leaned on a bulkhead, waiting for her pulse to slow.

Chapter 13

Wyse marched among the row of guns. "With the next shot we'll take out their rigging. Load!"

Staying back with Conor, Jamie watched the gun teams go through a well-rehearsed sequence of steps. The ship boys brought cases with gunpowder. Tobby hobbled among them. He gave Jamie a wide grin. "Your first battle!"

Jamie nodded. So far, he had nothing to brag about. Even though he participated in the gun exercises, he wasn't as efficient as the gunners and been told to stay out of the way. And during exercises, they only pretended to fire. He wasn't prepared for the immense boom those guns made.

A thud, a piercing scream, and a string of curses came from the end of the row. Wyse pivoted and sped in that direction. "Odds bodkins!" he cried, not for the first time that day. "Get those men below."

Jamie's stomach twisted. Whatever happened was likely gruesome.

With his lips tightened into a line, Wyse approached him and Conor. "Three men from the gun team are hurt, including the sergeant." His gaze rested on Conor. "You go to that gun. It's already loaded and aimed, but you must fire at my command. Have you done this before?"

"Aye, aye, sir. Lots of times." Conor's voice sounded confident, but his hands rubbed against clothing and his face paled a shade.

Wyse nodded. "Flowers, you go with him."

When they walked over to the gun, Conor stared at it.

"What am I supposed to do?" he whispered to Jamie.

"You don't know?"

"I... it's been a while. While you drilled with the men, I had to study."

"But..."

"Fire!" Wyse's voice roared into the horn.

There was no time to talk. With the help of the gun team, Jamie passed a pricker down the touchhole to pierce the powder cartridge and poured a small quantity of fine-grained powder. Standing well back, he jerked the long lanyard which fired the flintlock. The *booms* of other guns exploded in his ears. The world filled with smoke that made his eyes water and lungs constrict. The gun flew back with a mighty force.

For a moment, there was nothing but silence and the odor of rotten eggs. *I must have gone deaf,* he feared. Then the horrible blast returned, pounding in his head and chest. The deck under his feet shook, and more explosions filled the air, making Jamie grab his head. The enemy ship had fired back.

Finally, the noise died down, and he could hear voices of men around him. And then a scream chilled his blood.

He turned to see Conor and Wyse down. When he saw that both were moving, relief washed over him. But the string of curses that poured from Wyse's mouth and his bloodless face told him that the lieutenant was hurt.

"Odds bodkins! What were you thinking, standing where the gun would hit you?" he added to the many oaths and grunts.

Wide-eyed Conor rose to his feet. His mouth gaped but he seemed uninjured. Jamie rushed to Wyse and kneeled by him. The lieutenant's foot was a bloody mess. Sharp bones protruded through the skin, and blood pooled from the wound. Wyse was no longer screaming or cursing. His eyes were closed. For a moment, Jamie thought the man expired. Then Wyse's chest rose.

"He pushed me out of the way. I could've died." Conor stammered.

"You'll explain to me later why you know so little. Now, we must act." He glanced toward the gun port. The enemy ship was getting closer. "The captain will want to fire again. Order the men to get ready. I'll carry Mr. Wyse to the surgeon."

"Stay and help me." Conor grabbed Jamie's arm. "Please. Someone else can carry him."

Jamie shook his arm off. "I'm the least useful person here. These gun crews know their work. They just need your orders. I will tend to Mr. Wyse."

A group of boys appeared with the powder, including Tobby. Jamie called to Digby, a lad the size of a grown man. "Please help me carry Mr. Wyse to the orlop. And you two…" He nodded to a pair that appeared to be twins. "Run to the captain. Please report that Mr. Wyse is gravely injured, and Mr. Leach is commanding the guns." Tobby's face crumbled, likely because he wasn't chosen for the job, but Jamie knew he couldn't run as fast as the other boys.

His mind reeled. *What if said something wrong? I'm not supposed to give orders!*

He quieted the voice in his head and focused on getting Wyse to the surgeon.

With Digby's help, Jamie lifted Wyse by the shoulders. A moan escaped the lieutenant's bloodless lips. The men around him were loading the guns to Conor's commands. While the young man's voice sounded strong and confident, Jamie knew different. Conor must've embellished his experience. The notion made Jamie's teeth clench.

The captain trusts Conor. Others could get hurt because of Conor's lie. Mr. Wyse already has.

Crouched under Wyse's weight, Jamie and Digby descended the dark stairway. The iron stench of blood became stronger with every step. Heart wrenching moans resonated from below. As they neared the orlop, a woman's voice rang above those wails.

"Sully, hold his shoulders tighter. Thread the needle, Tyler. Faster! He's losing blood."

As they entered, a chilling scene came into view. On the operating table, a man lay with his guts spilling out of his belly. Ella, with her sleeves rolled up, was sewing up the terrible wound. Her assistants hovered by her, restraining the patient, and obeying her commands.

If she noticed them enter, she didn't spare them a glance. Jamie scanned the crammed space full of men. Some held their bandaged limbs or heads, others lay motionless. A few did their best to tend to their wounds while waiting for Ella or her assistants.

"There's space in the back," Digby said. "Let's take him there."

Even though they were as gentle as they could while transferring Wyse onto the mattress, the lieutenant moaned. Pain must've woken him up, because he opened his eyes. "Odds bodkins, how bad is it, lads?" he labored to ask.

With his stare on the bone fragments in the wound, Jamie bit his lip.

"Stop gaping and speak," Wyse snapped.

Jamie didn't have the heart to tell him the foot looked like it would need to be amputated.

"I'll fetch the surgeon. She was tending to a patient when we came in and likely didn't see you. I'll let you know you are here."

He made a move to go, but Wyse grabbed his arm. "Don't you dare disturb her. She'll get to me when she can, and not before tending to any man who needs her more than me." His eyes closed for a second, but then snapped open and stared at Digby. "What are you still doing here? Go carry the powder. This battle isn't won yet."

As if in confirmation, the berth shook from an impact of the shot somewhere above them.

"Aye, aye, sir." Digby hastened away. As he crossed the berth, he almost bumped into Ella, who was coming toward him. He pointed to Wyse and Jamie.

Her eyes widened as she approached them. She grabbed a lantern and brought it closer to examine Wyse's wound.

"If you have other patients, treat them first." Wyse said through clenched teeth. "That's an order. And don't even think of removing my leg. I don't need such a life."

She placed her hand on his forehead. "Trust me, you must be next. I will remove the foot, and thus save the rest of the leg. Marietta needs her husband and your boys their father." She fetched a small bottle and measured out a dose of medicine. By the distinctive scent, Jamie recognized laudanum, same as what his father occasionally gave his most difficult patients when extracting teeth. After administering the medicine, Ella studied Jamie.

"The blood on your shirt... Wyse's or yours?"

Jamie glanced at his clothes and noticed the blood on them for the first time. "Wyse's. I'm unhurt."

"Then stay here to help me. Find Tyler or Sully and bring Wyse to the operating table."

Jamie flagged down Sully to help him. As they carried Wyse, Sully prattled with excitement.

"A man I just bandaged told me our crew has boarded the French ship to fight. What would I give to hold a sword or a cutlass! Perhaps, after you help me with Mr. Wyse, you could still join the action."

A thrill tingled through Jamie. He had fencing lessons as a boy. His parents insisted that he rested every ten minutes to avoid overstraining his heart, but he always found practices exhilarating.

When they transitioned the patient onto the table, and Sully used straps to restrain him, Ella walked over. Beads of sweat glistened on her forehead.

"Sully, I need you to help Tyler. There are wounded in need of urgent treatment. Mr. Flowers can help me."

Jamie stared from the table where Ella prepared her instruments, to the ladder that would lead him to the deck. "I hear we are battling the French on their ship. My fencing teacher always praised me. I should go fight."

Her chest heaved as she gave him a hard stare. "Do you imagine that practicing with dull rapiers in the ballroom is anything like the bloody mess happening there now? It's bad enough that Wyse is badly hurt as are many other of my friends. Stay here and help me with the wounded. There are enough people battling. Never enough hands to care for the injuries that result from those fights."

In the flickering light of the lantern, her eyes glowed like fireflies. His objections abated.

She is right. Her work here is as important as the battle.

"What do you need me to do?" he asked, watching her secure the tourniquet on Wyse's leg.

"When I slice, hold down Wyse with all your strength. I gave him laudanum, but the pain will wake him."

Wyse, who seemed oblivious to the world for a while, half-opened his eyes. "Lad, don't let her take my foot."

Jamie looked at Ella for guidance.

Her shoulders slumped. "There's no choice. I must do it to save his life."

Jamie thought about what his parents or sisters would say if he could have a healthy heart but had to lose a foot. In his case, this would be a cost they would all gladly pay.

"You said he has a family?"

Her breath shuddered. "Yes. His wife Marietta. And two little sons."

After composing her face, she lifted a scalpel. Wyse struggled and cursed as she cut. Jamie grasped his shoulders to keep him down.

"Ella tells me that your wife Marietta is loving and loyal." He spoke to Wyse as he fought his grip. "And you have wee sons you are proud of."

"They don't need... a father... with no foot." Wyse bellowed as Ella cut further and blood poured.

"Yes, they do." Jamie used the weight of his body to hold Wyse down. "Dr. Parker, and then your wife, will nurse you back to health."

He paused because Ella grabbed the largest saw. Wyse thrashed as she severed the bones. Jamie tightened his grasp. "With one healthy foot, and a wooden peg, you will still walk. I bet you will chase those boys soon enough. Imagine, they'll be racing each other in the garden, and you surprise them, joining their game."

Jamie's chatter, or the loss of blood, eased Wyse's thrashing. He now lay with his eyes closed, his moans becoming quieter. The needle in Ella's fingers flew with great speed. Jamie marveled how fast she'd done the surgery.

"Keep telling that story." She sewed the skin on the stump. "I liked it. Took me away from all this..." She indicated with her head the terrible scene around them. "If only for a moment."

"In the evenings, you will tell your boys of the battles and your courageous actions. And your beautiful wife, her belly round with another baby, would say... um..."

"It's all worth it." Ella whispered as she dressed the stump. When Jamie furrowed his brow, Ella repeated. "Marietta had a nightmare of a delivery with each child. And yet she told me it was worth it."

He remembered Wendy's baby in Ella's arms—that moment when Ella awkwardly carried the baby and her bag at the same time, desperate to hold onto both.

"Not only the children, but being married to a naval officer, waiting for him to come home," Ella added.

"And what do you think?" Jamie half-whispered.

She stared at Wyse's stump, then at Jamie's bloodied shirt. "That you belong at home with your parents and sisters. Before something terrible happens to you."

As he contemplated his response, steps sounded from the stairs.

"Jamie, you are still here?" Conor walked in with a swagger. His clothes were covered with blood, but he showed no signs of injury. "You missed everything. The broadside shots, the fighting. We've taken the French ship. I killed two Frenchmen with my sword. Captain Grey was pleased."

"Good thing he didn't see you stand in the path of the gun." Jamie pointed to what was left of Wyse's leg. "Did you tell him the true extend of your naval experience?"

Conor stepped beside him and whispered in his ear. "My father wrote to Captain Grey that I served on his ship. He recorded my name in the ship books for years. I didn't know he did this, but I couldn't make my father look like a liar."

"You must tell the truth."

"Not right now." Conor leaned back. "With Wyse injured, he needs me. I am to take the prize ship back to England."

Jamie crossed his arms. "Be sure to steer it on the right course. Or you'll end up in India."

"You think I will blunder? We'll see about that." Conor grinned. "I kept the deal we made. After I told the captain how much you've helped me with the guns, he allowed you to come with me. Go put on your volunteer uniform. You'll be my second-in-command."

Ella, who was bent over her patient, straightened.

"What's happening?"

Conor's eyes gleamed. "Jamie and I are in command of the French ship. We'll sail it back to Plymouth."

Tobby, who walked in at that moment, opened his mouth wide. "I want to go with you."

"You are too little," Conor rebutted. "I will be given eight able men to go with us."

Jamie opened his arms to hug the boy. "We'll meet soon enough, little brother. Stay safe."

"I always get left behind," Tobby whispered and hung his head.

Ella gave Jamie a weary smile. "I will see you in England. Hopefully unharmed."

When Conor grabbed Jamie's arm to go, he wanted to shake it off and gaze into Ella's eyes one more time. To hold her hand and not let go. But Conor's grip and excited chatter pulled him away.

Chapter 14

"How am I to tell my wife in a letter that I'm a cripple?" Lieutenant Wyse's voice, normally sonorous and commanding, wheezed. A month has passed since he sustained his injury, but his face remained as ashen as right after the surgery. Ella suspected that his state of mind impaired the healing process.

She eased him back on his pillows. "Marietta loves you. She will not leave you. If you wish, you can dictate your message to me. But quickly because we only have an hour."

Wyse closed his eyes. A vein pulsed on his forehead, which was covered with scratches and wrinkles. "Let her find out when we return. I wish for her to be happy a little longer."

Ella's fingers caressed the stubble on his cheek. She knew how hard it was for her stubborn friend to tell his beloved Marietta about his injury. Yet an opportunity to send a letter home by a merchant ship heading back to England should not be squandered.

"Marietta must prepare the home to make it comfortable for you. Stock up on the foods to restore your strength." *Cry her tears before you arrive so she can greet you with a smile.*

"Write her yourself." He turned toward the bulkhead and closed his eyes.

With a sigh, Ella stood and strode to her cabin. There, she dipped her pen into the inkwell. What could she tell her childhood friend who was raising two little boys? How could she soften the blow? When she remembered Jamie talking to Wyse during the surgery, the words came to her. Her pen glided as she wrote how with Marietta's love Wyse will surely recover and soon play with his beloved sons. When she finished writing, the memory of Jamie's face as he rocked Wendy's baby in his arms stayed with her.

Jamie, where are you? Are you safely back in England?

Since Jamie left on the French ship, Ella found herself thinking of him many times each day. When she learned that Tobby snuck into the boat with the prize crew, a premonition stewed in her gut. And when a rumor that Conor wasn't as experienced as he boasted reached her, her sleep became disrupted with dreams of Jamie and Tobby chained in a dark, confined space that reminded her of a ship's hold. Or a prison.

***

When Ella stepped off the boat and surveyed the busy Plymouth harbor, the familiar smells of food and yells of peddlers surrounded her. It was good to feel firm land after three months at sea. The *Neptune* protected the Channel from the French ships reaching England, and, after a few battles, returned for supplies and repairs.

Ella craved to rest and refresh herself in her rented room, but there was much to do today. Help Marietta with getting her injured husband situated at home. See how Matilda held up in prison and check on the progress of the appeal. Tend to the sick and injured from her crew who were transferred to the naval hospital. Visit wives and mothers and speak with them of their husbands and sons who died of their injuries. Later, she also hoped to hold baby Wendy.

Thinking of the baby, whose birth brought Jamie back into her life, Ella scanned the harbor for her friends who'd left with the French ship. They should have arrived in Plymouth weeks ago. So far, she hadn't caught sight of them. Not that they would necessarily know of the *Neptune's* arrival, but she pictured Jamie keeping up with naval news and rushing with Tobby to the port to see the ship anchoring.

Perhaps he listened to my advice and returned to his family. The thought should have comforted her, but weight pressed on her body.

Her assistants were helping Lieutenant Wyse into the wooden wheelchair Marietta brought to the port. Ella thought to greet her and update her on Wyse's medicine regimen but decided to wait till later. The kiss her childhood friend bent down to give her beloved husband made Ella's heart melt.

A hand touched her shoulder, and she spun around to see Captain Grey's daughters, Bella and Cecilia. She beamed at them.

"Are you hosting a feast tonight in honor of your father's safe arrival?"

Both girls shifted their feet.

"We'd like to, but Father said he may be home late," Bella said after a silence.

"He went to speak with the port admiral. He may have to go to the Admiralty in London," Cecilia added.

"Why? What happened?" Ice slid down Ella's veins.

"Did you tell her?" Mrs. Grey wedged through the crowd.

Bella's shoulders dropped. "Not yet, Mother. I was just about to."

"What is it?" Ella clasped Bella's hand. The realization hit her like a stone falling onto her chest. "The prize ship? They didn't come back?"

The thought that Jamie, Tobby, Conor and eight more men drowned or met some other death made her want to sink to her knees. The memory of Tobby's smile squeezed her chest like a vine. And Jamie... His face when he rocked Wendy's baby...

Mrs. Grey's arms enveloped her. "Ella, did you hear me? By all accounts, they are alive. There was a substantial number of

French prisoners on the vessel, and it's suspected that they had overtaken the British crew and steered the ship to France."

"The seamen will be taken to a prison." Bella said. "It's terrible, but at least they will stay alive."

"The officers may have parole. They will live in a nearby town if they promise not to run away," Cecilia added.

Ella's head throbbed as she imagined her friends locked in a dark, dirty cell. Parole would apply to Conor, and possibly Jamie, but twelve-year-old Tobby would be among the common seamen.

"Would they be exchanged for the French captives?" Ella asked.

Mrs. Grey shook her head. "Only a handful of high ranked officers had been exchanged. Some men escaped and made it back to England, but I hear most runaways are recaptured and severely punished. Most likely, Mr. Flowers and other men taken with him will remain in prison until the end of the war. I feel terrible. As you probably guessed, it was I who helped your friend to get a position as my husband's servant. He made a lovely impression on me. I never meant for him to come to harm."

"Father will speak to the port admiral and learn all he can about the crew's whereabouts." Cecilia threw her shoulders back.

"I'm organizing a knitting circle to make warm socks and scarves for the British prisoners of war. Veronica and Henrietta already joined." Bella touched Ella's elbow. "Ella, can I count on you? Your friends say you are proficient with knitting needles."

As a young girl, Ella had spent many hours embroidering and knitting with her friends and their mothers. The handicraft made her fingers nimble, which later helped her master suturing. But the thought of Jamie and Tobby despairing in a crowded cell made her too restless for the work required.

She gave Bella an apologetic smile. "It's a wonderful endeavor, but I'm sorry, I don't think I can join you at this time."

"That's right." Cecilia raised her chin. "Ella will not knit mittens when she can go to France and help the crew escape. I bet she'll find the way to rescue Mr. Flowers and all the other prisoners."

"Cecilia, are you mad?" Her mother threw up her hands. "Don't put such notions into Ella's head."

Too late... Ella inhaled. *I wonder if I could travel to France. Risking myself to find my friends may be easier than waiting for their return.*

***

The group of British captives approached the tall walls of Verdot prison. Surveying the stone buildings looming over the walls, Jamie guessed that centuries ago, the fortress was used for military purposes and housed soldiers.

Tobby limped and held on to Jamie's shoulder. Jamie was glad that he had the means to hire the carriage for him and the men whose feet had been rubbed raw or whose skin burned in the scorching sun. With good shoes and a hat, Jamie managed to avoid injuries and walked the last twenty days. No matter what horrors their destination held, he was relieved to have reached it.

Conor whistled softly as he observed the height of the walls. "Hundred feet at least. But the mast is even higher. If I make a good rope…"

Tobby bit his lip. "I only climbed the ratlines. And I'm slow."

Jamie gave Conor and Tobby a strict look. "Don't even think of scaling these walls. You'll fall and break your legs. Or be caught in the act and punished."

Tobby's shoulders shook. "We'll be here forever."

"I'm not going to wait for the war to end. If not the walls, I heard a rumor that this fortress has underground tunnels. Perhaps…" A grin brightened Conor's face, and he glanced at Jamie. "Oh, how could I forget? Jamie, you and I are officers. We will receive parole and will have freedom of visiting the town and hopefully sleeping somewhere decent. There may be other officers here to play cards with. And French girls to meet."

"What about the rest of us?" Tobby's lips curved down.

The lad's crushed expression made Jamie's throat thicken. Because of their bond, the boy followed him to the French ship and became tangled in their failed mission. It was great fortune that none of them lost their lives when the French overtook the ship and imprisoned them in the hold. And now they were entering another prison.

"Remember what we promised each other in the hold?" Jamie clapped both of his friends on the back. "We stay together."

"Like brothers." The boy raised his head.

Conor frowned and swiveled his neck toward the picturesque town a short distance away.

The soldiers straightened and fell silent as a tall officer came out of the gates. Two guards accompanied him. By the gray in his mustache, Jamie guessed him to be in his fifties. His cold gaze studied the group.

"I am Jean-Luc Vignon, commander of Verdot prison." His English was excellent, but his stare on him and Conor made Jamie shiver. "Your uniforms distinguish you two as junior officers, which means I must give you parole. If you attempt to run or cause trouble, you will lose your privileges, and I will happily introduce you to my accommodations."

"Then we could run. If they lock us up, parole is canceled." Conor whispered in Jamie's ear.

"I assume you have money and soon will receive more from England," Vignon continued. "Go to the town and find a lodging. The rest, follow me. Your stay is not going to be so comfortable."

As the men trudged with their shoulders dropped, Tobby spun his head to Jamie and Conor. The boy's chin trembled.

Conor grabbed Jamie's arm. "This won't be so bad. I heard the town is famous for wine. I fancy to taste it with roasted chicken. Let's find a tavern."

Jamie shook off Conor's hold on him and sprinted after the guards. "Monsieur Vignon!"

The commander turned with a grimace. "What do you want?"

"The boy." Jamie pointed to Tobby. "His leg is in bad shape. He should go to the hospital or at least see a surgeon in town."

Vignon gave him an annoyed glance. "There's no surgeon or hospital in town. The Royal Navy is supposed to send someone. In the cell, he can rest his leg all he wants."

Stiffening, Jamie tried a different tactic. "The boy is my younger brother. He should have the same privileges as I."

The commander rolled his eyes. "Next thing you will tell me that all these men are your brothers or cousins. The boy is a common seaman and will go to the cell with the rest."

"It's all right, Jamie." Tobby blinked rapidly, tears welling in his eyes. "I won't be afraid."

"We promised each other that we will stay together. An officer and a brother keeps his promise." Jamie faced Vignon. "We will share the cell with our men."

His shipmates, Vignon, and Conor stared at him wide-eyed.

"Did I understand you correctly? You want to stay in the cell instead of the lodging in the town?" Vignon asked.

Conor grabbed Jamie's shoulder. "What are you doing?"

Jamie peered at him. "Don't you remember how we shook hands and said we stay together and take care of each other?"

"Yes, but..." Conor's face reddened. "I didn't expect this. I'm not sleeping on a stone floor when I can have a bed."

Just when I thought he was a good man, he chooses comfort over friendship.

"Suit yourself." He unhooked his money purse and put a handful of coins into Conor's palms. "Don't even think of gambling. You'll need money for lodging and food."

Conor gaped as he counted the coins. Jamie turned from him and positioned himself next to Tobby. His eyes met with Vignon's. "Lead on, sir."

The guards lit lanterns and led the prisoners down the stone stairs. The cold penetrated his uniform. Tobby didn't even have a coat.

When they stepped inside the cell, Jamie could hardly breathe the stagnant air. A tiny, barred window let in a bit of light. Twenty men or so spread themselves sitting or lying in a crammed space. The odors of unwashed bodies, urine, feces, and vomit, all mixed into a reek so strong Jamie's eyes watered.

The new arrivals found spots to lay down. Tobby pinched his nose. "How will we sleep here?"

"We'll get used to the smell. Let's find a good place to rest."

He showed Tobby the space below the window, thinking the sun would offer warmth and the air would be the freshest.

When they collapsed on the spot, the man who rested nearby shook his head. His face was scarred, and his hair long and matted. "You can't sit here."

Jamie forced a smile. "I don't mean to take someone's coveted space, but the boy is tired and cold. Let him rest here for a few minutes."

He rubbed Tobby's shoulders to warm him.

"Who's in my spot?" a loud voice boomed. "I go for a piss and someone takes it!" The large, red-faced man who was hollering had a few teeth missing.

Jamie rose. "Sir, we just arrived and didn't know it was yours. But please let the lad rest his legs and get warm."

Tobby gasped and bolted to his feet. "I know him! His name is Simkins. He was on the *Neptune* before."

"And I know you!" The man's face turned into a horrible grimace with bulging eyes and gaping mouth. "You are that boy who always hid behind that witch woman, Ella Parker! Is she here?"

"Thank heavens, no," Jamie answered. For a moment he saw Ella in this place, and horror stole his breath.

Please let Ella be safe in England.

"Shame..." Simkins licked his lips. "The French know what to do with witches."

"Doctor Parker is not a witch, and you know it." Tobby stomped his foot. "She even treated you after you fell overboard."

"What? Did a rat squeak?" Simkins put a hand to his ear. Men near him laughed. Then he bared the few teeth he had and peered at Jamie. "Listen, bugger. I don't care who you are. You may wear an officer uniform, but it don't matter here. I rule this place. So, take your little pest and move somewhere else."

Jamie led Tobby away. "Don't worry. This man won't hurt you. But let's find a different spot."

Simkin's mean laugh echoed through the cell as they crouched in dingy corner, a couple of steps from the piss bucket.

"You should go find Conor and get a room in town," Tobby whispered. "I'll be all right."

Jamie wrapped his arm around him. "That's not what a brother does."

Chapter 15

Ella's stomach soured as she breathed in the heavy air of dark corridors. Her hand clutched her basket, filled with meat pies and current scones. The guard's key ring clinked with every step. She expected him to take her to the cell she once shared with Matilda and the other women. Her toes curled in her shoes as she remembered Rose holding a knife to her neck. Instead, the wide shouldered guard stopped in front of a different cell at the end of the row and unlocked the door.

"Ten minutes," he barked.

Ella offered him a few coins. "Twenty."

He clenched the bribe and shined his lantern, illuminating a lone figure sprawled on the floor. Her heart in her throat, Ella rushed to her friend. Her first thought was that Matilda had fainted, but when she came closer, a loud snore came from the midwife's gaping mouth.

Ella kneeled by her friend and shook her by the shoulder. "Matilda, I hate to wake you, but I don't have much time. Eat some pie while it's still hot and listen to me. A terrible event occurred."

The older woman's arms stretched, and her eyes snapped open. She sat up. "I already know. The prize ship had been taken back by the French and the crew sent to prison."

"How could you know that?" Ella's mouth gaped.

Matilda chortled. "Plenty of women visit me to ask for advice and bring me news."

"You treat women even here? And the guards don't stop you?"

"Why would they?" Matilda spread her hands. "See? I have my own cell now. They first sent me here as a punishment, but I prefer it. The guards' wives consult with me about their maladies. And bring me food. Speaking of which, what's in your basket?" Matilda moved aside the cloth and grabbed a pie. Juice ran down her face as she ate. "How is Jack Wyse? Marietta came to see me after she received your letter."

"He was feeling poorly this morning. No doubt from anxiety about seeing Marietta's reaction to his injury. But she met him with embraces and kisses."

Matilda bit off another piece of the pie. "I'm sorry that I'm chewing, but these pies taste so good while they're hot."

"I hope Marietta will nurse her husband back to health." Ella shifted her knees, already aching from the hard stones that the straw failed to cushion. "I keep thinking about what she said, 'that it's all worth it.' And I can't get Jamie out of my mind. He's one of the men taken prisoner, along with Tobby. Am I mad to search for a way to get to France and find them?"

Matilda rose and walked to the tiny window. After staring into it for a moment, she faced Ella, who approached her.

"Do you believe he loves you?"

Ella fidgeted. "We didn't speak much on the ship. I pushed him away. But I believe I was the reason he came to Plymouth and sought the posting on the *Neptune*."

"And you don't perceive him to be a fortune hunter, like Mr. Weston?"

"No." Ella shook her head. "I don't believe he is interested in my inheritance. Unlike Robert, he never asks about my family's fortune."

"What about your profession? Did he express any notions against it?"

"No. He assisted me twice, with Wendy's baby and with Wyse's amputation. His face was white as paper, but he was helpful to me and compassionate to the patients. He spoke to Wyse about his boys to distract him from pain, and to Wendy's newborn as he held her." A smile at the memory formed on her face, then flew away. "Matilda, what am I to do?"

With a thoughtful expression, Matilda walked back to the basket and lifted it. "Those pies you brought me. They are irresistible when they are hot. Tomorrow they will not be so appetizing. In three days, they will be stale. In a week, they will rot."

"The pies?" Ella fidgeted, for a moment afraid that her friend had gone mad. But then the meaning came to her. "Oh, yes. You are saying that over time my feelings will fade. You are quite right. I will keep my head focused on work and let time pass to calm my heart."

Matilda tilted her head. "That's what I did for much of my life. Acted reasonably. Stayed practical. But you are a woman who takes risks and pursues adventure. I wish I was more like you. Life is too short to eat stale pies."

"What happened to you, my careful advisor?"

The older woman shrugged. "Too much time with nothing to do but think over my life. The chances I didn't take. The opportunities I denied myself. I don't want this for you. If you believe this man is worthy, find a way to see him. Wives and daughters of some imprisoned officers had gone to France to be with their men. Perhaps you could do the same."

Could I search for Jamie in France? But what about my ship crew? I cannot leave my work.

"I don't know, Matilda. I'll think on it." She gave her friend a hug.

The door opened. The guard let in a large woman who held her abdomen and cringed. "Mistress Pesce! What do you suggest for a bellyache? The pie I ate last night must've been too old."

"See what happens?" Matilda gave Ella a light shove. "Eat your pies piping hot."

"I'll leave you to tend to your patient." Ella smiled at her friend. "And next time I see you, I hope it will be at your shop."

"And I hope you will be telling me your plan how you will rescue that handsome young man." Matilda gave her a wink and hurried to her visitor.

***

Late at night, Jamie tossed and turned on the cold and dirty straw. His stomach growled, unsatisfied by a meager dinner of bread and overcooked vegetables. Tobby cuddled up next to him, covered by Jamie's coat. Several men coughed and wheezed in their sleep. Many scratched their skin and hair.

The man on his other side sat up. After a long coughing fit, he spit in Jamie's direction.

"Don't do that," Jamie whispered to avoid waking his sleeping neighbors. "I'm sorry you are unwell, but please don't spit on me or the boy. If you need water, I have some in my cup."

The man accepted the cup and drank it in one gulp.

"I'm sorry," the man said after catching his breath. He tried to hand the cup back, but Jamie waved it away. "The phlegm is clogging my throat. I can't spit in the other direction. The man sleeping there is a friend of Simkins. One word from him, and I'm dead."

Jamie bit the inside of his cheek. "You are too sick to be here, in a crowded cell. Diseases must spread here like fire."

"Aye. Many have died. But the French don't care. We are the enemy."

"Are there no British officers to stand up to Vignon and advocate for the sick?"

"No, sir. I hear there are officers living in the town. But none have taken any interest in our lot."

Too busy playing cards and meeting with French women, Jamie thought of Conor with bitterness.

"What is your name, friend?"

The man unrolled his shoulders. "Silas Culpepper."

"Perhaps I can ask Commander Vignon to organize an infirmary with warm beds."

Culpepper doubled over from hacking. His gaze dashed from Jamie to a man on his other side. He spit thick saliva into his hands and wiped them on his breeches.

"Vignon would never do a kind thing for any of us. He hates us."

When Culpepper's hacking quieted, and he wheezed in his sleep, Jamie was still awake and mulling over his situation. In days or weeks, he'll likely catch a disease and die in this cell. Most likely, Tobby will as well. In such conditions, only strong built men, like Simkins, could last long. And he and his cronies use their strength to bully the weaker men.

I can use my parole and live in comfort. Tobby's head rested on his shoulder. He could never betray the boy and leave him in this place.

I can accept my fate and welcome illness and death. My heart cannot last much longer anyway. That was an easy choice. But then Tobby and Culpepper will die because there's no one to advocate for them.

The last challenge was the hardest one. *I need to change these conditions. Persuade Vignon to make improvements. But how?*

In the morning, the guards brought breakfast of porridge and bread. There were not enough spoons, and most prisoners ate like dogs with their heads in a bowl. Nothing was brought for men to wash themselves.

The porridge was bland and watery, but Jamie was glad to have something hot in his belly.

Tobby bit into his hard roll and cried out. Wincing, he spit out a tooth.

Jamie gasped in horror. Could the boy have developed scurvy already? Was his mouth filled with sores, making his teeth loose enough to fall out?

"That baby tooth was wiggling for a while. Finally, it fell out. It's easier to eat without it," Tobby said, smiling.

Relieved, Jamie patted the boy's back.

"What are we going to do all day?" Tobby asked. He finished his food, and his eyes were glued to Jamie's uneaten bread.

Jamie broke his roll in half and gave the other half to Tobby. "I don't know. Perhaps, the guards will let us out to the yard. A walk in the sunshine would be nice."

"We haven't been out for walks in month," Culpepper croaked, clearing his throat.

"What about church? It's Sunday, isn't it?" Jamie asked. Like the rest of his family, he was not a churchgoing man, but hearing a sermon or singing a hymn seemed like a nice diversion from sitting the gloomy cell.

Culpepper grunted. "We had a chaplain, but he returned to England. There was a surgeon too, but he disappeared somewhere. Likely left for England as well. No one else came to minister to us since."

With nothing to do, the day was long. Some men slept; others huddled in small groups and talked among themselves. In a loud voice, Simkins regaled his cronies with a story that made Jamie want to cover Tobby's ears. The captives who came with Jamie clustered in the corner. Their slouched backs spoke of sorrow and defeat.

"I miss the ship," Tobby said. "There I played with my friends. Doctor Ella read us stories and gave us lessons."

"Hmm... Perhaps I can retell you a book I read. It was about a man named Robinson Crusoe, who was shipwrecked on a small island, far from any other land. He was the only man there and had to survive all alone."

Tobby scratched his cheek. "An island where it was only him. If he couldn't leave it, was it a prison?"

"I suppose so." Jamie smiled at the boy's cleverness. "A prison with no walls or guards, but still a prison."

"I wouldn't want to be in prison like that." The boy hugged his knees.

"Even if the island is lovely, with colorful plants and exotic animals?"

The boy ran his hands over the straw floor, then touched the stone wall. He turned his face to the tiny window, then back to Jamie. "No. There he was all alone. We are with other men. They may not all be nice, but they are people we can talk to. And I have my brother with me."

Jamie wrapped his arm around the boy's shoulders.

When the dinner was brought, Jamie's nose wrinkled in disgust as he sniffed it. The meat was rancid.

He grabbed Tobby's hand as the boy brought a piece to his mouth. "Don't eat it. Your belly will hurt."

He stood up and made his voice loud. "Don't touch the meat. It will make you sick."

A round of laughter came from Simkins and his cronies. "The food here is not fine enough for the new lad. He wants a fresh beefsteak," Simkins said in a mocking voice. He shoved a large piece of meat into his mouth and his followers did the same.

Tobby stared at the plate. "I'm hungry. Can I eat just a few bites? Then my belly will hurt only a little."

Jamie grabbed Tobby's plate and his own and threw the meat into a corner where a couple of rats scurried. One of Simkin's friends rushed over and grabbed it.

"We won't get anything else to eat until night," Culpepper whispered. He sniffed the meat and set his plate aside. "I don't have an appetite anyway. Everything tastes like metal."

"Must be a fever. We need to get you broth, my friend." Jamie stood. "Tobby, I'm sorry, but I need my coat back. Just for an hour or so."

"What are you doing, Jamie?" Tobby asked.

"I'm going to speak to Commander Vignon."

Chapter 16

The hard chair in the port admiral's waiting room caused Ella's back to ache. During the hour she waited, a couple of people had been called into the room beyond the door, and many more remained. To pass the time, she tried to guess why the others had come to see the port admiral or his clerks. The woman in mourning black … probably a widow with an issue regarding her late husband's pension. An officer in a wrinkled uniform … could be inquiring about a new commission. Without it, he'd be on half pay. An elderly man with his arm missing may be asking for permission to stay at Greenwich hospital in London, a permanent home for retired seamen.

She shifted in her seat. *And what am I doing here? All Captain Grey said in his note was for me to come to this building. Who am I supposed to speak to, and does it involve Jamie and Tobby?*

She hoped the modest but pleasant blue dress was the right choice of clothing. Breeches or a fancy gown would likely be out of place in such a setting.

"Miss Ella Parker," a uniformed officer called.

Following him, she stepped into a spacious room with a soft rug under her feet. Charts and ship drawings adorned the walls. A man in a gray coat stood by the desk. Neither handsome nor ugly. A face one would forget an hour after a chance meeting.

Ella waited for him to introduce himself and why he wanted to see her.

The man paused long enough for Ella to fidget, then spoke. "Captain Grey told me much about you, Miss Parker. But when he praised your skill as a surgeon, he made me think you were older. He also failed to mention your beauty."

Her skin tingled and she sprang back.

"Sir, I don't know you. I'm not sure if I should thank you for a compliment or leave immediately."

The man cracked a small smile. "He did mention your spirit. My name is John Greville. That's not likely to tell you anything. But you don't need to know much more than my name. And I already know enough about you to see that you would be perfect for my mission."

"A mission? I'm beginning to understand. Are you a spymaster?"

Mr. Greville tilted his head. "Something like that. Although I prefer the word 'intelligencer'."

"In that case, a mistake must've occurred. I am a surgeon, not a spy." Ella turned to the door.

"Don't you want to hear me out, Miss Parker? The mission concerns your friends. Tobby Hill. Jamie Flowers. Conor Leach. Captain Grey said they mean a great deal to you, and to him."

When Ella spun around, Mr. Greville pointed to a chair.

Ella shook her head and planted her feet firmly. "What is the mission? How can it benefit the captured men?"

"Officially, it's a posting I imagine you would be eager to take. The Naval Board is sending a surgeon and a chaplain to Verdot, the prison where your friends are most likely held. You would be that surgeon."

I would see Jamie and Tobby. Take care of them if they are sick. But what about the rest of my crew? I cannot leave them.

She suppressed a sigh. "Sir, I thank you for the offer. But my place is on the *Neptune* as its surgeon. I worked hard to earn that place."

"You forget that I've already spoken to Captain Grey. He gives you leave. Another surgeon and your assistants will care for the crew. When you return, your captain will hire you back."

But why would a spymaster want me for this mission? Why is he involved at all?

"If the Naval Board needed a surgeon to send to France, they'd have many men to choose from. They don't even know me and would be appalled if they learned of my gender. Captain

Grey must've told you how I disguised myself as a man to pass their exam. How could I be chosen for this position? And why me?"

Mr. Greville showed no emotion except for a small spark in his eyes. "There's a second part to the mission. And it was my idea to recruit a woman to accomplish it. First, I thought she would be a surgeon's daughter coming to assist her father. But then rumors reached me about a trial of a midwife and a female witness who claimed to be a ship surgeon. I investigated and liked what I learned about you. I interviewed Captain Grey, and finally I have the pleasure of meeting you. Everything I noticed about you today makes me think you are well-suited for both parts of this assignment."

Ella wrung her hands. "Why do I have a feeling I will be less comfortable with the second part than the first?"

Mr. Greville kept his face blank. "Some information that we have about Verdot prison does not add up. The man we sent there to investigate had disappeared. And there were others who seemed to disappear as well."

"Perhaps they have escaped?"

"That's what Commander Vignon said in his reports. But those men had never made it to England or been recaptured. And there's been enough of such incidents to raise suspicion. We believe the French commander is lying."

Ella's lungs filled with air. "You want me to learn what happened to the missing prisoners. Why do you believe I will succeed?" She suspected she already knew the answer. Women spies were used in all wars to get close to powerful men and learn their secrets. And that closeness usually involved lovemaking. Her blood boiled.

I'm not a spy! And certainly not a courtesan!

She adopted a frosty tone. "If you believe I would accept such a mission, you must be misinformed about my character. I care about my crew, but I can make my own way to France. If wives of imprisoned officers have done it, so can I." She strode toward the door.

"Yes, with money and courage you could travel to France. But could you free your friend Matilda Pesce?"

Gaping, Ella turned slowly. "And you can?"

Mr. Greville's charcoal eyes bore into her. "Yes. There're reasons to appeal the verdict and remove the corrupt judge. With my connections, Mistress Pesce could go home immediately, and her possessions restored to her. Without my assistance... justice is slow to come... and your friend is not young."

He has me. I must save Matilda.

Her shoulders dropped. "I must set Mistress Pesce free. And I want to go to France and care for my crew and other British captives. If there is some sinister plot, and the prisoners are disappearing, I am most concerned for my friends. But the price I must pay... I am a Christian woman."

"How you obtain the information is up to you. You may be clever enough to divulge Vignon's secrets without overstepping your principles. And you will not be alone. Hired guards and two companions will travel with you."

"Two companions? Who are they?"

"You know them. One is a chaplain. While you tend to the prisoners' bodies, he would heal their souls. He shouldn't know of your secret assignment. His name is Mr. Doolittle."

"Nooo." Ella groaned. "He used to be the chaplain on the *Neptune*. That man cannot be trusted." The memory of the clergyman's dishonest act churned her insides, as he tried to deceive her into giving her assets to the church for his own gain.

Mr. Greville averted his eyes. "His superiors chose him for the posting. He seems like a dull and greedy but harmless man. His presence may prove beneficial."

"Fine." Ella rocked on her heels. "At least I know what to expect from him. Who is my second companion?"

Mr. Greville crossed the room and opened a small door Ella didn't notice before. A striking woman wearing a burgundy dress that revealed her shoulders stepped in.

"We meet again, Duchess." She laughed.

Ella shrunk away. "This woman... Rose... she threatened me with a knife. I cannot go with her."

"I only scratched you." Rose rolled her eyes. "If I wanted to kill you, I would have done it."

Rose had a secret dispatch with her that she only let Captain Grey see. Unlike me, she must be a trained agent. A woman like that could murder me if it suits her.

Mr. Greville turned to Ella. "It is good for you to remember that Rose can be dangerous. But she's useful and has proven her loyalty. Now, Rose..." he said as his head swiveled to the mysterious woman, "you will accompany Miss Parker to Verdot before you start your own assignment. For propriety, you will play the role of her maid."

Rose stomped her foot. "Again? You promised to let me be a rich woman with servants of my own."

"Perhaps next time." Mr. Greville shrugged. "For this mission, we must send a surgeon. Miss Parker is who we need. While you are skillful in many areas, medicine is not one of them."

Rose paced from one side of the room to another. Then she came nose to nose with Ella. "Fine. I will go with you. But don't expect me to do your bidding."

Ella forced her legs to become firm and not shake. *I cannot let her hold the upper hand or show my fear.*

Chin raised and spine rigid, she conjured the strict tone of her father's housekeeper, a no-nonsense woman who commanded a dozen maids.

"To play the role convincingly, you will need to attend to me when we are in public. Besides that, I expect my servants to bathe. The offending odor you omit will reflect poorly on both of us."

Rose's face turned the burgundy shade of the dress she wore. Her hands reached for Ella's throat, then balled in front of her face. "Duchess, you will regret this. I promise you."

Mr. Greville drew closer. "Ladies, please stop this quarrel. You both have important missions, and I count on your good sense. Next week you will receive documents for travel and a message about the ship that will take you to France. Do not share that information with anyone."

Ella hugged herself. "Can I say goodbye to my shipmates and friends?"

"Please use discretion. And no one should know of your secret mission."

An icy chill slid to the pit of her back. *I'm going to France with an untrustworthy chaplain and a pretender maid that could kill me in my sleep. This seems like my maddest decision ever. And for a woman who disguised herself as a man to study medicine and then boarded a ship to become a surgeon, that's saying something!*

Chapter 17

Jamie called to the fresh-faced guard, a dark-haired man about his age, who stood on the other side of the bars. "I must speak to Commander Vignon. Please take me to him."

The guard blinked. "No order for that."

Jamie handed him a coin. "Remember, I'm on parole. I am free to walk about this town. I take it that the commander's quarters are within the boundary. Why don't you ask Monsieur Vignon if he is available to speak to me?"

The young guard walked away, but soon returned with two more, another youth and an older man. He stayed at his post, while the others flanked Jamie as they escorted him up the stairs and through a maze of narrow corridors.

While they walked, Jamie practiced his French and asked the guard's name and where he lived. The young guard told him that his name is Adrien Renaud, and that his father is a bookseller, when the older guard ordered him to stop chatting with a prisoner.

The older guard knocked on a heavy wooden door.

"Commander Vignon lives here? Right in the fortress?" Jamie asked Renaud.

"Yes. He has no family. He made this chamber his sleeping quarters."

The other sentry gave him a look of fury, and Renaud blushed.

"Bring him in," Vignon grumbled through the door.

Jamie found himself in a small chamber with simple furniture. There was a cot by the wall and a cheerful fire in the hearth. Vignon sat at the table and was cutting into a large piece of meat. The aroma that came from his dinner was mouthwatering.

Vignon dismissed the guards with a flick of his hand. Chewing the meat, he studied Jamie. "Mr. Flowers. This is quite irregular, but I was curious to hear you out. You were offered lodging in the town. Staying here was your choice. I'm sure you weren't expecting luxury."

Jamie crossed his arms. "I am here to speak on behalf of the men. They received rancid meat today. It will make them ill. Many are already sick with lung disease as well."

"As I said before, I don't have a surgeon. Your government is supposed to take care of that." He sipped his wine. "There's an apothecary in the town. If you want to buy his remedies, you can spend your own money. And I give the prisoners the required rations."

"Spoiled meat is not a ration. They also need fresh air. Daily walks in the yard."

Vignon's face stayed passive. "Why should I care? You had the ill fortune of becoming prisoners of war. I hear my countrymen are held in ship prisons in England."

Jamie rocked back and forth, thinking of a convincing argument. A lesson from a ship book came to his mind.

He leaned on the table, getting his face closer to Vignon.

"It is easier to control the men who are treated well. Discipline and morale improve. Fewer will attempt to run."

Vignon tilted his head in thought.

A sudden idea came to Jamie. He straightened and brought his chest out.

"Why do you think I chose to eat and sleep with the men instead of taking advantage of my parole?"

The Frenchman twisted his lips. "A foolish act of loyalty by a romantic soul."

"No. I was specifically sent to learn of the conditions. There were reports... of..."

Vignon dropped his fork. It gave a clink as it hit his plate.

"Reports about this prison?" Vignon's face paled a shade. He stood and paced to the wall then back. Then he halted. "What did they say?"

"Exactly what I witnessed. Dirty and overcrowded cells. Inedible food. No walks outside. Diseases spreading."

Vignon's rigid posture slacked. His eyes glanced up to the cracked ceiling, as if thanking Heaven. He walked back to the table and drummed his fingers.

"What do you want me to do?"

Jamie balled his fists to spur his courage. "I want better food for the prisoners. Fresh straw to sleep on. Time in the yard every day when the weather allows, as well as an hour in the church."

Vignon jotted down something with his feather pen. "It will be done."

Jamie's jaw dropped. *So easy? Or is he so afraid of the reports that I made up?*

Encouraged, he continued. "Sick men must be separated from the healthy. They need an infirmary with warm beds and more sunlight. Perhaps at the top floor..."

"No." Vignon barked. "It's... uninhabitable. The ceiling leaks and may even drop. No one goes there for safety reasons. Instead... The empty barracks can serve as the infirmary." He scratched his beard. "They need repairs, and I don't have men for that."

"Put the prisoners to work. When the surgeon arrives, the infirmary would be ready."

Vignon waved his hand in a dismissive gesture. "They are lazy. Or they will steal the tools to use for their escape."

"They will toil, knowing the infirmary is for their own benefit. I will supervise them."

"No." Vignon shook his head. "They will taste freedom and run."

"If you give them all you promised, not a single man will run. I give you my word." He offered his hand to Vignon. The commander's cold gray eyes stared into his.

"What if someone escapes? What good is your word then?"

Bile crept up Jamie's throat. The men needed decent food, fresh air, and an infirmary to survive. He could not think of anything else to offer.

"Then do with me what you will. I'm sure you have a dungeon or another way to punish me."

Vignon shook his hand. "I will remember what you said."

This was almost too easy, Jamie thought as he walked back to his cell.

Convincing the prisoners turned out to be harder.

Jamie's voice grew hoarse from repeating the same arguments. "This is for all of us. Without an infirmary, disease runs unchecked, and more people catch it and die. You must know this from living on the ship."

"We are not working for Vignon." Simkins spat on the floor. "I rule here. I tell these dogs what to do."

Tobby wedged his way forward. "Mr. Flowers is a better leader than you. He'll get us better food and make sure we don't get sick."

"Perhaps we should listen to Mr. Flowers. He was right about the meat," one of Simkin's friends said in weak voice. He lay in a fetal position and held his stomach. Several men sprawled next to him in a similar state. Other crowded by the buckets. The stench of human waste was becoming unbearable.

"It's a trick. He and Vignon planned this." Simkins' face reddened and sweat poured down his forehead. Jamie wondered if the man ran a fever.

"I will go to the apothecary for something to settle your stomachs and for a cough remedy as well. But everyone who is healthy tomorrow will start on the work."

Three guards walked in carrying fresh smelling straw. They stared at Jamie with awe.

"Clean straw for everyone?" Jamie asked.

They nodded. "There's a lot more," Renaut said.

Jamie chose two men who didn't cough or hold their bellies. "Friends, will you help? You are welcome to make your own beds first."

He bent down to lift an armful of straw. The men did the same.

***

Ella could hardly contain a giggle as she and the midwife neared Matilda's home.

"Close your eyes, Matilda."

Matilda shook her head. "Ella, this is silly. I'm too old for games. And considering the ruckus I'm left to cleanup, I'm not in the mood."

"Please. Only for a minute."

When Matilda obliged, Ella led her inside. Whispers hushed as they entered the sitting room, but as soon as Ella told Matilda to open her eyes, a dozen women and several children cheered, waved, and danced for joy. Henrietta squealed and hopped like a little girl. Veronica attempted to jump with her, but then patted her growing belly and lounged on the sofa. Marietta rocked her infant who cried from the sudden noise.

Blinking away tears, Matilda scanned the fresh plants and vibrant bouquets that perfumed the air. A new table boasted plates with fruit and pastries.

"Thank you," she mouthed and wiped her eyes.

"You must see the shop next," Ella said and led Matilda there.

The herb shop was back to its former glory. Ella and her friends finished cleaning up this morning. Matilda would need to replenish some supplies, but she would be able to receive customers starting tomorrow.

With a sob, Matilda opened her arms to embrace her guests. As the women took turns hugging her, she thanked each one and inquired about her children or her health. Ella approached her last.

"We won't stay long. I'm sure you wish to finally sleep in your own bed. And I'm getting ready to leave tomorrow."

"Already?" Matilda gaped. "I was hoping you would come for breakfast and finally tell me how you managed to free me."

Ella winked. "I have friends in high places. You take care of yourself. And of these women who couldn't wait for you to return. Meanwhile, I need to help someone else."

Matilda peered into her face. "Are you going to France?"

Ella nodded. "I'm going to heal the British detainees. Jamie and Tobby should be in the prison I'm sent to."

"Before my arrest, I would've urged you not to go. But I see things differently now. Safe journey, my dear."

They embraced and kissed. Ella backed away, overwhelmed with love for her older friend.

Veronica caught her hand and led her to the kitchen where Henrietta was fixing more plates with tarts while Marietta nursed her baby. Even though the food appeared delicious, Ella couldn't eat anymore. Before this gathering, she said goodbyes to her crew at the Cooked Goose. While her stomach was heavy from beefsteak and beer, her heart was even fuller from toasts and well wishes of the seamen. The hard men who previously refused to accept her did not want to let her go.

"Ella, we have something for you." Veronica offered her a package wrapped in brown paper. "Happy belated birthday."

"Oh goodness. Thank you." Ella said.

"We had to guess your measurements, but I believe we got them right. I have a professional eye for those things," Henrietta said.

"Is that a new gown? While I appreciate your efforts, I wear breeches more often than skirts."

"You never know when you need a new outfit." Veronica tilted her head. "I still hope to make your wedding dress."

"Perhaps someday." Ella rolled her eyes.

"Ah, so it's no longer 'never ever'," Marietta said, shifting her baby.

Ella bid her friends goodbye with more hugs and kisses and rushed toward the door.

There she almost bumped into a woman who was walking in with a baby in her arms and several children trailing her.

"Mrs. Moore," Ella exclaimed. "I must leave in a moment, but may I see little Wendy? It would make me so happy to hold her."

Mrs. Moore's expression was somber as she passed her the baby. "I keep thinking that my poor daughter died in this house alone. And I was the one who made her leave. But the child she left me to raise turned out to be the greatest gift."

"She is beautiful." Hugging the baby to her chest, Ella remembered Jamie holding the newborn in this very room. "I'm going to France to find our friend. He will be pleased to know you are in good health," she whispered into the baby's ear. Baby Wendy cooed and gave a joyful whimper.

Chapter 18

"Get up, Duchess," Rose hollered as she knocked on the door of Ella's room. Ella blinked and rubbed her eyes. The curtainless window of the room she rented above a bakery, in some tiny French town in Brittany, allowed the light of a crescent. Dawn had not come yet.

"Rose, it's still night. Why are we up so early?"

Ella stretched in her bed. The mattress was hard, but after the swaying ship and a bumpy wagon ride on the hilly road, Ella could use more rest.

"We need to get a start and cover as much distance as we can during the day," Rose said, walking in. "The roads are dangerous at night."

"Surely we are safe with our escorts." Two guards, sent by Mr. Greville, accompanied them. "And we haven't had breakfast."

Rose gave her a look that could turn the water in the jug by her bed to ice. "We must be in the carriage in twenty minutes."

Ella bolted upright and gaped at her companion. "A carriage? We were riding in a wagon."

"I told you I'm not traveling another minute in that wreck. After you went to sleep, I spoke with the innkeeper. Her brother is a carriage driver. He is happy to take us."

"All the way to Verdot?"

"Yes, for the right price, which I negotiated. See? I get things done."

"When you want to," Ella grumbled. She had to admit that since they entered France and passed inspection by gendarmes, Rose became more cooperative and cheerful. But at times too efficient.

Is Rose British or French? Ella wondered. *She is fluent in both languages, and I don't detect an accent.*

"I'm not going to fetch your hair comb, Duchess. Get yourself ready."

In twenty minutes, Ella came out and climbed into the carriage next to Rose. Mr. Doolittle sat across from them. Their belongings were inside, packed and ready to go. The guards positioned themselves on the upper level, where they could observe the surroundings for any sign of danger.

"Go," Rose urged. Ella was unsure if the woman couldn't wait to leave the inn or was anxious to get to their destination.

Perhaps she's tired of our company and wants to deliver us to Verdot as quickly as possible, Ella reasoned.

Mr. Doolittle scratched the stubble of his beard. "Pardon me, ladies, I didn't get a chance to shave this morning. And I haven't said my morning prayers. Perhaps you care to join me?"

Rose rolled her eyes. "No, thank you."

Ella folded her palms. "Let's pray for the prisoners, for their health and safety." Her thoughts were with Jamie and Tobby.

The shaking of the carriage and Mr. Doolittle's lengthy prayer made her sleepy. The sun lit the window, and she watched the hills and fields with hedgerows pass by.

When they drove by a farm that appeared abandoned and overrun by tall weeds, Rose's neck snapped to the window. Mr. Doolittle finished his prayers and watched the countryside.

"I noticed many farms are abandoned. Why is that?" Ella asked. She meant her question for Mr. Doolittle, but Rose spoke.

"Napoleon." Her nostrils flared. "His policies devastated these lands. The men conscripted into the army. Farmers ruined by the levies and taxes."

"You know these lands well?" Ella asked.

Rose tightened her lips into a line, as if she regretted what she said.

"Did you live here?"

"That's none of your business, Duchess." Rose crossed her arms.

After the modest breakfast, the three of them fell into silence. Mr. Doolittle snoozed with his mouth open, the Bible in his lap. Ella opened *Candide*, her favorite book in French. Rose's posture stayed rigid, her eyes fixed on the window.

After a couple of hours of shaking in the carriage, Ella's back hurt. She removed the map Mr. Greville gave her from her valise. Perhaps they were nearing a village. She would insist they stop and stretch their legs.

Their route on the map did go through several villages. But outside their window, the forest drew near. A refreshing scent of pine drifted through the air. She checked the map. The forest was south of their way.

"Rose," Ella waved to get the woman's attention. "Why are we passing near the forest?"

Rose sucked in her cheeks. "We are going on the right road. Don't you worry." She rummaged for something in her bag.

"I don't think so." Ella leaned to the window. "Driver, stop!"

In that moment, Rose's hand gripped Ella's shoulder and the cold barrel of the pistol was at Ella's temple. "Took you long enough to catch on. The pistol is loaded, so keep quiet."

Ella's insides froze. Her pulse thumped in her ears.

"Keep driving, Jacques!" Rose yelled. "Faster!"

"What's happening?" Mr. Doolittle's eyes fluttered. Then they snapped open. He gasped and dropped the Bible on his foot.

Rose's voice was colder than the metal pressing into Ella's head. "One word or move and I will blow her head off."

Mr. Doolittle paled and raised his palms up. "Please spare me! I'm doing God's work!"

Ella's heart dropped. "What do you want, Rose? Money? Take what I have and let me go. I must get to Verdot."

A piercing whistle came from the distance.

Rose laughed. "We have arrived, Duchess."

The carriage came to a sudden halt. Two shots, then clank of steel on steel, mixed with yells and screams sounded from outside. Their escorts must have been fighting Rose's accomplices, whoever they were. Ella wanted to hit herself for letting Rose fool her.

Another pistol shot made Doolittle jump. He crouched on the floor to protect himself from a stray bullet. Ella did not dare to stir. When all grew quiet, Rose pushed Ella out of the carriage. Her pistol barrel was still tight at Ella's temple. She yelled to Doolittle to follow.

"You run and I shoot her!" Rose warned.

What happened to our guards? Are they dead? Ella thought with horror.

Doolittle clambered out, holding his money bag to his chest. When his legs touched the ground, he sprang to the thick trees with a surprising agility. A musket round hit a large tree that hid his escape.

Rose gaped. "He just left you to die? Who does that?" Her grip on Ella weakened. Perhaps on her pistol as well.

Mustering her strength, Ella struck Rose with her elbow into her abdomen. Rose doubled over and dropped the pistol.

Ella lifted her skirt and ran, desperately missing her trousers. Before she could make ten steps, another pistol barrel aimed at her chest, held by a tall man in black. He was coming straight at her, his finger on the trigger. She froze and raised her hands.

Chapter 19

Jamie stopped hammering to wipe the sweat off his face. His body ached after a long day of work. Overall, he was pleased with their progress. Last week, they cleaned the chapel and started using it for prayer, led by one prisoner who was a vicar's son. Jamie also used the chapel to offer lessons in reading and writing. So far only Tobby, Culpepper and his old crew had shown interest.

Today, they began turning the old barracks into the infirmary. With the remedies Jamie bought from the apothecary, more men became well enough to toil. Surprisingly, even Simkins and his cronies came out to work even though they scowled any time Jamie approached them. The guards watched from a distance without interfering or helping. Jamie was unsure how much English they understood.

The pink shadows in the clouds reminded him that their time outside was nearly over. They did not spend all day in the cell, but they were still prisoners. The tall walls that blocked the view reminded him of that.

"Stop. Everyone, turn in your tools," he called. The hammering seized and the whisper of a flowing river resonated from beyond the walls.

Perhaps Conor is taking a swim while we labor. Jamie's mouth turned down, but then he dismissed the envious thought. *It's my choice to be here and help these men. Besides, Conor said he's a poor swimmer.*

When men finished gathering the tools, he checked the bag and counted every piece.

"A hammer and a saw missing. Who has them?"

When no one spoke up, Jamie's spine stiffened.

"All tools must be turned in or guards will think we are stashing them away for an escape attempt. Look for them."

While men bent their heads to search, Jamie met eyes with grinning Simkins.

"This better not be your trick."

"Here is the hammer!" Tobby lifted the heavy instrument. "I found it behind the bushes."

The grin disappeared from Simkins' face and his piglike eyes became menacing.

"Simkins held it earlier." Culpepper said. "I saw him."

"Liar!" Simkins waved his fist in front of Culpepper's face. "I had nothing to do with this."

"Simkins, where is the saw?" Jamie asked with his arms crossed.

"Don't know."

"Then ask your friends. We cannot lose it."

Simkins grabbed Jamie's collar. His foul breath hit Jamie's nose. "And what will you do? Tell the guards?"

"If I must—"

"Did you hear that, you dogs?" Simkins shoved Jamie and addressed the men around him. "Flowers is ready to tell the Frogs. Shall we show him what we do to snitches?"

Jamie raised his hands. "A missing tool jeopardizes our plans."

"Perhaps I can make better plans." Simkins lowered his voice. "You can listen to Flowers as he orders you to fix a hospital and church, and perhaps... plant some flowers, since that's his name..." Simkin's cronies snickered at that.

"I like the suggestion," Jamie answered. "I was just thinking the yard is too bare and could use something to please the eye." Flowers reminded him of his mother and sisters, avid gardeners.

A cold shiver passed through him in that moment, as if someone's hateful stare fixed on the back of his neck. It wasn't the first time he experienced this strange sensation when he worked outside. *Perhaps it's a reminder that death is not too far, and I won't see my family.*

"You hear that!" Simkins jeered. "He'll have you plant bloody flowers. Only fools would listen to that snotty boy." He dropped his voice to a whisper again. "Those who are with me will soon taste freedom."

"I can't have that, Simkins." Jamie said. "The whole reason we received better conditions is because I promised Vignon that no one runs. Now bring back the saw."

Simkins thrust his fist beneath Jamie's nostrils. "You will have to fight me for it, lad."

Jamie's palms balled, and he stepped back, ready to duck a punch. "Is that a threat?"

"No, it's a challenge." Simkins cracked the knuckles of his heavy fists. "Whoever wins, gets to keep that saw."

***

The ropes cut into Ella's arms. Tied to the tree, she watched the robbers open her cases and valises. They didn't annunciate like her French tutor, but she understood them well enough.

"The guards likely had only a few coins on them, but the holy man cradled that bag to his chest. All three ran into the woods. Next time we shoot to kill," the driver grumbled. His name was Jacques. Of the group of three robbers, he appeared the oldest, with a gray mustache and hair.

"It doesn't matter," Rose said. "The woman has plenty of money and expensive things we can sell."

"Shame on you, Rose." Ella said in English. "You were given a mission. Instead, you involve yourself with bandits."

"I will gag you if you are not quiet," Rose said as she opened Ella's valise that contained her clothes. A surprised laugh came from her throat. "Shirt and trousers? Do you wear that, Duchess?"

Ella wished to have her arms or legs free, so she could've kicked herself. Having strangers go through her things, deciding what to keep and what to discard, was sickening. And how would she get to Verdot without money or documents?

The man who prevented her escape brought her medical bag out of the coach. Ella learned that his name was Louis. "What's this?" he asked as he studied the contents.

Ella groaned. They would take her scalpels and saws and use those as weapons instead of the life-saving instruments they were meant to be.

"We can sell these," Rosa said. "They look almost new."

"Does she know how to use those things?" Louis asked her.

Rose shrugged. "She's sent to work in a prison as a surgeon. Why do we care?"

"Because of Albert. He received a ball to his shoulder two days ago. The wound festers."

Rose's hand flew to her mouth. "I thought you made him stay behind because you wanted to keep him safe. Why didn't you say he was hurt?"

All eyes went to Ella. The three men laid down her valises. Rose stared at her, shielding herself with her crossed arms.

Louis approached, holding Ella's bag. He was quite tall, with overgrown hair that touched his shoulders. When he was pointing his pistol at Ella, he made her blood turn to ice. Now his chin had dropped to his chest.

They want me to care for their wounded mate, Ella guessed. *What if I can't save that man? Will they kill me?*

"My brother Albert is wounded," Louis spoke slowly, in French. "We'll set you free if you save his life." His voice did not carry menace. It carried... fear.

She scanned her attackers. Their gazes were averted, afraid to meet hers.

Of course she would care for the wounded, whoever he was. But she would take advantage of the situation.

"Untie me." She made her voice strong. Louis removed a knife from his belt and cut the ropes. Ella rubbed her wrists and shook her legs. Part of her wondered if she should dash for the trees.

"I need guarantees first. I give you my word that I will do what I can to save your brother. But no matter what happens, you will return my things and let me go."

"Only if you save him," Rose objected. But her posture, with dropped shoulders and her hands folded on her belly, lacked confidence.

"When it comes to Albert, I decide," Louis snapped at Rose. "Agreed," he said to Ella. "I trust you with my brother. You can trust us."

Ironic thing for a bandit to say. Yet his pleading expression touched her. *He may be a criminal, but he loves his brother.*

Encouraged, Ella raised her chin. "One more condition. I want—"

"Save Albert first, then we'll discuss your conditions," Jacques's grumbling interrupted her. "We may need you, but you need us, too. Alone, you won't make it wherever you are going."

A knot was in Ella's throat. Her life was in bandits' hands. And she had no guarantee they would keep their part of the bargain.

Chapter 20

J amie spotted Conor at the table in the corner of the half-empty tavern. Judging by the unpleasant smells of stale fish and oysters, Jamie doubted that roasted chicken his friend mentioned was served here. Four British officers called their wagers in the card game they were playing. When Jamie passed them by and sat across from Conor, they bent their heads and whispered to each other.

Conor leaned in, as if trying to hear them.

"You want to join them?" Jamie asked.

His friend's lips pouted. "Don't have the money. But I heard something interesting from them earlier. Supposedly, a couple of drunk French guards talked."

Jamie waved to the burly server and asked for bread and cheese. "About what?"

Conor sipped his wine and winced. Perhaps the drink was too sour. "That a British volunteer organized the prisoners to build an infirmary. When some tools disappeared, and a seaman prisoner was caught red-handed, that sailor challenged the volunteer to a fight. A scandalous thing to our officers. Gentlemen can duel, and jack tars can wrestle, but a fight between a gentleman and a common sailor... they don't approve."

"We are not on the ship, and not in England." Jamie shrugged.

"True. Rules are laxer here. Especially considering that the same volunteer had been sharing the cell with the men since he arrived."

"I'm sure they don't approve of that either. But why should I care what they think?"

Conor surveyed the tavern with a bored expression. "There are too few amusements here. Everyone is tired of gambling and drinking. And since a couple of fellows caught syphilis, they stopped visiting the nearby brothel."

Jamie winced. "That ailment is named French disease for a reason."

"The officers want to watch the fight. And they are taking wagers. Rumor is the seaman is a much larger man than the young volunteer. They are betting on the giant to win."

"He's not quite a giant, but they are choosing a safer bet. Who do you want to wager on?"

Conor rubbed his forehead. "On you. I already paid. But now that I see you, I realize it wasn't my brightest moment. Have you ever been in a fight?"

"Not like the one I got myself into. I had fencing lessons, and I read a book about boxing. Oh, I was in one fight as a boy. It wasn't much of a fight because my ma interfered."

"There goes the last of my money." Conor groaned.

"Perhaps you can give me advice."

"Advice." Conor drummed his fingers on the table. "Did you finish repairing that infirmary?"

"No, we just started."

"That's too bad. You'll need it after that fight. Broken ribs hurt something awful. I speak from experience." Conor's shoulders shivered.

"Teach me what to do."

"Didn't you hear me?" Conor threw up his hands. "I lost that fight. It was over a card debt. The men I fought with left me for dead. I crawled home, spitting up blood on the way."

"Jesus!" Jamie brought his hand to his mouth. "Who cared for you?"

Conor shifted on his seat. "My father came home from his voyage two days later. He bound my injuries."

"And you say that you hardly know your father. He came in time to save you."

Conor's chin trembled. "He said he'd whip me if he could find a spot on me that wasn't black and blue already. Then he paid the landlady to care for me and left. I waited for him to return. I wanted to talk to him, ask him for some fatherly advice.

Even a whipping would be better than thinking that he despises me."

"Did he come back?"

"No." Conor made a noise in his throat as if stifling a sigh. "A couple of months later I received a message from him. It came on my seventeenth birthday. I got excited, thinking he wrote to congratulate me. There was not a mention of my birthday or a concern about my injuries. He said that he asked a fellow captain for a favor, something he should have done years ago. He ordered me to report to the *Neptune.*"

"He cares about you. He likely didn't want to ask for favors, yet he did it for you. Perhaps he hoped you would learn discipline and find your purpose on the ship."

Conor cringed. "Enough about my troubles. I need you to win that fight. Do you still have your knife?"

"Yes, but I won't use weapons. It would not be fair."

"You think your opponent will fight fair?" Conor raised an eyebrow.

"I may be fighting with my fists, but I will fight with honor. And I must win to become an undisputed leader among the prisoners. Many are squarely on my side, but Simkins has his followers. This is a fight for leadership. Besides, I'm responsible for the tools, and Simkins stole a saw."

"I sure hope you thrash that Simkins. Not only to win my bet, but... He sounds like a man who broke my ribs for not paying the debt on time."

Jamie licked his dried lips. "I've had this book about boxing with illustrations. But it was only a book. I haven't applied what it taught."

Conor pushed himself away from the table. "Let's go outside. You'll show me what you remember."

***

Rose and Louis flanked Ella, while the other bandits walked in front and behind her. They were deep in the woods, with little sunshine seeping through the trees. Chilly air and anxiety made her shiver.

Jacques, who led the group, changed direction to the right and disappeared. Ella squinted into a pile of branches and dry grass before she realized they hid a shack.

The robbers' den. Ella's breath caught.

There was no chance for her to run. In the thick of the forest, she would be lost. Attacked by wild animals. If her pursuers didn't catch her first.

Straw and leaves rustled under her feet as she followed Louis and Rose. A lantern illuminated the makeshift shelter, roughly the size of her cabin.

"I'll make a fire." Jacques said and stumbled out of the crowded space.

"Please bring me some water," Ella called after him. "I'll need it to wash my instruments and clean the wound."

Would they get angry at me for commanding them? But I must have their assistance.

Louis stepped next to a man who lay under a wool blanket. Until that moment, Ella imagined that her patient would be a tall, intimidating man, like Louis. But the dim light revealed a face of a man too young to shave. His eyes were closed, and face was flushed with fever.

Rose's hand circled Ella's wrist. It was icy cold.

"Albert." Louis kneeled by his brother. "We brought you a surgeon. She'll tend to your wound."

The injured bandit stirred but didn't open his eyes. "Too late. You should've brought a priest instead."

Ella's brows flew up. *A robber who wants last rites?*

"Don't you speak like that." Louis felt his brother's forehead and winced.

Crouching, Ella moved down the blanket, exposing the patient's shoulder, tied with a scarf. When her fingers removed the bandage, they touched warm skin. An entry wound was clearly visible, with red flesh and dried blood around the hole. The ball was likely stuck in the muscle. Perhaps it shattered a bone, but it didn't break a major artery, or the man would've bled to death.

She brought the stained scarf to her nose, inhaling the metallic smell of dry blood. It did not reek of rot or pus that accompanied festered wounds. Nor could she see the greenish discharge.

"How did you keep his wound clean?" she asked Louis.

"I washed it with water several times a day. And changed his bandages."

"Don't we have vinegar?" Rose interjected.

Louis muttered something under his breath. "I forgot about vinegar."

"If you have it, we'll pour it on the wound after I remove the ball," Ella said. "Now, I need more light and my bag."

Rose handed her the medical bag, and Louis brought the lantern closer.

Ella removed a small bottle of laudanum, wrapped in several layers of fabric. Weakened by blood loss, Albert would likely faint during surgery, but she believed in making treatment as painless as possible. She poured the dose into a vial and let Louis coax his brother into drinking it.

As her patient's breathing deepened from drugged sleep, she removed a scalpel, forceps, needle and catgut from her bag. She also prepared all the bandages she brought. Hopefully, along the way, she would be able to replenish her supplies. If they let her continue her way.

"Are you getting started?" Rose asked. She hugged her knees to her belly.

"There are a few more steps to prepare," Ella answered. She inserted a strap into Albert's mouth to protect his tongue. "Someone will need to hold him down. Rose, why don't you hold his head, while Louis holds his legs."

Louis kneeled by the patient's legs, but Rose winced and grabbed her abdomen. Her complexion turned a greenish hue.

Ella gave her a sharp look. "If you are feeling sick, you better leave and ask someone else to help. Your weakness may impair the surgery."

"I'll ask Jacques." She hastened out, holding her palm to her mouth.

A minute later, Jacques squeezed in and dropped on his knees by the patient's head. A bucket with water was in his hand.

"Rose is retching like she never saw blood before," he grumbled to Louis. "The girl used to deliver calves with me."

Louis did not reply. His gaze was glued to his brother's face.

Why would an agent deliver calves? Ella wondered. She shook her head and lifted the sounder.

"Hold him tight and don't speak. I'm going to look for the ball."

Both men grew so quiet, Ella suspected they held their breaths. As she inserted her instrument into the wound, Albert moaned and writhed. The two assistants held him down. Her movements were precise and careful. Metal clinked on metal. As she suspected, the ball was deep in the muscle tissue, near major arteries. One careless move and the patient could bleed to death. That would likely lead to her own demise, as Louis and the others would kill her, despite the prior assurance. She had to remove the ball without causing harm to the young robber.

Chapter 21

"Jamie!" Tobby slipped inside the church followed by Culpepper. "We want to wish you good luck."

Jamie stood from the pew. He wasn't a religious man and didn't use the time before the fight to pray. He just needed a quiet place to get his thoughts together.

"Thank you, my friends."

He studied Culpepper's ashen face. The remedies Jamie purchased from the apothecary made Culpepper well enough to leave the cell, but he still coughed profusely.

I need to win this fight so we can work as one and finish the infirmary.

Tobby bounced on his toes. "You will win, Jamie. I just know it." Jamie offered him his hand, but the boy jumped into an embrace.

"Sir," Culpepper lowered his voice. "I think Simkins will fight dirty. You should be prepared for his tricks."

"He doesn't need tricks. He's larger and stronger than me. But I did my best to prepare."

Jamie stepped out into the yard. Almost all the prisoners were gathered there. Most men appeared cheerful, with eyes shining. The guards were here as well, as were the British officers from the town. Conor was among them, his face tense and his forehead creased.

Simkins was surrounded by his followers as usual. "Look, he was hiding in the church. Were you praying for a miracle, Flowers? That's your only chance to win." His friends chortled.

Jamie ignored the taunt. He stepped forward to the middle of the yard. As he walked, he noticed the ground was slightly muddy after yesterday's rain. When Simkins came close, Jamie offered him a hand to shake.

"We fight fair. If you lose, you must give back the saw. And I must warn you, the ground may be slippery."

Simkins crossed his arms, refusing to shake Jamie's hand or to acknowledge the warning.

Commander Vignon approached. "The tools are mine. Even if Mr. Flowers loses the fight, he must get the saw back somehow, by our agreement."

Jamie stared Simkins in the eye. "Last chance for you to tell me where you hid the saw."

Simkins stepped forward with his arm raised. Jamie thought he wanted to shake hands after all. But when Simkin's face froze into a grimace, Jamie instinctively jerked back and ducked. The punch just missed him. Then Simkins threw himself at him. He jumped out of the way, but Simkins's arm and shoulder caught him. Jamie fell backwards. The sailor lowered and pressed a knee to his right side, constricting air in Jamie's lungs. Conor's warning about broken ribs echoed in his mind.

Simkins raised his fist, aiming to punch Jamie in the eye. Jamie blocked the punch by crossing his arms over his face. Then he brought his left leg around, wedging it between his chest and his opponent's throat. The heavy man shifted off Jamie's side, and Jamie rolled onto his abdomen.

Breathing hard, Jamie rose to his feet and assumed a boxing stance.

"Punch him," men yelled. He hoped the encouragement was for him and not his opponent.

Jamie filled his lungs with air and charged. He landed a couple of quick punches on Simkin's chest. The large man showed no reaction. Then his blow glanced the side of Jamie's neck. Jamie's next punch hit his opponent on the nose. With a grunt, Simkins stepped back. A fountain of blood sprayed from the nostrils.

"Do you want to stop? With first blood?" Jamie offered.

"Not a chance," Simkins roared.

He lunged at Jamie again. This time Jamie jumped out the way like a toreador evading the charging bull.

Simkins's head jerked in surprise. He sprang after Jamie, but slipped and fell forward with his face hitting the muddy ground.

Jamie clenched and unclenched his fists as he waited for Simkins to rise. As he rolled his shoulders, a shiver passed through him like an icy wind. A movement caught his eye. Jamie glanced up to the highest floor of the citadel. A face, framed by the small window, stared back. Something about that face made his blood chill.

Yells of many voices at once brought him back into the fight. Simkins leapt at him—a knife clenched in his hand.

Jamie ducked, his instincts saving him. The knife struck the air above his shoulder.

"You didn't know I have a knife, did you?" Simkins hissed. "You are dead."

Don't I know it. Which is why I have nothing to lose.

His heart hammered so fast it dizzied him.

Simkins's next strike aimed at Jamie's chest. Jamie crouched and punched Simkins's knee. The large man waved his hands as if trying to grab on to air. Off balance, he fell backwards. The knife flew in Jamie's direction.

A sharp pain made Jamie cry out. The blade struck his ankle. Blood colored his stocking. He bent down, lifted the knife, and threw it to Renaut. Simkins bared his clenched teeth as the guard hid his weapon.

"Ready to end this, Simkins?" Jamie wiped the sweat off his face. "We both are tired and need to clean our wounds. Tell me where the saw is, and we'll call it a draw."

With a bloodcurdling cry, Simkins threw himself at him. Jamie poured his strength into his legs, but the charge forced him to step back. His foot slipped on the mud, and he dropped onto his side. Simkins, with the momentum behind him, fell onto his belly. Jamie kneeled on his opponent's back and pulled on his leg, twisting it. Conor taught him this maneuver. It was supposed to give the adversary intense pain. Before the fight, Jamie resolved not to use it. But ending the struggle could save both from more injuries.

"Stop! Aaah!" Simkins heaved.

"Give up?" Jamie asked.

Simkins's voice diminished from a roar to a shriek.

"Where is the saw?"

"Someone bring it." Simkins croaked. "Let go, you bugger."

Jamie released Simkins and straightened. One of Simkin's friends disappeared inside for a moment. He brought the saw and laid it on the ground in the middle of the yard.

The men and the guards clapped and cheered. Tobby jumped with his hands up. Officers wore sour expressions as Conor collected his winnings. He grinned at Jamie and winked.

A feeling of warmth washed over him as he flashed a smile at the men. But in contrast, a cold breath touched the back of his neck. He spun and again glimpsed a face in the window of the top floor.

"Watch out!" someone warned.

Simkins was running at him, his body bent at the waist. This time Jamie acted like his book on boxing taught him. His punch hit Simkins under the jaw. The large man collapsed as if struck by a rock. Seconds passed, but Simkins lay motionless.

"You knocked him out, sir," Culpepper said, approaching.

Stunned by what he did, Jamie shook himself. He bent down to Simkins. To his relief, the man's chest rose and dropped, but he didn't respond to Jamie calling his name or touching his bloodied face.

Conor's hand patted his back. "You did it, Jamie. We must celebrate with my winnings."

Jamie ignored him and addressed a couple of strongest prisoners who gathered around him. "Please take Simkins inside. It's too bad the infirmary isn't finished. But if we all work together, it will be in a few days."

When the men carried Simkins away, Tobby's hand touched Jamie's. "Your leg is bleeding."

The pain he temporarily forgot cut into him. His body shook from weariness.

Conor gave him his arm. "Sit by the wall."

Each step gave Jamie pain that resonated throughout his body. When he reached the wall, he sat and pulled off his shoe and stocking. Renaut handed him a flask of water. Jamie washed off the dirt and blood and inspected the cut.

"It doesn't look too bad," Conor said. "Keep it clean and it should heal fast."

Conor removed his neck scarf. As he was tying it around the wound, the world swayed before Jamie's eyes. The face he earlier saw in the window appeared before him. It was a woman with pale skin and disheveled long hair. Her eyes were full of loathing as she stared at him. The hair on the back of his neck lifted from her furious gaze.

"Jamie, are you asleep?" Conor shook him by the shoulder. "How does your leg feel?"

He glanced down at his leg, tightly wrapped.

"Feels fine. Thank you." His tongue grew sluggish.

"You need some rest."

Conor gave Jamie a hand to stand; many eyes followed his movement.

The men need to see that I'm not badly hurt.

Gingerly putting weight on his leg, Jamie made himself walk slowly but without assistance.

"Let's all rest for an hour. Then we work on the infirmary," he said in his full voice.

"Aye, aye, sir," replied every prisoner present.

Chapter 22

Louis fetched some rags, and Ella tucked them under Albert's shoulder. The cushion would make her patient more comfortable and absorb spilled blood. Then she checked the tourniquet one more time. It was as tight as she could make it. Her instruments, cleaned with sand and water, reflected the dim light of the lantern. All was ready. With a deep breath, she lifted her scalpel.

"Must you cut him? Can't you take it out with those?" Jacques pointed at the forceps.

"I use the scalpel to clear the way. Then I can use the forceps to remove the ball."

Jacques scratched his mustache. "But won't he bleed? He lost much blood already. And pain?"

"Jacques, *arrêt*. Let her do what she must," Louis said in a hoarse voice.

"No." Jacques glared at Louis and then at Ella. "I've never heard of a woman surgeon before. What if she's a pretender? We can't let her cut Albert. She must tell us how she knows what she's doing first."

Ella lay down the scalpel. Her insides stewed. Of all the people she had to prove her credentials to she never imagined that she'd be questioned by bandits.

"Like Rose told you, I was on my way to treat British prisoners. Do you think the Naval Board would send me if I weren't qualified? I've served as a ship surgeon for over two years."

Jacques tilted his head. "Tell us how you plan to remove the ball without hurting him more." He spoke in a quieter voice, which somehow sounded more threatening than a holler.

Her heart was in her throat. If the patient screamed in pain, as he well might, they'd think she was harming him. If he lost too much blood... Her bladder threatened to loosen at the thought what these men may do to her.

I've answered challenging questions before. In medical school I raised my hand to answer at every chance to impress Dr. Miller.

Her memories returned her into the hospital ward, and she spoke as if she was in front of her esteemed professor.

"This tourniquet will restrict the flow of blood. I will proceed carefully not to nick the artery beneath his arm." She traced its route with her finger. If she were speaking before her instructor, she'd name and point out the six branches of that artery. For the bandits, she thought she was being detailed enough. "I will start with the scalpel to slice the skin. Then a lancet to cut through fat and muscle tissues." She paused because Jacques shivered.

"That should remove all obstructions to extract the musket ball with the forceps. Once I manage that, I will clean the wound and apply sutures. As for pain, I had administered laudanum, as much as I could give him. And I will work as fast as I can. I'm known to amputate limbs in under two minutes."

Jacque jerked back. "Rose scares me at times. But she's nothing compared to this British woman and her knives," he said to Louis.

Is he afraid of me? She held her breath to stifle a laugh.

"The faster this is over, the better," Louis croaked with a pained expression.

"I agree." Ella breathed and peered at Jacques. "Did I convince you?"

"Convinced me enough to give me nightmares. What do you want us to do?"

To keep your mouth shut.

"Hold him tight. He's nearly senseless, but pain may still cause him to thrash."

When Jacques pressed his calloused hands into the patient's healthy shoulder, she gripped her scalpel. Blood pooled under the blade as she made the incision. Albert moaned and arched his back, but her assistants held him tight. The red stream ran down the shoulder.

I must work faster, or he'll lose too much blood.

Sweat formed on her forehead and trickled down her cheeks.

She couldn't stop to wipe it. Her left hand was swabbing the blood, her other was cutting into the flesh with the lancet. Yet, she feared that drops of sweat may fall into the cavity and cause an inflammation deep inside. Dr. Miller would laugh at her concern, as he used instruments crusted with blood, but she believed in the theory her friend Oli formed that clean hands and instruments could prevent festering.

"Please. Wipe the sweat off my brow," she whispered to Louis. When he gave her a bewildered look, she explained. "I don't want it to drip inside the open wound. But don't use any of the bandages I prepared."

He glanced around, then removed his coat. Ella realized that he planned to use the sleeve to wipe her forehead. It was soiled with dirt and smelled of smoke.

"I have a handkerchief in my pocket."

Ella froze as the man thrust his hand into the slit in her gown. The pouch hung low, touching her thigh. She bristled as he rummaged there.

Serves me right for not helping Rose when someone had to retrieve the letter from her petticoats.

Louis retrieved the handkerchief and gently wiped her forehead. Her hands were stained with blood halfway up to elbows, but they never stopped moving. Albert was losing blood. With forceps, she dug around for the ball that was hidden under the dark stream.

When she felt something hard and was about to clench the object, Albert shuddered and moaned. His head rocked from side to side, as if he was trapped in a nightmare. Jacques and Louis held him down. Her hand trembled, but she managed to grip the ball. Once she secured it in the jaws of her forceps, she pulled. Blood flowed, staining her skirt. The ball was trapped in the tissues. She had to cut the way for it.

The dose of laudanum must've worn out, because when she sliced the thick muscles, Albert cried out. The boy's agony twisted her gut. Jacques's furious glare made the hair on her arms stand. But the ball was free, and she brought it out. A long breath escaped her chest, followed by a noisy exhale from Louis.

With warm water and strips of bandages, she cleaned the wound. Then she poured vinegar to prevent inflammation. It didn't always work, but many surgeons she knew favored it. The vinegar must've stung, because Albert opened his eyes, dull from laudanum. His face cringed into a grimace of pain and fear.

"*Mamm*," he called.

Louis's chip trembled. "But our mother has been dead for ten years."

Furrowing his brow, Jacques touched Albert's face. "His forehead is burning."

"It will take time to bring the fever down." Ella said. She was threading the needle to apply sutures. "Comfort him however you can. Whatever you think he wishes to hear."

Louis spoke in a language Ella didn't know but guessed to be Breton. Albert's face, ashen with blood loss, calmed. As Louis kept speaking, the shadow of a smile appeared on the lad's cracked lips. His muscles relaxed, allowing Ella to close the incision. By the time she finished dressing the wound, her patient was asleep again.

"I used to tell him the story of Yann the Fool when he was a little boy," Louis said and patted his brother's head with affection.

People are not so different, whoever they are, Ella thought. *Rich or poor, French or English, when we are ill, we want our mothers or a story that comforted us in our childhoods.*

Ella lifted the patient's wrist to count his pulse. Despite the blood loss and fever, it was steady and even.

"How is he, *médecin*?" Despite the hint of irony in Jacques's tone, his expression warmed.

"He should recover. I will monitor his fever. His rest is imperative, so best only one of us stays with him to avoid disturbing him."

Jacques stood and rubbed his knees. "Let's go make dinner, Louis. I'm famished."

Louis hesitated and turned to her. "*Merci*, Miss Ella. We are in your debt."

Ella let her head fall back. *Perhaps they will keep their word and spare my life.*

***

"Ella! Sit with us and have some food." Rose called. The aroma of gamy meat cooked on the bonfire made Ella's mouth water. As cool sweat trickled down his forehead, Albert slept with a peaceful expression. His fever had broken. She covered him with another blanket and approached the bonfire where Louis, Rose, Jacques, and the other two men assembled in a semicircle. As soon as she sat, Louis sped back to the shelter to check on his brother.

The bandits ate the juicy meat with their hands, chasing it down with a drink in a flask they passed to one another.

I'm about to share a meal with thieves, who also happen to be French, my country's enemies. The thought left her amused rather than shocked. Her teeth sank into the pink chunk of meat. Juice ran down her face, making her chin greasy. When Jacques passed her the flask, she expected a strong drink to burn her throat, but the sweetness of apples refreshed her.

"This is delicious," she said.

"My cider was always the best in all of Brittany." Rose threw her shoulders back. "*Maman* and I would prepare it all winter."

"How is Albert?" Jacques lifted a massive hunting knife which he used to cut another piece of meat.

"Better. His wound needs to be kept clean, but he should recover."

Jacques passed the generous portion to her. "You have our thanks."

"Louis already lost one brother. He was also shot." Rose remarked. "When I saw Albert's wound, it was like seeing his brother's ghost. So please don't think I'm easy to rattle."

"Another robbery gone bad?" Ella asked.

Eyes pierced her, and she suspected that the cider loosened her tongue and made her say a wrong thing.

"None of us wanted this life." Jacques stared down at the ground. "It's all Napoleon. We were conscripted to fight for him. What for? We were peaceful farmers."

"Only Pierre, Louis's and Albert's other brother, wished to give his life for Emperor Bonaparte." Rose spread her hands wide. "He did just so. But he was only a boy, much too young to see the cruelty and unfairness of Napoleon's rule. He made it home gravely injured and died the same night he returned."

Ella swallowed. "These wars between our countries have gone on so long and cost so many lives. It's one of the reasons I became a ship surgeon. I wanted to heal the wounded."

"Losing Pierre was the final blow." Rose balled her fists. Her cheeks flushed from cider and perhaps anger she bottled inside too long. "I tended to the farm since I was little. Papa said it would be my inheritance. But taxes and levies left us in poverty. Then we learned that army recruiters were on their way, and the farmhands hid in the woods. When soldiers came, they took horses, livestock, and our stores of food. We were left to starve. My parents caught an illness in the winter and died. After Pierre perished in my arms, I joined my farmhands in the forest."

"First we survived by hunting and fishing," Jacques said. "But then Rose came up with various schemes. But when we are in a dire need of money... It's shameful, but we turn to robbery."

"Sorry, Duchess, but you and the holy man made easy targets." Rose gave her a weak smile. "I should stop calling you that. You are not what I expected you to be."

"Neither are you." Ella tilted her head. "But don't you spy for England?"

Rose pursed her lips. "England is an important ally. We won't be rid of Napoleon without it. But I don't serve your king. I serve my own cause."

"My cause is an important one," Ella said. "I am going to tend to British prisoners." At the thought of Jamie, her heart sped up. She wanted to tell him about today's adventure. "And I have another mission I must fulfill."

"I have a mission as well." Rose shifted in her seat. "Jacques will take us to Verdot, but once we reach town, we'll go separate ways. It's best that Commander Vignon doesn't know that we are acquainted, or he may become suspicious."

As she contemplated her secret mission, Ella's stomach, full of rich food and sweet alcohol, roiled. *What will I have to do to uncover how the prisoners disappeared?*

Branches cracked and steps pounded as if a large animal was nearby. Ella and the bandits sprang to their feet. Jacques loaded his pistol.

"Help! For Heaven's sake help me!" A male voice shrilled in English. "I'm thirsty and hungry."

"That's Mr. Doolittle." Ella guessed. She wasn't particularly pleased to see the chaplain after he left her to fend bandits alone, but she didn't wish for him to die in the forest either.

"We are steps away from a creek, and he ate breakfast this morning," Rose muttered. "He's so pitiful, I'm tempted to shoot him."

"He should still have that money purse that he clutched when he ran away," Jacques said.

"Please save me." Mr. Doolittle's voice quivered. "I need medical aid."

"Oh, no. I must help." Ella raised her voice. "Come out here, Mr. Doolittle."

With his pistol in hand, Jacques strode behind the clearing and soon returned with Mr. Doolittle. When the chaplain stepped up to the bonfire, he dropped onto his knees. His clothes were ripped and covered with thorns, and his hands shook. "Thank you, Lord for saving me from vicious animals and starvation and for bringing me to safety." He studied Ella with a guilty expression. "Dr. Parker, I need your help. A splinter lodged itself into my palm."

"A splinter." Ella rolled her eyes. "You must be dying."

"Please don't laugh at me." Mr. Doolittle brought his hands to his chest. "I've suffered a horrible day, alone in the forest. I searched for the guards, our brave companions, but never found them. And you, I thought you were long lost."

Ella crossed her arms. "That's because you left me with the bandits to save yourself. But now, these people are my friends."

Chapter 23

Culpepper's face had taken on more color when Jamie checked on him. The fire in the chimney kept the newly fixed infirmary warm. Four other sick men were also here, looking comfortable in their beds. All were afflicted with cough, and Jamie hoped that better air, warmth, and rest would cure these men. Or at least keep them alive until the surgeon arrives. Despite Jamie's efforts and the medicines from the apothecary, three men had perished of lung illness.

"How are you feeling, my friends?" Jamie asked

"Better, sir." Culpepper answered. He rubbed his head. "Just wish that hammering outside would stop."

"We are almost finished. Tomorrow, after a good night's sleep, you will be able to sit on the benches in the sun."

A man stepped in and saluted him. "We are done, sir."

When Jamie followed him outside, two wooden benches, sturdy and well built, stood before them. The men stretched their shoulders and shook out their hands, smiling. Even Simkins's friends surveyed the results of everyone's labor with nods of respect. Simkins hadn't left the cell since the fight two weeks ago. While he sulked over his defeat, Jamie and all able-bodied prisoners worked together and finished the infirmary.

Jamie sat down on the bench and ran his hand over the smooth wood. "Well, it can hold me." He laughed and men grinned back. "Great work, everyone. I have something to reward you." He removed tobacco from his pouch. "Enjoy, my friends."

While the men chewed the tobacco with pleasure written all over their faces, Tobby perched next to Jamie. "How soon will the flowers grow?" he asked, staring at the sprouts Renaut brought them to plant.

"Soon enough," Jamie replied. Flowers would remind him of his mother and sisters tending to their garden. "Perhaps later we'll plant vegetables, so we have even better food."

The deal with Vignon brought the results Jamie hoped for. The men received fresh straw and better sustenance. The guards emptied the waste buckets more frequently and brought water for washing. The prisoners did useful work and listened to Jamie's reading or sung hymns in the church. On the days the weather kept them indoors, Jamie led them in fitness exercises his fencing teacher taught him. With better diet, healthier conditions, and activities to work their bodies and minds, the men no longer looked hopeless and defeated.

The setting sun and the grumbling in his stomach reminded him it was time for supper. He called for the men to go inside. As they crossed the yard, a strange sensation, like a breath of winter chill, made the hair on his back stand.

My nineteenth birthday was last week. This must be death reminding me that it is coming soon enough.

After the long day of work, most fell asleep right after the supper of hearty soup that emitted an unfamiliar but aromatic scent. Jamie was too tired to enjoy it and only drank a mouthful. Tobby also pushed away his bowl and complained that the soup was too bitter. But the others were famished and emptied their plates with eagerness, except for Simkins, who complained of a severe headache and demanded to be taken to the infirmary.

The throb in his almost healed cut, as well as cramps in arms and back, kept Jamie awake. He closed his eyes, hoping for sleep to finally take him. After a while, Ella's slender figure appeared. She was staring at the flowers he planted by the infirmary. They'd grown and blossomed, making a lush garden.

"Why did you plant flowers?" she asked him.

"I thought you and my sisters would like them. Even if you'll never see them."

A light shined into his face and the dream disappeared. He cringed, frustrated that Ella had vanished. He so longed to see her smile. But the light stayed on his face, bringing him back to his cell. When his eyes snapped open, a woman stood before him, holding a flickering candle. Her hair was down to her knees and disheveled. She was barefoot and wore nothing but a shift that clung to her bony figure.

Jamie gasped. He wanted to throw his blanket on the woman's shoulders to protect her from the frigid air and men's eyes. But everyone seemed dead to the world except him. And there was something ghostlike in this woman's sallow skin and emaciated figure. If he did throw a blanket over her, it might find nothing but air.

She brought the candle closer to his face, as if to inspect his features better. Breath caught in his throat as her face became a terrible mask fury with bared teeth and black eyes.

It's a nightmare. I need to wake.

"It's you," she hissed like a snake. She spoke English, if such voice could be called human.

Cold sweat formed on Jamie's forehead. "What do you want of me?"

She threw her head back and laughed—a chilling sound that made his skin tingle. "Your death."

His heart hammered against his ribs, as if trying to break free. The room spun in front of him.

It's happening. She must be here to take my life. I'm finally dying.

The faces of his family appeared to him. In his mind he said a loving goodbye to his parents and sisters. Guilt choked him as he thought of Ella.

I never told her about my heart. Perhaps she expected me to return from France and build a future with her.

The night visitor lit the faces of men slumbering next to him, studying them. Her voice rustled like dried leaves. "Are the others here?"

He bolted upright. Whatever was to happen, it was meant for him only. He couldn't allow this spirit or whoever she was to steal anyone else's life. Blinking to stop the world from spinning, he scrambled to stand. Her gaze was fixed on Tobby, who slept with his palms folded under his cheek. The boy's eyes fluttered in the light of the candle. Jamie clapped his hands to make the visitor turn to him.

"I'm ready. Do what you must."

The woman, if she was a woman, gestured for him to follow out of the prison door. The guard snored on his chair as they crept by him. With his eyes fixed on the flickering candle, Jamie staggered through the winding passageways of the old fortress. A narrow stairway brought them into a tunnel that was likely constructed to provide a covert escape route out of the citadel in the event of a siege. The air grew colder and mustier, reminding Jamie of the orlop deck on the ship.

Their path wound and forked, yet the woman showed no hesitancy when choosing the way. Her head almost touched the ceiling. Jamie had to crouch and suffer the throbbing in his leg.

To keep his wits together and not let himself give in to panic brewing inside him, he made himself count the turns they made and note their direction. This was like a game he played with Caroline when they were younger. He would bury a treasure, a pretty shell or a colorful rock, and draw a map with instructions for his sister to find it.

Something crunched under his foot. He gasped. The flicker of the light revealed what looked like bones. Did someone die in this passage while searching for the way out? Jamie shuddered as he thought of death from hunger and thirst.

Several turns later they stumbled upon a full skeleton that slumped against the wall. "What happened here?" he dared to ask. His guide didn't respond.

After many more turns, which Jamie etched in his mind, she pushed on a rock. It retreated into the wall, creating an opening one could crawl into. Jamie squeezed after his guide and finally straightened to his full height. He inhaled lungs full of air, but the foul stench of rotting flesh made him cough. The candle illuminated at least a dozen corpses spread among the room. Worms crawled in empty eye sockets and feasted on the remains. Some corpses wore rags. Others were only bones. And one was wrapped in a navy frock coat of the Royal Navy just like the one Jamie was wearing.

Jamie grabbed onto the wall to prevent his knees from buckling. The woman faced him with bulging eyes. Her lips turned up as if she tried to smile, but the effect was terrifying.

"You recognize your friends?"

Words refused to form on his tongue. "I don't understand."

"Liar!" Saliva foamed at her mouth. "They too tried to deny it. Said they've never been to Quiberon Bay. Never saw me before. Never hurt a woman in their lives. All lies!"

He spurred himself to recall what his father told him of the invasion of Quiberon Bay by England. From what he remembered, it happened in 1795, seventeen years ago. He was a small child then.

A cold shiver traveled down his spine. *This is not a spirit of death. She is a woman, and she's seeking someone who hurt her.*

"Ah, your face betrays you. You recognized me. Your wicked tongue may deny your crimes, but I know you were there, with all these men." She coughed and winced, as if speech hurt her throat. "You shelled my home, destroyed it to the ground. My mother died in the rubble. You looted what you could salvage, and then you found me, hiding in the cellar. Do you remember what you did to me? What your comrades did?"

She believes that I, a British officer, could've been there. Her harmed mind cannot comprehend the passage of time and her attackers growing older since that battle.

Obviously, she was raving mad. And extremely dangerous. Yet his heart squeezed for her. If French soldiers attacked his town, destroyed his home. Violated his sisters... His eyes welled with tears, but his arms grew tense, as if he wanted to throttle anyone who'd threatened them.

Despite his compassion for a woman hurt by his countrymen and his desire to tell her that he loved his mother and sisters and would never intentionally hurt a woman, he had to stop her. Her vengeance must end with him.

"It was me." He deepened his voice to sound convincing. "I take full responsibility for all you accuse me of. I was the leader of these men. You've found them all. Now you can kill me, and your revenge will be complete."

Her features softened. The grimace transformed into a tired face of a gaunt woman with wrinkles near her eyes. Her thin lips stretched into a smile. "Yes, I will avenge myself and my mother. I feel her joy."

Jamie rubbed his hands from the chill. *How does she plan to kill me? Or will she bind me so I die of thirst? Such death is supposed to be agonizing.*

"It's presumptuous of me to ask for a quick death from you. You deserve justice, but please be merciful."

The woman's smile grew wider. She twirled like a young girl during a dance. "I long chose a method of death just for you. It's said that Cleopatra used it to kill her enemies."

She dashed to a wooden trunk Jamie didn't notice before and retrieved something. "Here you are, my pet."

A hiss made Jamie's back melt into the cold wall. The woman held a snake in her arms.

"You don't deserve a quick or easy death," she said stroking a gray snake with triangular flattened head. "This will be slow and painful."

The memory of a mean boy sneaking a snake into his clothes iced his veins.

It was my plan to die and save others.

"Remember, you found us all. I'm your last offender. My death will complete your revenge."

With all his heart, he hoped the woman would find peace and be satisfied.

I wanted to sacrifice myself in a meaningful way. If after my death she stops killing prisoners, I've saved many lives. My plan came to a perfect conclusion. And if the pain becomes terrible, a knife in my pocket can help me end it.

He slid against the wall and closed his eyes. When burning spread from his ankle to his thigh, as if his leg was on fire, he welcomed the sensation. Cold sweat drenched his forehead. His heart raced. *Please, break now. Make my death a quick one.*

The woman's light footsteps sounded farther and farther away. He was left in the company of corpses, soon to join them in death.

A dizzying spell overtook his body. His stomach cramped. Breathing became harder.

Perhaps death will not wait long.

Someone's hand shook his shoulders. He forced his eyes open, but it was too dark to see.

"Jamie, it's me, Tobby. I followed you. Please don't die. I tied my handkerchief on the bite. I'll get help."

"Get out of here, lad. Run after the woman or you'll be lost." Jamie tried to say these words, but his tongue no longer worked. Consciousness slipped away. A gripping fear that the boy would not find his way back and die in the maze of tunnels was his last thought before darkness swallowed him.

Chapter 24

The tall, mustached commander, Jean-Luc Vignon, led Ella and Mr. Doolittle inside the citadel. Two guards followed them, carrying their belongings. Gripping her medical bag, Ella glanced into the maze of corridors.

"Where are the prisoners being held?"

"A level below us," Vignon answered.

She gasped. "In the dungeon?"

The guards snickered but quieted under the commander's glare.

"No, Mademoiselle Parker, the dungeon is even further below. This fortress is several centuries old and holds many awful places. But don't worry, none of your countrymen are being held there."

"That's a relief."

Jamie, are you here somewhere?

"Your French is almost perfect, mademoiselle. And that's only one of many extraordinary qualities I noticed about you." Vignon smiled as he ushered them into his office, with papers piled on the desk. Ella wondered if those papers contained the names of her friends, but she thought it would be unwise to ask about specific prisoners.

A half-empty bottle of wine stood on a small table with two chairs by the fireplace. The commander pointed to it and snapped his fingers, and one of the guards rushed away.

Vignon invited Ella and the chaplain to sit. After several days of riding in the carriage, Ella found pleasure in reclining onto a cushioned chair. When the guard returned with goblets and a bowl of grapes and oranges, Vignon poured the pungent red wine. Offering her a goblet filled to the brim, he caught her hand and studied it.

"Such a small, delicate palm. How can this be the hand of a surgeon? These graceful fingers should grip nothing but flower bouquets or wine glass stems. If I'd known that the British were sending me such a gift, I'd have prepared a grander reception."

Ella's neck heated under the commander's admiring gaze. His silky voice and manner made her fidget, especially in front of Mr. Doolittle and the guards. But Vignon was eating her up with his eyes like she was a dish he craved and didn't seem to care about being observed by a clergyman or his subordinates.

"Please eat and drink. You must be famished after your long journey," Vignon added when Doolittle clasped a branch of purple grapes and stuffed his mouth. Ella sipped wine to soothe her thirst. It was delicious, but she didn't let herself indulge. She was here for the patients.

Her eyes studied a portrait on the wall of two beautiful women, one older and one younger.

"Your wife and daughter?" Ella asked in English for Mr. Doolittle's benefit. She also wondered how well Vignon spoke the language.

Vignon sighed. "Yes. My wife Sophie and my daughter Isabelle. Sophie died during the invasion on the Bay of Quiberon." His English sounded fluent.

Doolittle crossed himself while chewing a mouthful of food. "I will pray for her soul."

"I'm so sorry." Ella bowed her head. "And your daughter?"

The commander blinked as if trying to hold his tears. "Please, let's not speak of the terrible things that occurred that day. You've endured a perilous journey and surely need rest. I can recommend an excellent lodging in town."

"Yes, that would be most agreeable." Doolittle emptied his wine.

"I'll have one of my subordinates show you the way and bring your things." Vignon turned to the door.

"Thank you, but that can wait till later." Ella rose and set aside her almost full goblet. When Vignon spun around, she added. "I wish to check on the sick, and I'm sure Mr. Doolittle wants to meet his flock."

"But..." Mr. Doolittle's lips turned down. "We just arrived..."

Vignon bowed. "What passion for your work. Perhaps you'll visit me for dinner and tell me more about ... your experience as a surgeon. I'll order a roasted duck to tempt your appetite."

The commander's gaze lingered on the curves of her dress, as if he was thinking what could follow the dinner. Ella's stomach lurched.

"I wouldn't dream of having such a feast without my friend." She grinned at Mr. Doolittle.

The chaplain patted his belly. "Duck would be delicious. Why don't we rest in our lodging, as Mr. Vignon suggested and..."

"No. We are here to alleviate suffering." Ella lifted her medical bag. "Where do you house the sick? Please don't tell me they stay with the rest of the prisoners."

Vignon tilted his head. "I believe you will be impressed with the infirmary. It was finished only two days ago." He clasped her hand and escorted her out. Doolittle's panting sounded behind them.

They stepped into the yard, where the July sunshine warmed the grass.

"Do the men come out here for a walk?" Ella asked.

Vignon nodded. "Every day when it's not raining. They take air and even do physical exercises as well as work."

Ella raised an eyebrow. "Good. I'm glad to hear it."

"And do they pray?" Doolittle asked. "At least on Sundays?"

"Yes. This is the chapel." Vignon pointed to a wooden building nearby. "After their walk, they usually gather there."

"How marvelous!" Doolittle folded his hands in a praying position. "Prison life must have made them turn to God."

"Who leads the prayers?" Ella asked.

"One of the men, a vicar's son. And there was an officer who read out loud and taught men how to read and write. The prisoners seemed in better spirits afterwards."

An officer who read to the men and taught them... Could that be Jamie? But why did Vignon say "taught" instead of "teaches"? Perhaps he misspoke.

"My sermons will lift their spirits even higher." Mr. Doolittle beamed.

"Why don't the men meet Mr. Doolittle in the chapel and hear a word of God, while I inspect the infirmary," Ella suggested.

Vignon bowed. "The guards will summon the prisoners to the church while I gladly show you the infirmary. I think you will be most satisfied. Please mention my efforts in your reports to the authorities."

Holding her hand, he led her out of the yard. When they were beyond the gazes of guards, Vignon stopped and faced her. Her neck heated under his ogling eyes.

"I do hope you visit me tonight, Miss Ella. I missed a woman's company. We can share a most pleasant evening, just the two of us. Mr. Doolittle can dine somewhere else."

This is why Mr. Greville sent me. He must've known of Vignon's lustfulness. But... No, I can't...

Sickened to her stomach, Ella freed her hand from his grasp. "I'm afraid I must decline. A lady cannot dine with a gentleman alone in his chamber. That would ruin her reputation."

Vignon's face soured. "Oh, I thought a woman who chose such an unladylike profession would be above preconceptions. I'm only asking for your company to brighten my lonely evening. Perhaps you'll reconsider." His fingers brushed her neck. "After all, I have the power over all those unfortunate British prisoners."

Ella's breath constricted in her chest. *Could he manipulate me by hurting the prisoners? Then he mustn't know that Jamie and Tobby are dear to me, or he'll use them to make me comply.*

"Let me think about it." Ella forced a smile. "Right now, I'm anxious to see the patients." Please show me to the infirmary."

"Yes, my English Beauty." Vignon rested his hand on the small of her back as he led the way. They neared the walls of the prison perimeter when he pointed to a few low buildings. "These were soldiers' barracks recently fixed up to house the sick. I hope you will find the conditions satisfactory."

The swept path led to a wooden building with makeshift curtains on the windows. Two benches in front of it made a pleasant spot for recovering patients.

"Did the guards do the work?"

"No. The prisoners made the improvements themselves. The British officer, the same one who read to the men, led the effort and purchased most of the materials."

"And the benches?" Ella touched the smooth wood.

"Yes. He wanted the sick to enjoy some sun."

"How kind."

Something else caught her eye. Green blooms emerged from ruffled soil of a flower bed.

Jamie, did you plant flowers?

Before she could ask about the gardener's identity, Vignon invited her inside.

A row of beds came into her view; six of them occupied with patients.

Ella turned to the commander. "Thank you, Monsieur Vignon. I'm sure you have work to do. I will need some time to examine the patients."

"If you don't mind, I will stay a bit longer to ensure all is well." He planted his feet wide. "I won't be in the way."

Perhaps he wants to make sure I truly am a surgeon and not a spy, Ella guessed.

She expected that the prison conditions would result in lung maladies for the prisoners. As confirmation, the first three men wheezed and coughed. But it was only three of them; not a massive outbreak she feared. The fourth man cringed and held his belly, while his neighbor shivered under two blankets, likely from a fever. Her jaw dropped when she recognized the last man.

"Simkins!" Her legs weakened. That man almost drowned her once.

"You!" Simkins leaped out of bed. He thrusted his arms forward, as if holding back an evil spirit. "Don't come near me, witch."

Ella threw her shoulders back. "I thought your test already proved that I'm no witch. But seeing how quickly you move, it's clear that you don't need to be here. Are you pretending to be sick? I won't put up with that."

"I was beaten! Viciously beaten!" Simkins yelled and pointed to a bruise on his chin and a swollen nose. "Flowers will pay for what he's done."

Ella forced her face to stay blank and not to beam at hearing Jamie's name.

Jamie is here. He built this infirmary and reads to the men to improve their morale. Oh, I can't wait to see him and tell him how proud I am of him.

"That was two weeks ago," one of the men said between his coughs.

"So what? I won't let him forget." Simkins waved his fist.

Ella glared at Simkins. "Keep your voice down. There are people here who truly are sick and need quiet."

"That's right, Simkins. You of all people should hold his tongue." The man with the fever said. "You picked a fight and lost. You didn't help build the infirmary, but now you want to lie in a bed."

"Since you look quite recovered, I suggest you visit the chapel," Ella said to Simkins. "Mr. Doolittle, who you may remember, is starting his sermon."

Simkins's nostrils flared. "You watch it, witch. The captain isn't here to protect you."

He shuffled out. Vignon tilted his head. "Seems like you are used to a company of rough men, Mademoiselle Parker. But sometimes, you may need protection. Which I'm happy to give you whenever you need it."

Ella made her voice as casual as she could. "If I need protection, perhaps I could ask that officer everyone mentions, Mr. Flowers. Is he in the chapel with other prisoners?"

Vignon shifted his feet and pulled on the button of his coat. "No. Two days ago, Mr. Flowers and a young boy, Tobby Hill, escaped. Mr. Flowers shamefully violated his parole. I announced a reward, and the locals organized a search. Even the British officers on parole had joined the effort. Unfortunately, Mr. Flowers and the boy have vanished."

Ella's heart fell into her stomach.

After toiling so hard to help the prisoners, why would Jamie run? This must be the mystery Mr. Greville wanted to solve. The prisoners are disappearing, and Jamie and Tobby are now among their number.

Chapter 25

Vignon finally left Ella when a guard came to give a report. As their steps sounded further away, Ella exhaled a long sigh. Without the commander's stare unnerving her, she could give her full attention to her patients. After administering grains for calomel for Mr. Price, the man with an upset stomach, and the powder from Jesuit bark for Mr. Jacobs, the patient with the fever, Ella sat near one of the coughing patients.

"What is your name, sir?"

"Culpepper."

He turned away and curved into a ball from a coughing fit.

Ella passed him a bowl to spit. "How long have you had this cough?"

"A few months. It used to be even worse, but Mr. Flowers bought me medicine to ease it."

Ella pressed her ear to the man's chest. The bubbling sound indicated that the patient had fluid in the air sacs. Pneumonia.

"It's fortunate that Mr. Flowers took such good care of you."

If not for Jamie's efforts, he'd likely be dead.

Culpepper dropped his gaze. "I'm worried about what happened to him."

"You don't believe he ran?"

Culpepper shook his head. "No."

The patient with an upset stomach, Mr. Price, massaged his belly and cringed. "Mr. Flowers would not do such a thing. He could've lived in the town and enjoyed a comfortable life. Instead, he stayed with us and worked to improve our lot." He gasped and ran out of the room holding his abdomen. The medication produced the desired effect. Ella only hoped the man made it to the latrine in time.

"What could've happened to Mr. Flowers?" she asked Culpepper as she gave him water.

"Don't know. I would've suspected Simkins, but he slept at the infirmary the night Mr. Flowers disappeared. Cough kept me up much of the night. I know Simkins never left the room. And the boy is gone as well. He never left Mr. Flowers's side."

Tobby, my sweet boy. What happened to you and Jamie?

"Perhaps Simkin's men took revenge on Mr. Flowers for winning the fight," one of the cough patients said.

Jacobs, the patient with a fever, shook his head, sending drips of sweat down his face. "Simkins's men don't know where their own heads are without their leader. It's a strange business. Vignon said the British officers are searching for him as well. Surely, they do not suspect their compatriots would have attempted an escape—had they, they'd likely aid them."

"Vignon posts a large reward for finding runaways," Culpepper said. "They may be in it for the money."

Mr. Price returned and collapsed on his bed. "Please don't give me any more of that medicine. It left nothing inside me."

"Let's hope so, Mr. Price." Ella palpated his abdomen, pleased to see the patient no longer winced at her touch. "Do you often suffer such stomachaches?"

"Yes. The guards used to feed us rancid meat, and it made me sick. Since Mr. Flowers had a talk with Vignon, the food had improved, but my stomach hadn't fully settled."

What did Jamie say to Vignon that the commander provided better food and let him fix the infirmary?

The door swung open, and Conor appeared with Tobby limp in his arms.

"Miss Ella, is it you?" Conor's jaw dropped. "Oh, thank God."

The patients sat up on their cots.

"Tobby! He's been found."

"What's wrong with the lad?"

"Where is Mr. Flowers?"

Ella ran to Conor and cupped Tobby's bloodless face. The boy's eyes remained closed, but his chest rose. "Bring him to a bed."

Conor laid Tobby down on a cot by the wall. Bracing herself, Ella put her ear to the boy's chest. His skin was ice-cold. But the steady beat of Tobby's heart made her exhale with relief.

"Where did you find him?" she asked Conor as she continued examining her patient.

"In the tunnels." Conor pulled on his coat. "When I heard that Jamie went missing, I wandered all around this prison. I suspected that the commander lied, and Jamie was in a dungeon or some other horrid place. After many hours of searching, I stumbled upon a door that opened into a series of tunnels. I roamed there for a bit, calling Jamie's name, but I was afraid to go too far and get lost. On my way back, I found Tobby. First, I thought he was dead, but then I noticed that he was still breathing."

Ella's hand flew to her mouth. "He likely spent a day or more in those tunnels. And Jamie may be still there."

She lifted Tobby's head and poured a spoonful of water down his throat. Prolonged thirst would be the biggest danger to his life. The cold of the tunnels could give him pneumonia. Bites from rats or other vermin could cause terrible illnesses.

Rubbing Tobby's arms and legs to bring blood to them, she looked for signs of such bites. When she touched the swelling on the leg Tobby injured in battle two years ago, the boy jerked and opened his eyes.

"Tobby, it's me, Ella." She stroked his sticky hair and dirty cheeks. "You are safe now."

The boy's eyes opened wide, but they stared at something above her head. His cracked lips trembled. "The ghost woman. Her candle," he whispered. "A snake." Then his scream made Ella shudder. "Death." His eyes rolled to the back of his head.

"His mind must be broken," Conor said, hugging himself.

Her hand caressed the boy's forehead. "Temporarily, I pray. If he was lost in a maze of tunnels without food or water... He may be in shock or suffering from brain fever."

She opened her bag to prepare valerian root to calm the boy's nerves if he got more agitated. And a lancet to bleed him, if the medicine would not be enough.

"Jamie is likely in these tunnels, possibly in a similar condition." She locked eyes with Conor. "You must tell Vignon to send a search party and find him—before it's too late."

Chapter 26

Ella was measuring the dose of valerian root to give to Tobby when Conor returned. Her other patients were resting after the medications she administered.

"Commander Vignon wants you to see him." Conor tugged on a button of his coat.

Ella almost spilled the pungent-smelling liquid. "Pardon?"

"I told Vignon that I found Tobby and that you said he must organize a search party. He wants you to come and talk to him first."

Her brow knit as she bent over Tobby. The boy tossed violently, as if trapped in a nightmare. "Hold him while I give him medicine." Conor's arms pressed on the squirming patient, while Ella lifted the boy's head and poured the valerian root into his mouth. "I hope that calms him and lets his nerves rest. Now, why did you need to speak about me with Vignon? Couldn't the idea to send the search party come from you?"

Conor shifted his feet. "I relayed what you said. What's wrong with that?"

"Did Vignon say *why* he needs to see me?" Ella stood crossed her arms.

"He... He asked if you knew Mr. Flowers. If you were particularly worried about him."

Ella's face squeezed as if she tasted vinegar. "You told him that Jamie is my friend, didn't you?"

Conor cleared his throat. "I thought 'betrothed' would sound better. I didn't stretch the truth, did I? You traveled to be with him, that must mean you planned to ..." He halted speaking as Ella planted her hands on her hips and glared at him.

"I did not come here for Jamie. The Naval Board sent me here as a surgeon to care for the prisoners."

His lips rounded. "That never crossed my mind. When I saw you, I thought you were here because of Jamie. And perhaps Tobby as well."

He's not completely wrong. But now Vignon knows that Jamie is important to me.

The idea of Vignon wanting her to submit to his will made her feel sick to her stomach. But the fear for Jamie spurred her to act.

She wiped Tobby's sweaty brow. "Stay with him and keep giving him water. He must drink."

Conor's lips trembled. "He's not dying, is he?"

"Heaven forbid! He suffered a great deal, but diligent care should restore his body and mind. I'll ask Mr. Doolittle, the chaplain who came with me, to pray for his recovery."

Conor's face crumbled. "Neither diligent care nor prayers were enough to save my brother. He was just older than Tobby. And my sisters were four and two when they died days before him."

The pain written across his face was so raw, Ella's breath caught. The place in her heart that was hollow from losing her mother and brother resonated with misery. Conor Leach, though insufferable and selfish at times, shared a common bond of unspeakable tragedy with her.

"I'm sorry." Her hand brushed Conor's arm. "I wish I could heal your pain... and my own. My mother died in childbirth with my brother. Anytime I must attend a delivery, I want to curl into a ball and weep."

"Yet, you carry on? I don't think I can stand to be at anyone's sickbed." He winced as Tobby tossed and threw off his blanket.

Ella covered the boy and caressed his head. "He needs you to watch over him while I speak to Vignon. When I return, you can go to the tunnels and join the search for Jamie."

"That sounds less nerve-racking," Conor muttered.

Outside, Ella paused to reflect on the situation. To enter Vignon's chamber alone would be like stepping into the wolf's lair. In hope that the chaplain's authority would protect her, she hastened to the chapel. To her disappointment, it was empty except for two men sweeping the floor under the watchful eye of a guard.

"Is the sermon over? Where's Mr. Doolittle?" she asked.

"I believe he went to the town to eat dinner," one of the men replied. "After reciting 'Our Father', he said that while caring for the spirit was vital, the body shouldn't be neglected too long."

Ella grunted. As usual, Mr. Doolittle prioritized his comfort above all. Her shoulders sank. Without the chaplain, she would have to go to the commander alone.

"Is there something I can help you with, mademoiselle?" the young guard asked.

He had an agreeable and honest face. Perhaps Vignon would behave in front of his man.

"Yes. Please escort me to Commander Vignon."

The guard leaned from one foot to another. "I must ask on what matter. Commander does not like to be disturbed over anything trivial."

"Trivial?" The word made Ella's blood heat. "Jamie Flowers is likely dying in the tunnels. And your commander said he wants to see me before he sends a search party. Does that seem 'trivial' to you?"

The guard stepped back. "The tunnels? It would take days to search through them." His head snapped to the prisoners. "I must take them back to their cell. Please wait here."

When he left, Ella collapsed onto the pew and buried her head in her hands.

Jamie, I traveled so far. Please stay alive. And you, Tobby. Please get better and tell me where Jamie is.

A hand touched her shoulder. The young guard stood before her.

"My name is Renaut. Mr. Flowers was ... well, we are not supposed to fraternize with the prisoners... but I wished to be his friend. Why does Vignon want you to go to him?"

Ella lowered her eyes. "You can guess why."

"Other guards will not go to the tunnels without a direct order. But if Vignon does not send them, I will go on my own."

Ella's palms clasped the guard's hand. "*Merci*. But will it be enough?"

Renaut shook his head. "Only if we are lucky."

"Then I must ask Vignon to send a large party." She took Renaut's hand to rise.

Upon entering Vignon's chamber, they were greeted by the sight of the commander, dressed in an ornate coat of emerald and gold, pacing beside the hearth. Ella guessed this room to be his sleeping quarters, because besides the table covered with a white tablecloth and boasting a large pot of aromatic stew, there was a bed large enough for two. A scent of lavender wafted from the pillows.

The commander gestured to Renaut. "Stand outside the door."

"I would prefer him in the room while we speak," Ella protested, blocking Renaut's way.

Vignon gave her a salacious smile. "You showed great composure with the boorish sailor today. And you said that you don't need protection. You have nothing to fear from me."

"Then perhaps this guard would be of better use to search for Jamie Flowers. As well as the rest of your men."

Renaut straightened and raised his chin. "I volunteer to search the tunnels, monsieur. How many men can I bring with me?"

Vignon cringed. "Pick one partner and go. Be careful not to get lost."

When Renaut left, Ella wrung her hands. "Only two men? I hear the tunnels are extensive."

Vignon poured wine. "I cannot spare many men for the search. There wouldn't be enough to guard the prisoners. They would take advantage of the situation and escape."

Ella threw her head back. "But if he's not found soon, he may die."

"My heart breaks for you, Miss Parker." Vignon demonstratively brought his hand on his breast. "You came all this way to learn that your betrothed is in mortal danger. Please eat and drink to keep up your strength. I didn't have a chance to order the duck I promised, but the stew is decent, while the wine is excellent."

He offered her the goblet and bid her to sit, taking the chair next to her. "What should we drink to?"

"Whatever you wish. My thoughts are with Mr. Flowers and Tobby. The child is in dire condition."

"To their health, then." Vignon raised his goblet. "I was wondering if Tobby said anything that may give a clue to where Mr. Flowers is or what had occurred to them."

"His mind is damaged, I'm afraid." Ella bit her lip. "He said something about a woman ghost, a snake, and death. Nothing else that I could discern."

Vignon's hand trembled slightly. He brought the goblet to his lips and drained it in one gulp.

His anxiety did not escape Ella. "Are there any women here?"

"No." Vignon averted his gaze from her. "Poor boy lost his mind. As I told you, it's been a long time since a woman visited these walls. Please, dine with me while we wait for the news about Mr. Flowers." He gestured toward the stew.

Ella forced herself to lift her fork. She hadn't eaten since morning and didn't wish to risk a swoon from hunger. Taking her time, she ate with small bites and chewed as if her strictest governess was watching. The stew was fatty to her taste and sunk in her stomach like lead. Vignon ate as well, but his eyes seemed to devour her.

He licked his greasy lips. "Would you like a pastry?"

Ella touched her belly. "Thank you, but I cannot eat more. Everything inside me is in knots as I fear for my betrothed. Perhaps you could send more men to search for him."

The commander shook his finger and laughed. "Ah, you want to play games, little vixen. How charming! But you must do better. Why should I care if you eat dessert or not?"

Ella jerked back. "Pardon?"

He leaned closer and circled his finger on her lips. "This pretty mouth is made for most charming kisses. One kiss, one more man to help the search. Two kisses, two men. You understand the game now?"

Trembling, Ella forced down bile. In her nineteen years, she only kissed Robert, and she loved him. To allow this disgusting man to kiss her...

I must. To save Jamie.

Cringing, Ella rose, folded her lips and squeezed her eyes shot. "I'm ready."

His lips covered hers. "One." He said after planting the first kiss. His hands hugged her waist, and he pulled her closer. "Two."

Ella gasped, ill to her stomach.

His hands cupped her bosom. "Let's make the game more fun, shall we? For two more men, the next two kisses will be on your nipples. I can help you remove the dress."

Horrified, Ella sprang back. Not even Robert kissed her like that. Her heart palpitated, making her feel faint.

She wrapped her arms protectively around herself. "No."

"No? But don't you want to win the game?" He stepped closer and his hands circled her. Caressed her back. Undone a button.

Her stomach spasmed. Its contents flew out of her throat and landed all over Vignon's boots.

While he cursed and raged, her hands clasped the door handle and her legs sprinted down the corridor before her head knew what she was doing. Outside, she fell on the grass and retched. When nothing but bitter bile came up, she stayed on her belly, breathing in and out to calm her shaking limbs.

"You lost the game, Mademoiselle Ella." Vignon's voice sounded above her. She looked up to see his taunting grin in the window. "You are welcome to a rematch. I play fair. With the kisses you allowed me, I will send two more guards."

"Damn you, scoundrel!" She shook her fist. "I will report you."

Vignon chuckled. "Something tells me you will be too ashamed to write about our *rendezvous* to your authorities. Even if you send a report, I have the means to intercept it. And the local gendarmes won't care. Mr. Flowers's life is in my hands. Remember that."

Ella held her abdomen as she staggered into the door of the infirmary. Price and Jacobs were sleeping, while Culpepper and two other patients were drinking tea. When she approached Tobby's bed, the boy's eyes fluttered, and he muttered incoherently. Conor, who perched at edge of the bed, jumped to his feet.

"Miss Ella, are you all right? You look awful."

She poured herself a cup of water to cleanse her mouth from the taste of vomit. "He will send four guards to search for Jamie... He would've sent more if I..." She covered her burning cheeks with her hands.

"Old devil," Culpepper muttered from his cot.

Conor's eyes widened. "He wanted you to submit to him in exchange for sending a search party? I will challenge him. Jamie would want me to." He straightened his coat, as if to appear more presentable when throwing the gauntlet.

Ella clenched her hands. "No stupid duel! We need to search for Jamie. One of the guards said it may take days. If Jamie is hurt or without water, he doesn't have such time."

"The British officers are searching in the nearby woods. I'll direct them to the tunnels."

"I forgot about them. Yes, please show them the way." She touched Tobby's sweaty brow as the boy tossed in his sleep. "How is he?"

Conor scratched his cheek. "No change, I think. I gave him water like you told me. He opened his eyes once and muttered the same words again."

"I think he is trying to tell us something. When I asked Vignon if there's a woman here anywhere, he was so startled he almost spilled his wine. There's a mystery here, and it has to do with a woman."

"No time for some mindboggling mysteries." Conor stepped to the door. "I'll gather the officers, and we'll comb through the tunnels. Jamie will be found alive."

When the door slammed shut after Conor's leave, Culpepper cleared his throat. "I believe you are right, Dr. Parker. Strange things like this have happened before. I came here with Lieutenant Knox, who was always kind to me. After an argument with Vignon, he was confined in the citadel overnight, on the higher level that they use to punish officers. Next morning, he was gone. Everyone assumed that he escaped and were glad for him, but I didn't believe it. He wouldn't run without me. And I heard rumors that other fellows had disappeared during nights when everyone slept soundly. Just like the night Mr. Flowers and Tobby vanished."

Ella paced. "Perhaps something was added to food or drink?"

"That may be." He sat up and shook Price. "Wake up you sleepy head."

Price opened his eyes. "What? I finally slumber without the urge to run to the latrine. Let me enjoy some proper sleep."

"Aha! Normally, you can't sleep. You go to the bucket several times a night. What about the night Mr. Flowers disappeared?"

Price gave Ella a side glance. "I don't want to say in front of a lady."

"I'm a surgeon first, Mr. Price. You are unlikely to shock me. Please speak because it could aid us in finding Mr. Flowers."

"I woke up in a pool of my own shit." Price reddened. "That never happened before."

"It does seem someone mixed in a sleep remedy into your meal." Ella continued to pace. "Perhaps it was done to conceal an abduction. But an abduction conducted by a woman? It's hard to imagine her taking Jamie by force, unless she had accomplices."

"If she asked for help, Mr. Flowers might've gone with her willingly," Culpepper said. "And Tobby followed out of curiosity."

Price sat up. "I just remembered. I had a strange dream that night."

"So strange that it made you shit yourself?" Culpepper laughed.

"Please, Mr. Culpepper. This is nothing to taunt Mr. Price about." Ella walked over to Price's bed. "What was it?"

"This very thin woman with long hair, walked into the cell, wearing nothing but a night dress and holding a candle. She wondered among the men, shining light in their faces, then moving on. Like she was looking for someone. When she approached me, she glared with such hatred that my guts trembled. Worse than usual, I mean. When I woke up, covered in you-know-what, I was relieved that it was all a dream. That woman frightened me so awfully, I thought she may be a spirit of death."

"Your dream sounds like Tobby's muttering about a ghost of a woman." Ella touched her face. "But if she's not a spirit but a being of flesh and blood, the guards must know of her. Someone may be bringing her food or emptying her chamber pot. Which guard should I ask? The wrong person may snitch to Vignon."

"The young one is the kindest one of them. Renaut." Culpepper clicked his tongue. "He'd likely tell you if he knows."

"He's not here. He went to search for Mr. Flowers. Anyone else?"

Culpepper scratched his unshaven cheek. "If the woman is Vignon's secret, then he trusts it only to those who served under him the longest. The old guard. I heard he fought with Vignon in the previous war. You know his name, Price?"

"No. Why would I know a Frog's name?" Price crossed his arms.

"Because Mr. Flowers knew all the guards' names and greeted them when they brought us food."

"Batiste is his name. He made me remember it when he found a rope I was weaving." Everyone turned to Jacobs, who sat up on his cot and grunted. "Your chatter woke me up. But I think I'm feeling better. The fever broke."

Ella checked his forehead. "Indeed. I need to find someone to care for Tobby. Then I will go speak to this Batiste."

Jacobs reached for his cup with water. "We all seem better and can take care of the boy. But what do you want Batiste for? He's a mean old dog."

"Didn't you hear? He may be the only one who knows about the mysterious woman."

"The woman? The one who lives on the top floor?" When everyone's mouths gaped and eyes bulged, Jacobs shrugged. "What? I thought everyone knew about her. There's a ladder that leads to her room."

Chapter 27

Enveloped in the moonlight, Ella leaned on a large tree and let Jacobs catch up to her. The man huffed and panted as he walked. When he reached the tree, he grabbed it to stay upright.

"That bloody fever weakened me."

Ella offered her arm to steady him. "You should go back to the infirmary. I'm sure I can find the ladder myself."

"I doubt it. This fortress is ancient and full of hidden passages."

"Then how do you know it so well?"

"Because I've been trying to escape it since the day I got here. When we were locked up all the time, it was much harder. But I owe a debt to Mr. Flowers. While he had others work on the infirmary or gathered them for lessons, I would slip away and explore various passageways."

"The tunnels as well?"

He shivered. "I was planning to go into the tunnels, but I became ill and delayed my escape. A good thing, seeing what happened to Tobby."

They hid behind the tree as a guard walked by. He carried a tray with food toward the infirmary.

After he passed, Jacobs urged her to keep moving. They walked out into the prison yard. Another guard blocked their way.

Speaking in French, Ella said the words Jacobs and she agreed on. "I'm escorting Mr. Jacobs back to his cell. He has recovered from his fever. I will also meet the other prisoners and check on their condition."

As they crossed the yard, Ella heard the guards' voices behind her.

"Jacobs was not in his bed at the infirmary when I brought supper."

"He's here with the woman surgeon. He's going back to the cell."

"Phew, I thought he ran."

"They thought you escaped," Ella whispered.

"I will at the first opportunity," Jacobs replied. "Mr. Flowers had made our lives here better, but he was wrong to speak for us and promise that we wouldn't run. Simkins is a despicable scum, but if he organizes an escape, I will follow him."

A portly guard was standing at the door of the citadel. Jacobs flashed a smile when he saw him.

"That one is a fool."

Ella stepped up to the guard. "Mr. Jacobs is feeling better. Please take him to his cell. I will come with you and see the prisoners' sleeping conditions."

"What? This late?" The guard yawned.

"I said I'm inspecting the prisoners' sleeping condition. So, it must be done when they sleep."

"I suppose that makes sense." The guard scratched his head and started down the stairs. He only made it a few steps when Jacobs's fist collided with his head, knocking him out.

"I may be weak from the fever, but I can still land a punch." Jacobs grinned.

Ella checked on the unconscious guard. "He'll wake up any second. Let's hurry."

Jacobs motioned for her to follow back up the stairs. Stepping almost soundlessly, he led Ella through several corridors until they reached a kitchen. A large kettle simmered on the stove. Two guards sat on stools and chewed on bread.

"Batiste is the older one." Jacobs breathed. "We must wait here till they leave."

"Can't I just talk to him?" Ella scratched her face, nervous that the guards would see them.

Jacobs shook his head and pointed at the door in the kitchen. "There are stairs behind the door, leading up. Don't talk to the guards. They will call Vignon."

Afraid to breathe, Ella waited for the sentries to finish their meal.

"I need to bring a tray up for her," Batiste said.

"Would she eat? Or will you have to force her?" the younger guard asked.

Perhaps Batiste isn't being as cautious as he should be, Ella wondered. *Secrets, such as a mysterious woman living inside a prison, are hard to keep.*

"The last two days she's been singing, laughing, and eating everything I bring her."

"After all those weeks of hollering and weeping? Perhaps she's regaining her wits."

Batiste shook his head. "No. It means something else."

To Ella's horror, her nose itched. The chill and dust of the corridor caused her to make a deafening sneeze.

"What was that?" the younger guard asked.

"Let's check." They stood.

Jacobs gasped. "I can't outrun them."

Ella brought her hand to her hammering heart. "Pretend you have fainted."

Jacobs understood her plan just in time. When the guards came out of the kitchen, he sank to the floor.

"Help!" Ella screamed. "Please help him!"

A couple more guards appeared from another corridor.

Ella frantically gestured to Jacobs. "This is my fault. I thought he was only pretending to be ill and made him return to his cell. He must be taken back to the infirmary!"

"He looks flushed with fever," one of the guards observed.

"But what was he doing here, by the kitchen?" another sentry asked.

"He wandered around in delirium." Ella threw her hands up. "Please, take him to a bed before he dies! Hurry!"

When the guards carried Jacobs away, she ran into the kitchen. In a rush, she flung one door open but found a pantry. Then she grasped the handle of another door, but it was locked. Her eyes were scanning the space for where a key could be hidden, when someone's forceful hand clenched hers.

"What are you doing?"

She spun to face Batiste.

"Looking for the willow bark for Mr. Jacobs's fever. Do you have any?"

"Do you take me for a fool? Vignon shall hear of your snooping." He slid handcuffs on her wrists.

Ella's knees hit the floor. "Please. Let me go. I'll give you money."

The guard cringed. "I won't take your bribes. Get up or I'll carry you."

"No." Her voice quivered. "Lock me in a cell if you wish. Just don't take me to Vignon. He will force himself on me. I'd rather die." Tears flooded her face. She crouched on the floor and bawled. When Batiste's hand touched her shoulder, it was not the painful clench that she expected, but a gentle stroke.

"If you are an actress, you are convincing. But I'm inclined to believe you. Vignon has done such things before. A young wife of a British captain came to live with her husband in town. Then Vignon arrested him for no reason, and the wife came to beg for mercy. He had me guard the door. I'll never forget her eyes when she staggered out of his chamber. Shame on him. His daughter went mad after the British soldiers violated her, yet he does the same."

Ella sat up on her knees and met Batiste's furious gaze. "The woman living upstairs is his daughter? What's her name?"

"Isabelle. She was only fifteen when the British invaded Quiberon Bay. Her mother and her maid died from an explosive shell that hit their home. She survived and hid herself, but the soldiers found her when they looted the home. Vignon and I were defending the town and came too late to save her."

"Please. Let me talk to her. Perhaps I can help her as a doctor."

"She's been mad for seventeen years. I doubt there's anything can be done for her."

Ella shifted on her throbbing knees. "You were right. I was trying to find a way into her room. I need to know what she has to do with prisoners disappearing."

"Some things are better not to know." Batiste helped her rise and removed the handcuffs from her throbbing hands. "Go away. I won't tell Vignon this time, but don't let me catch you here again."

Her feet didn't budge. "If she's doing something nefarious, she must be stopped."

Batiste's face darkened. "She deserves revenge for what was done to her."

"But if the tragedy happened seventeen years ago, the prisoners are unlikely to be the culprits. Certainly not Jamie Flowers, who is only nineteen. What does she do?"

He averted his gaze. "None of my business. And none of yours."

She remembered how Culpepper said that Jamie greeted the guards when they brought meals.

"You saw the good Mr. Flowers has done. He treated everyone with kindness. Why should she be allowed to hurt him?"

The old guard's face remained a stone. "He was a navy officer and fired at our ships. Killed my countrymen. I don't pity the enemies of France."

Ella bit her lip. *He pitied the wife of a captain who came to be with her husband. Perhaps he has a softer side for women and admires spousal loyalty.*

"Mr. Flowers is my betrothed. I came to Verdot to be with him. Please let me ask her where he is."

Batiste did not respond, but his features softened. He sighed and put a buttered roll on the tray. "You followed me when

I brought this tray to her. I never saw you. You understand?"

When Ella nodded, he gave her the tray and unlocked the door.

Chapter 28

Ella ascended cautiously, clutching her tray, mentally preparing for a horrifying sight. A woman so frightening, that the men thought she was a spirit of death. Would she jump on her, scratch and bite? Ella braced herself for the attack.

Much to her astonishment, upon reaching the top of the stairs and entering the room, she discovered a beautifully decorated space, illuminated by elegant candelabra. There was a large canopy bed with silky sheets and a chest of drawers with a large mirror. If not for the bars on the windows, Ella could forget she was inside a prison.

A fragile figure sat on the bed facing away from her, wearing a dirty shift that exposed bony shoulders. The long fingers held a comb and struggled to untangle a knot in the unkempt hair. The glass reflected a sallow face of an emaciated woman, young if not for the lines near the eyes and on the forehead.

"Mademoiselle Isabelle," Ella called, still holding the tray and the bag. "I've come to talk to you."

The woman rose and spun around. The silver comb fell out of her fingers.

"Madeleine! You've returned."

Who's Madeleine? How do I play along?

Ella gave a weak smile. "Yes, I have returned."

Isabelle's eyes opened wider, likely seeing things beyond her surroundings. "He said that he was the last one. I avenged us, and you are here. This means *Maman* will return as well."

Ella's throat constricted with pain. Like her, this woman lost her mother. In a way, Isabelle was fortunate, because her ill mind believed that she would see her mother.

"Well, don't just stand there." Isabelle pouted. "What did you bring me to eat? I'm hungry."

Madeleine must be her maid, Ella guessed. *Batiste said she also died in the explosion.*

With a curtsy, Ella brought the tray to Isabelle, who stuffed the bread into her mouth.

"Would you like me to help you dress for bed and comb your hair?" Ella opened the drawers under the mirror and found a lovely blue gown. She set it aside and looked for something more suitable for bedtime, but Isabelle gasped.

"I want to put on this dress. Maman said I should save it for my sixteenth birthday, but I'll be careful and not get it dirty."

She genuinely believes she's still a young girl.

Ella's heart throbbed as she helped Isabelle into the dress much too loose for her. With a comb she ripped through Isabelle's matted hair, streaked with gray before its time. There were knots the size of walnuts and pieces of food stuck in them. Despite the pain the untangling must've caused, Isabelle hummed as song as Ella brushed her.

How do I get her to tell me what she has done to Jamie? One wrong word and all may be ruined.

"You seem to be in a cheerful mood," Ella said carefully.

"I am so happy. And you should be, too. We are avenged. You, me, Maman. Soon we'll return to our home."

"How did you avenge us?"

"Those men who hurt me, they come here. When I see one of them, I rage and scream until Papa lets me out and gives me a key to their cell. I slip a sleeping potion into their food. It's a bottle Papa bought for me, but I hid it. Late at night, I go to the cell and find my attacker. If he follows me, I lead him to the tunnels."

"Where in the tunnels? How do you know the way?" Ella whispered. Her pulse beat in her ears.

"Oh, you think I could get lost there? I won't. When Papa brought me here, I wandered in and been lost there for many days and nights. I drank water from puddles and caught rats and worms to eat."

And lost the rest of your damaged wits. Ella winced from the bitterness in her mouth.

"I explored every passage in those tunnels. In that darkness, I told myself that I would bring my enemies there to kill them. When I came out to the sunlight, my father's guards screamed and ran. Papa later said they all thought I was long dead." She tossed her head back and laughed with a piercing sound that made Ella's knees weak.

"Would you take me there?"

Isabelle clenched her hand. "You want to see their remains? I will show you."

A tightness constricted Ella's breath. *She lures drugged prisoners into the tunnels and kills them. This is why they disappear. Jamie was her latest victim.*

"Yes." She forced her mouth to speak. "Show me."

Grasping Ella's arm with one hand and a candle with the other, the madwoman led her down the stairs. Ella's hand clutched her medical bag. When they reached the kitchen, Batiste's hooded eyes met with Ella's. Isabelle passed by him as if he wasn't there.

As they walked through winding corridors, the footfalls behind them reassured Ella that Batiste was following. After many turns, Isabelle opened a small door and pulled Ella inside the dark passage.

Why didn't Vignon seal this door, especially after his daughter got lost?

Her hand entwined with Isabelle's, Ella walked through the twists and turns of the labyrinth. The frigid air and gripping fear chilled her to the bone. Her chest ached at the thought of Tobby's terror of being lost in this maze. No wonder the child became ill. And Jamie... Ella braced herself for finding his body in one of these narrow passageways.

A gasp left her mouth when bones and a skull were illuminated by the candle. She wanted to say a prayer. Another skeleton lay a short distance away. Isabelle kept walking as if not seeing the bones. Ella could not hear Batiste's footsteps anymore. Her skin broke into goose-pimples.

He lost us in the maze!

After a good hour of walking, Isabelle pushed on a rock. To Ella's surprise it moved, opening an entrance. She ducked to enter.

The stench of rot made her gag. A dozen corpses and skeletons lay around the circular space.

Isabelle's candle illuminated the body on the floor. A scream pierced Ella's convulsing throat. Jamie was on the ground, steps away from her.

"Batiste! Someone help!" she screamed.

Her knees hit the stony surface, but she ignored the pain. Her hands searched for a pulse on Jamie's neck. When she found it, she wanted to fall on his chest and cry with relief.

"Is he still alive?" Isabelle's voice hissed with displeasure. Her candle shone over Jamie's prostrated body. "Oh yes. He's still breathing. I must kill him again."

"No!" Ella gasped.

"Right. You should have your turn." Isabelle wrenched a knife out of Jamie's fingers. "Stab it into his heart."

In despair that she didn't bring water, Ella stroked Jamie's cheeks. "Jamie, wake up."

"Do you feel sorry for him?" Isabelle's voice rose. "He was the leader. He hurt me the most."

"He certainly did not." Ella's anger erupted. "The invasion of Quiberon Bay happened seventeen years ago. Look at his face. He's hardly more than a boy. He was a small child when the British destroyed your home."

"You lie!" Isabelle pointed the knife at Ella's throat.

"Help!" Ella called again, but no sound of rescue came.

I must save Jamie and myself.

"Are you going to kill me, like you killed these innocent men?" She gestured at the corpses.

"He is not innocent. I saw him punch a man till he bled and cause him pain. That's when I became sure it was him."

"You saw him fight fairly against a vile opponent. Jamie is a good man. He fixed up the infirmary and cleaned the chapel. Even planted flowers. Does that sound like an evil man who hurt you?"

Isabelle's nostrils flared. "Why are you lying to me, Madeleine?"

"I am not Madeleine. Your maid is long dead. Your mother as well. They've been dead for seventeen years." Ella raised her open hands. "You are sick, Isabelle. And instead of treating you, or at least preventing you from hurting people, your father encourages your madness and lets you kill innocent men."

The knife slipped out from Isabelle's trembling hands. She stumbled to the wall, where she curled into a ball and wailed.

No time to deal with her. Shouting for help, Ella grabbed a candle and ran toward the opening.

This time, her plea was answered. A light shone in the distance. She raised her candle. Batiste, Conor, and Renaut approached.

She waved to them and showed them the way into the room with the corpses.

"Jamie is still alive," she urged. "Someone, give him water."

While Conor and Renaut bent over Jamie to let him drink, Batiste scanned the space with bulging eyes and his hand on the heart. "I didn't know there were this many. She must be stopped."

Ella spun around to the wall where Isabelle crouched minutes ago. The woman was gone.

"You must find her later. Right now, we take Jamie to the infirmary."

"We'll carry him, while you lead the way, Ella," Conor said.

"I don't know the way." She turned to Batiste. "Do you?"

"My head is still spinning from all those turns."

Renaut swallowed and shook his head.

Her heart dropped. "We must find Isabelle, or we'll all be lost."

"Jamie, wake up." Conor beat Jamie on the cheeks.

If only Jamie would awaken. He might've memorized the way here. When he was a boy, he played games with secret codes and treasure maps.

With a candle in her grip, Ella walked around the space, searching for any mark that Jamie could've left. She avoided examining the corpses too closely, although she had seen many in her work. An old chest, with half of its lid missing, caught her eye. Wondering what it concealed, Ella opened the lid.

A snake hissed at her, making Ella jump back with a scream.

Chapter 29

Ella froze, afraid to move. *This must be the snake Tobby muttered about.* No wonder he was frightened out of his wits. The three grown men and she shrieked until Batiste loaded his pistol and shot the hissing snake dead.

When the old guard lifted the limp serpent, Ella tiptoed to see it closer.

"Is it a venomous snake?" Conor asked. "Did it bite Jamie?"

"I think it's an asp viper," Ella said. "Venomous."

"Yes." Renaut spoke up. "My brother was bitten once. He barely survived."

Ella kneeled by Jamie to search for bite marks on his arms and legs. The handkerchief she once gave Tobby was bound around Jamie's leg. She untied it and felt swollen, hot skin. Conor brought the candle closer. A blistering bite mark came to the view.

"Yes. He's been bitten." Ella's mouth dried. "Perhaps that was the method Isabelle chose to murder him."

"That's why he didn't return with Tobby," Conor said. "He was too sick."

Ella wanted to punch the ground. *We are stuck in this maze when Jamie needs to be treated.*

"Look what I found!" Renaut exclaimed and shone his lantern at the wall. "Those marks are made with a knife."

Conor squinted at the marks. "Rs and Ls."

"Right and left?" Ella suggested.

Conor gasped. "Jamie must've taken notice each time they turned right or left. I bet if we followed in reverse order, we would find the way out."

Ella squeezed Jamie's cold hand. "You saved us. Now hold on a bit more so we can save you."

Time came to a standstill as they blundered through the tunnels, guided by Jamie's marks and their recollections. Ella took the lead, with the three men carrying Jamie behind her. Along the way, they encountered Renaut's partner, who joined them. As they wondered, they found more bones and remains. Jamie's directions ended, but they were still inside the tunnels. Their path forked.

"Which way do we try?" Renaut asked.

"Shh. I heard something." Ella strained to listen, and everyone froze. Steps resonated from a distance.

"This way. After me," a hushed voice said in English.

"Help!" Ella shouted. "We are over here."

The pounding of many feet echoed, but the sound grew quieter.

"Who was it? Did they run from us?" Conor asked.

"I don't know, but I think the sound came from over there." Ella pointed left. After a few minutes of stumbling through the path, the steps to the door appeared.

Conor whooped. "That's the way out."

When the group finally walked out into the corridor of the citadel and from there to the prison yard, Ella gulped air with relief. The scarlet clouds hinted at the coming sunrise.

Someone stepped out of the shadows and blocked their way with his legs spread wide apart. *Vignon*, Ella gasped. In the eerie light of the breaking dawn, his face was a mask of fury.

"Batiste, Renaut, report to my office at once," he barked.

"Keep going! Bring Jamie to the infirmary," she shouted to Conor and the two guards. "I will speak to him."

She drew herself up and stepped toe to toe with the commander. "You are a monster, Vignon. Do you know how many men you've allowed your daughter to kill? She's hiding somewhere in the tunnels, but the gendarmes will find her, and I will report you to the authorities."

He grunted and bared his teeth. "Isabelle had returned to her room. She always comes back after she satisfies her desire for revenge. Now the poor girl will have peace, at least for a while. I will always protect her. The British men are my enemies.

They destroyed my family and my home and deserve Isabelle's vengeance. The gendarme will not interfere with me, and your authorities are far away. And when we catch the runaways, they will have no mercy."

Ella frowned. "The runaways?"

Vignon's gaze burned her. "Was that your plan? To distract the guards with the search for Mr. Flowers while staging a mass escape? Most of the prisoners are gone."

Her jaw dropped. She was unsure if she should be glad or not. *What if they are caught?*

As if reading her thoughts, Vignon stomped his foot. "They killed one guard and wounded another. Once they are caught, they will be hanged."

"No!" Ella gasped.

"They must pay. I'm throwing all remaining prisoners into the dungeon. Including that nasty boy, Tobby. His friends from the infirmary joined the runaways."

Ella swallowed her pride and dropped to her knees. "Please. Have mercy on the prisoners. Especially the boy. The dungeon would be the death of him. I will tend to the wounded guard. Please show compassion."

His fingers ran down her trembling neck. Ella swallowed the bile that rushed into her mouth.

"You know I have a soft spot for you, my English Beauty. Tend to my man and your betrothed. When they are out of danger, you will come to me. No more games. Or I will change my mind, and Mr. Flowers and the boy will find themselves in the dungeon."

Ella grabbed her roiling belly.

Vignon marched away toward the citadel, while Ella bunched her skirts and ran to the infirmary.

When she swung the door open, she gasped. Tobby perched on the edge of his bed with his eyes fixed on Jamie. The other cots were empty. Ella's neck stiffened as she worried about her patients.

They are still ill. They could die before they reach England—and that's if they're not caught first.

"Ella!" Tobby shrieked. "I saw you before, but I thought I was dreaming. Are you going to make Jamie better? I called his name, but he didn't answer."

She hugged the boy's shoulders. "I'm glad to see *you* are better. Get back to bed. I'll examine you after I tend to Jamie."

Conor paced next to Jamie's bed. "I poured some more water into his mouth, but he's not waking up."

She pressed her head to Jamie's chest. The beat was rapid, and his breath labored.

With careful movements to avoid causing pain, she untied the bandage. The crimson bite marks made her throat clench.

I have no experience with snake bites. But likely I should make a small incision and drain the venom.

She opened her bag and removed the scalpel. As she washed it, Conor halted his pacing and stared. "Are you going to amputate his leg?"

"I pray it won't come to that. But I need to cut the skin and squeeze the venom from the wound."

Conor paled. "I just remembered about the British officers who are searching the tunnels. We broke into groups to explore in different directions. I should make sure they all know that Jamie's been found."

"Be careful not to get lost. There's been a mass escape. When we heard steps in the tunnels, that was likely the runaways. After I called, they might've chosen a different hideout."

"An escape? That's brilliant." Conor grinned.

Ella did not share his excitement and breathed a sigh of relief when he left. His nervous energy spread to her.

"I can help you, Dr. Ella." Tobby cried. "I tied my handkerchief around Jamie's leg."

"That was good thinking. But for now, you must stay in bed."

Ella prepared her instruments and clean linens for the procedure. When she sliced with her scalpel into the inflamed skin, Jamie didn't react. Pressing on the wound, she drained the venom and pus, along with some blood, into a bowl. Then she cleaned the wound and bandaged it. If only she knew any remedies that would neutralize the venom and aid the healing.

Without them, she had no confidence that the procedure would be effective.

The door opened, and Renaud and Batiste led in the wounded guard. With blood seeping from his head, he moaned as they helped him recline on the bed. Ella left Jamie's side and grabbed the bandages.

"It took us a while to convince him to bring him here," Batiste said. He persisted in trying to walk home. His name is Gabriel."

From Ella's assessment, Gabriel received a hit with a rock on the top of his head. She washed the wound as the patient groaned. After bandaging his head, she asked him about dizziness, but he waved her off.

"I can go home now."

"No, not yet. After a hit like that, you need diligent care and rest." She fluffed his pillows to make him more comfortable.

Catching Renaut's worried gaze, she reassured the guards Gabriel would recover. Batiste nodded and left.

"I'm more worried about Mr. Flowers," the young guard said. "Has he regained consciousness?"

"No." She clenched her hands. "I drained the venom from the wound, but it's in his bloodstream. I don't know how to treat it."

"When my brother was bitten by a snake, he became terribly ill, but he was only a little boy. Fortunately, he got better."

"Do you remember how he was treated?"

Renaut scratched his head. "I'm sorry. I don't remember. I was still a boy as well."

Ella's heart fell.

"I need to return to my duties. The prisoner escape..."

"Of course. Please be careful."

She turned from him and walked back to Jamie's bed. Her hand brushed his hair, matted with sweat.

"I remembered. My father sent me to fetch the poultice from the apothecary," Renaut exclaimed.

Ella curled her feet in her shoes. "The apothecary in the town?"

"Yes, and he still runs his shop. You will find him on the main street."

When Renaut left, she approached Tobby and examined him thoroughly. Apart from his pale face, she didn't find anything wrong with the boy. Sleep in a warm bed cured him.

"I must go to the apothecary and purchase medicine for Jamie," she said as she pulled the blanket to the boy's chin.

"Take me with you," Tobby begged. "I want to see the town. Maybe the guards will let me."

"Out of the question. You need more rest."

He thrusted his lower lip forward. "Please let me do something for Jamie."

"All right. You are in charge of my two patients while I'm gone."

Tobby bolted up and clapped his hands. "Did you promote me to a loblolly boy?"

"Yes. Make sure Mr. Gabriel eats his breakfast and rests. And you can sit with Jamie and talk to him. But not too long. You need to eat and rest as well."

"Aye, aye." He saluted her with a fist on his forehead.

She kissed his soft cheek and sped out.

Vignon's heavy steps made her halt near the gates.

"Going somewhere, Mademoiselle Parker?"

Ella jumped back. "Please don't delay me, Monsignor. I must purchase medicine for Mr. Flowers."

Vignon's lips stretched into a smile. "When you return, I expect you to visit me. After all, I've been merciful and kept the remaining prisoners in their cells. But there's room for them in the dungeon."

As he marched away, his heavy steps resonated inside Ella's shaking body. She wanted to crawl into a hole and howl.

Chapter 30

Most shops were not open yet and only a few people walked through the town when Ella searched for the apothecary. The smell of bread from the bakery made her mouth water, but she wasted no time ogling rolls and pastries. The sign on a small wooden house next to it, depicting mortar and pestle, told her she had found her destination.

A woman wearing a cloak and a veil knocked at the door. "Open up! I know you are there," she yelled. There was something familiar in her voice.

Ella stepped back into the shadows to see if the apothecary would let in the early customer.

The door flew open and a head in a nightcap appeared. The face belonged to a bearded man with curled lips. "You again. I told you to stop coming here when I'm not open."

The woman grunted. "When else can I come? You can't sell me those herbs when your shop is full of people."

The apothecary placed a finger on his lips and waved her in. Ella rushed after the cloaked woman. "Monsignor, please let me in as well. It's extremely urgent."

His eyes narrowed and his jaw set. He half-closed the door. "This better not be about ending a pregnancy, madam. I don't deal in such things."

"No." Ella's breath shuddered. "My friend had been bitten by a snake."

"Ah, that's different." The man ushered her in.

As she entered, the smells of medicinal herbs comforted her, reminding her of Matilda's shop. Vials and jars with small labels in curved handwriting filled the shelves.

"You will need to wait," the apothecary said to the veiled woman.

"I can't wait. I'll take what I need and leave the money on the table."

The apothecary gave her an impatient grunt. While he assembled knives, mortar, pestle, and other tools of his work, the veiled woman stepped to the shelves and grabbed a jar with pennyroyal. Ella averted her eyes. Matilda taught her that pennyroyal had many medicinal properties, such as aiding digestion and stimulating the monthly flow, but some women ingested large doses to induce abortions.

The apothecary glanced up at Ella. "Do you know what kind of snake bit him?"

"I believe it's an asp viper."

"Describe his symptoms."

"Swelling at the place of the bite on his leg. Loss of consciousness. Sweating. Irregular heartbeat and difficulty breathing."

"You are very observant, mademoiselle. Almost sound like a physician." He gave her an indulgent smile.

She swallowed a retort and thanked him.

When the apothecary turned to scan his shelves for ingredients, a hand touched Ella's shoulder. She spun around to face the mysterious customer, who lifted her veil. "Did you miss me, Duchess?"

"Rose." Ella brought her hand to the heart. "You scared me. Why are you purchasing pennyroyal?"

"It's not for me. More importantly, why do you need a snake bite remedy?"

Ella watched as the apothecary crushed mug wort and yarrow. His confident movements eased her worry a bit. "It's for Jamie. My friend. He's in bad shape. And Vignon..."

She blinked to hold back tears as she thought of the commander's advances on her.

Rose's hand touched her elbow. "If you need me, I will help. You saved Albert. I will do what I can for you or your friend. Here's where you can find me." Rose whispered in her ear.

Meanwhile, the apothecary poured the prepared poultice into a vial.

"Rub it on the place of the bite. It should reduce the swelling and relieve pain," he told Ella.

"That's all the poultice would do?" Ella bit the inside of her cheek. "His reaction to the bite is so severe that he's unconscious. Can more be done for him?"

The apothecary shrugged. "I'm afraid not. But don't lose hope. Most adult victims survive viper bites. If their constitution is strong, that is."

Jamie is a strong, healthy young man, she reassured herself. *He will recover.*

Despite her reasoning, her chest tightened.

As she trudged back to the infirmary, the weariness and lack of sleep caught up to her. Her body ached and eyes wanted to close, but she pushed on.

This poultice may not do much, but it's all I have. The rest is up to Jamie.

When Ella pushed the door of the infirmary, the melodic voice of Mr. Doolittle startled her. The chaplain bent over Jamie's bed. Tobby sobbed as he watched him. The injured guard, Gabriel, slept in his bed.

"Now, Lord, you let your servant go in peace," Mr. Doolittle intoned.

"No." Ella gasped.

The chaplain turned. "Ah, Miss Parker. You still have time to say goodbye. I'm almost done with giving last rites."

She flew to Jamie's bed, shouldering the chaplain out of her way. Her head dropped to his chest to listen to Jamie's breathing. It was more labored than before she left.

"The Lord shall keep watch over your going out," Mr. Doolittle continued to pray.

"He is not dying. Please let me do my work." Ella glared at the clergyman.

Mr. Doolittle pursed his lips and walked out.

Ella sat on the bed and unwrapped Jamie's leg. The inflamed skin seared her hand. Wincing, she applied the poultice, hoping it would reduce the inflammation. Then she wiped the sweat off Jamie's forehead.

"Jamie." She caressed his shoulders. "You need to live. Please…"

Her tears streamed. She buried her face into his pillow, letting her wet cheek touch his clammy skin.

"Jamie… I love you. I was afraid to fall in love again, but I did anyway. I love you."

***

"Ella, trust me, it's better this way." Jamie scanned the beach. A ship out in the distance swayed with all sails raised. They were in Seatown, at the same beach where they met as children. Once again, they were alone.

Her coral lips trembled. "Why are you leaving me?"

"Because I completed my plan. I found you. I've made great friends. I even learned to lead people and did some good."

"What about your family?"

"I left because of them. I didn't want them to cry over my deathbed."

"I'm crying by your deathbed right now."

A black cloud swallowed the sun. The summer breeze became a chilling gale.

He stepped back and stared into her eyes, which were full of anguish.

"No. You are supposed to be on the ship or in England."

Drops of rain fell, each pricking his skin. A chill, cold as death, pierced his chest.

"I'm dying, and you are there? No. You've suffered enough pain, and you don't need more because of me."

Her hands wrapped him, preventing him from leaving. "I am there. I found you. Don't leave me." Tears seeped through her voice.

"Ella, are you crying? Please don't. I didn't want anyone to cry over me. Especially you."

"How can I not? Don't you hear me?" The wind became so strong it was shaking him. "I just said that I love you."

His heart sped wildly, and he took a long breath.

Chapter 31

Dryness parched his tongue and throat. Then came the throbbing in his leg. These painful sensations told Jamie he was alive.

He forced his eyes open. The dim light of the sunset streamed through the windows. The window also let in the scent of grass and the earthly smell of the nearby river, which slightly neutralized the less pleasant odors of poultices and ointments.

Something heavy pressed on his shoulder. He turned to see Ella lounging next to him. He blinked, thinking that he was dreaming, but the warmth of her body and breaths convinced him she truly was next him. Her closed eyes and slightly gaping mouth told him she fell asleep resting on his shoulder and holding his hand. Warmth spread through him.

"Look, *garçon*. Your friend has opened his eyes," a man's voice said in French.

Feet tapped, and Tobby's face appeared over his. The boy yelped.

Jamie put a finger to his lips and turned his neck toward Ella. "Don't wake her. She must be tired."

His sluggish mind couldn't comprehend how she could be here. The risks and dangers she likely faced as she traveled to France and found the prison.

The boy ignored his whisper and nudged Ella. "Dr. Ella, wake up!"

Ella's eyes flew open. Jamie lost himself in their emerald light.

She gasped and jumped to her feet. Her gaze went to Tobby and then to the guard who lay in the nearby bed, but he turned away, feigning sleep.

"I believe he's on the mend," Tobby said in an important tone and touched Jamie's forehead. "Yuk, he's sweaty."

Ella laughed and brought water to Jamie's lips. He gulped to relieve the awful thirst.

"You gave us a scare," Tobby said with complaint in his tone. "Mr. Doolittle even wanted to give you last rights. But Dr. Ella said you will live."

Jamie smiled and touched the boy's face. "I wanted to make sure you found your way out of the tunnel."

A vague memory of Tobby's voice crying that he was lost and couldn't find the way out came to him. Jamie remembered that he made himself rise, and squinting in the dark, edged the list of turns he and the woman made onto the wall. He was sure that after that effort he would finally die.

"I tried to follow your Ls and Rs but kept getting lost." Tobby dropped his head. "I was so thirsty and hungry. My leg hurt and I couldn't walk anymore. I fell and everything went dark. But Mr. Leach found me and brought me here for Dr. Ella to heal me."

"Thank goodness for Ella." Jamie beamed at her blushing cheeks. "And for Conor. Where's he? I want to shake his hand."

She knit her brow. "I haven't seen him since morning. He went to tell the others you've been found."

The frown remained on her face and her eyes became unfocused.

"Is something the matter?" Jamie asked.

"You mean aside from you following Vignon's mad daughter, getting bitten by a snake, and almost dying from the venom? I say that's enough to have me slightly worried." She gave an uneasy chuckle.

"Should I bring some broth for Jamie?" Tobby asked. "That's loblolly's job."

"Yes, he needs to get his strength back. But I will go myself."

Tobby whined. "Please. I can't stay in bed anymore. My leg hurts when I'm bored."

"Fine. Bring the broth if they have it. *Bouillon* in French."

The lad hurried away, limping slightly.

Ella moved the blanket from Jamie's leg and unwrapped the bandages. "It's better. The swelling is going down."

He winced from her touch to the wound, but the pain eased as she applied a thick coating of the medicine.

"One of the guards, Renaut, directed me to the apothecary to buy the poultice," she said as she rubbed in the remedy.

"He's a good friend." Jamie grinned. "Brought us books so I could teach the seamen to read and write. These guards are good people."

"Well, most of them," Ella murmured and dropped her gaze.

Jamie tensed. "Was someone unkind to you?"

She kept her eyes down as she dressed his leg with a clean bandage and didn't answer.

After a minute of silence, she asked. "Why did you plant flowers?"

"I thought it would be nice to admire them. A reminder that even in prison we can make something beautiful. The flower doesn't even know it is growing inside a prison. It's enjoying the sunshine and the rain just like the flowers blooming in my mother's garden."

Ella tilted her head. "How wise... It reminds me of Shakespeare. 'There is nothing either good or bad but thinking makes it so. To me, it is a prison.'"

"I think I read that one. *Hamlet*?"

Ella raised her eyebrow. "Yes. I'm impressed. When we were rehearsing *Romeo and Juliet*, you were not too keen to learn your lines."

He laughed. "I was only a boy. But I found my favorite line that I wanted to recite to you. I never got a chance because you left."

"What was it?" Her eyes sparkled.

He paused for a moment so he could say the line with just the right tone. That line, treasured inside his soul for seven years, carried everything he had to say to the girl who had never left his mind since the day he met her.

"My bounty is as boundless as the sea."

His heart galloped. *Could it break in such a moment?*

She clasped his hands. "My love as deep; the more I give to thee."

"The more I have, for both are infinite," they said together.

Her finger traced his neck. "Jamie, I said something earlier. Something I didn't think I would say to any man ever again. I want to make sure you heard it. Jamie Flowers, I love you."

He grabbed her palm and kissed it. "Ella Parker, I love you more than life itself."

Now I will surely die of happiness, he thought as her lips covered his. A melting sensation ran from his neck to his chest.

The door screeched. "Mademoiselle Parker, Commander Vignon is requesting your presence." Jamie studied the guard. Of all his jailers, he was the only one Jamie didn't care for.

Ella straightened like a drawn arrow. Her cheeks, rosy a moment ago, paled.

"What's wrong, my love?" Jamie asked.

Her smile didn't reach her eyes. "Nothing. I will go see what Commander Vignon wants. Most likely a report on the patients."

Tobby walked in, holding the tray with a bowl. "I told the guards it's for you, and they looked mighty pleased that you are well enough to eat," the boy reported. "They understood me even though I forgot how to say 'broth' in French."

The guard glared at Ella. "Would you please come, mademoiselle? Vignon doesn't like to wait."

Ella stood from the chair, letting Tobby take her place. "Make sure Jamie eats everything."

Her voice quivered as if on the verge of tears.

Jamie sat up too fast and winced at the spinning in his head. "Ella, please, tell me what's wrong."

"Nothing. I will be back in a jiffy." She sped out of the room as if she could not stand being there another moment.

***

Ella's chest constricted as she walked toward Vignon's sleeping chamber. She'd just told Jamie she loved him. Found the courage to trust him. Now she will be forced to betray him.

The guard marched next to her, and his gaze needled her. He didn't seem the type she could bribe or stir pity to let her go.

It's a sacrifice for Jamie.

Tears flowed down her cheeks, and a sneer appeared on the guard's face. When they neared Vignon's door, the guard slapped Ella's bottom.

"After the commander rides you, come to my bed," he hissed in her ear.

Ella raised her hand to slap him, but he grabbed and squeezed it. She gasped in pain.

"Do I hear my English Beauty?" Vignon said from beyond the door.

The guard pulled Ella inside. Vignon was leaning on a table covered with a white tablecloth. The spread included wine, fruit, and cheese served on porcelain dishes. He dismissed the guard with a gesture and pointed at the food.

"You see, I ordered a lighter fare. It shouldn't upset your delicate stomach."

Ella took a small bite from an apple. Eating could give her a delay needed to plan. Besides, she was hungry. The apple crunched in her teeth while she scanned the room for something that she could use to protect herself.

Vignon filled her goblet with wine. "How is your betrothed? I hear good news, yes?"

Ella swallowed. "It's too early to say."

"Surely you can be optimistic. Tobby told the guards that Mr. Flowers woke up and spoke, and even wanted some broth." Vignon towered over her. "I kept my part of the deal. Sent my men to rescue him. Gave you time to nurse him. Now it's time you keep your word."

With her breath caught in her throat, Ella dropped to her knees. "Please. I love him. I don't want to betray him."

"I'm sure you will keep our intimacy undisclosed. Our little *secrete* that kept your betrothed safe."

Vignon gave her a hand to stand. His fingers ran over her neck pausing on the scar her father gave her in a drunken rage.

Tears obscured her vision. "Please, let me go. Your daughter went mad after she was raped. Surely you would not hurt a woman in such an awful way."

His lips brushed her neck. "I would never commit such violence as my sweet daughter had endured at the hands of your countrymen. I will give you pleasure. Someday Mr. Flowers will be gratified when you show him what you've learned from me."

Vignon's fingers unbuttoned her dress. She stood frozen as he pulled it down, revealing her underclothes.

She covered herself with her hands and squeezed her eyes shut. Her dress hanged at her waist when someone knocked.

"Who the devil is this!" Vignon bellowed. "I said I will not be disturbed unless..."

"Monsieur, it's urgent," the voice called from beyond the door. "The escaped prisoners have been found and detained. The gendarmes from nearby town are bringing them."

"Excellent!" Vignon shook his fists. "I will teach those scoundrels a lesson for running away and killing my man."

He thew Ella an apologetic glance. "I'm sorry, *ma chérie*. I must attend to my work. But you will come later. Once I punish the runaways, I will celebrate with you." His finger ran over her lips.

"You mean to hang them? All of them?" Ella trembled.

"The ringleader must be hanged." Vignon made a gesture of a neck breaking. "The rest will spend months in the dungeon. Some will die there, surely."

"Please." Ella choked. "These men only wanted their freedom. To return to their families."

Vignon squeezed her cheek. "Do not tempt me, Beauty. I must be firm. Enough escapes."

"Most did not escape," Ella cried. "Your mad daughter killed the prisoners."

"She deserved to have her revenge," Vignon bellowed, but then his voice broke. "My poor girl. Do you know what you had done to her, telling her that the invasion happened long ago? She lies in her room, refusing to eat. Enough." The vein on his forehead bulged. "Don't forget that Mr. Flowers is in my grip. A mistake may happen, and he may find himself in the dungeon with the runaways. As well as the boy."

He donned his coat and charged out of the room. The boom of slamming door exploded through Ella's tightened nerves.

Chapter 32

Rattled from the scene with Vignon, Ella came outside. The sallow moon made the stone prison walls appear especially intimidating. She was on the way to the infirmary to check on her patients. The commander's harsh voice made her halt.

"I ask again, who planned the escape?" his voice carried from the front of the citadel. Ella hurried there.

About twenty men, with their arms tied, stood in front of the prison gates. Simkins was there, along with Culpepper, Price, and Jacobs. She gasped at seeing Conor, pale and swaying on his feet. His legs buckled, but a guard kicked him and made him rise.

How could Conor be with them? I saw him only this morning.

"I ask again, who is responsible for the death of one guard and an injury of another?" Vignon's voice boomed. He approached Conor. "You? You are an officer."

"No, sir." Conor spoke as if in pain. "I don't know what happened. I was with other officers after I told them that Mr. Flowers was found. I left them in the tavern and walked through the town. Then, I don't remember. My head hurts…"

"The rope can relieve you of that pain forever."

Ella wrung her hands as she approached Vignon. "Please. Mr. Leach could not have led them. The night of the escape, he was in the tunnels, searching for Mr. Flowers."

"Silence, mademoiselle. This is not your place," Vignon barked. "These men will be punished for their reckless deeds."

Culpepper coughed, which caught Vignon's attention. The commander pointed. "You. Tell me who led the escape."

"I know nothing, sir"

"I can make British sailors talk. Your bosuns have the cat'o nine tails. I have a whip. And I enjoy using it."

When a guard handed Vignon a long whip, a shiver passed through the men.

Ella covered her face with her hands. In her time on the ship, flogging happened infrequently, and she never witnessed the punishment.

To her horror, Vignon grabbed Culpepper. "I will start with you and continue until someone tells me who was the leader."

Culpepper trembled and doubled over from a coughing fit.

Ella rushed to Vignon and grabbed his arm that held the whip. "Please stop. This man was in the infirmary. He's not the leader."

"You dare aid them?" he roared in her face. "I will learn who led them."

He pushed her out of the way. Then, in a couple of movements, he ripped the shirt from Culpepper. When the whip struck his bare back, Culpepper gave a heart-wrenching scream.

Ella's own shriek pierced her throat. She was thankful they were away from the infirmary and Jamie and Tobby were unlikely to hear what was happening.

"Are you ready to tell me who is responsible?" Vignon roared at the men.

Everyone's heads were down. Vignon raised the whip again.

Ella couldn't watch anymore. Bunching up her skirts, she flew toward the town.

***

Following the directions she received from a young couple who walked through the main street holding hands, Ella hastened to the inn that Vignon recommended. Mr. Doolittle would likely be there. As a clergyman, he could make Vignon see reason and stop the unjust flogging. Perhaps even dissuade him from hanging the leader.

After accepting a coin, a smiling innkeeper pointed out the room upstairs. "I just brought supper for monsignor. He recently returned, breathing hard and sweating, like after great physical exertion. My kitchen staff were overwhelmed fulfilling his order."

Ella thanked the chatty innkeeper and hurried up the stairs. When she knocked, Mr. Doolittle opened the door with slight annoyance on his face. "It's quite late for a visit, Miss Parker. And not exactly appropriate. I was about to finish my humble meal and retire for the night. I must rest before tomorrow."

He wiped his greasy mouth with the back of his hand. The smell of mutton and potatoes wafted in the air. Ella also spied a plate with pastries and a bottle of wine. Humble meal indeed.

"I'm sorry to interrupt your feast, but a terrible event has occurred. You must've heard about the mass escape."

He bobbed his head impatiently.

"The prisoners have been caught and detained."

"I know. But why—"

Ella stepped back. "How could you know that? They were just brought to the prison."

His gaze dropped. "Why don't you come in. These matters are not for others' ears." He glanced at the innkeeper who was knocking on someone's door.

Once the door closed behind them, Ella glared at him. "What is it you know about the runaways, Mr. Doolittle?"

His gaze dropped. "Unfortunately, they killed a man. It's a terrible sin. May the Lord be merciful when he judges their souls." He crossed himself.

"But how could you know they were found?"

Mr. Doolittle drew himself up. "If you must know, I found them and turned them over to the authorities."

"You? Snitched on our friends?" She stomped her foot.

"They are no friends of mine." He thrusted his large belly forward. "A lodger told me about a beekeeper on the outskirts of the town. Wishing to buy some honey for my tea, I went to find him. On my way, I got lost and stumbled upon an abandoned farm. Imagine my surprise when the most disagreeable English cursing reached my ears. I immediately knew I happened upon the lair of the runaways. They posted lookouts, but I managed to avoid them and ran to the gendarmes."

Ella's spine chilled. "Why did you betray our countrymen? They were supposed to be your flock."

"Not when they killed a man. I cannot turn a blind eye to such a deed. They had to be brought to justice."

Air burned inside Ella's nostrils. "Perhaps the monetary reward had something to do with your efforts."

"Yes, for my heroic actions, I will receive a due reward." Doolittle fiddled with a cross on his chest.

Ella noticed that the chaplain exchanged his wooden cross for a gold one. Already splurging in anticipation of the money coming in. She itched to throttle the traitor with the new gold chain he was sporting.

"Vignon will make them pay with their lives. He's going to beat them until they confess who was their leader. Our men will die for this."

And Vignon will have his way with me if I plead for his mercy.

Doolittle grabbed his throat as if a lump was stuck in there. "Miss Ella, I'm leaving the first thing tomorrow. My reward allows me to travel comfortably. I invite you to join me."

"What?" Ella blinked. "Where are you going?"

"To England, of course. There's no reason to stay in this terrible place."

Ella's eyes went wide. "Didn't you come to lift the prisoners' spirits?"

Mr. Doolittle made a dismissive gesture with his hands. "It was an assignment inflicted on me. And if the prisoners learn that I was the one who alerted the authorities to the runaways' hideout... They may not understand the goodness of my deed. But thanks to the reward, I can settle in a quaint town by the sea and preach to worthy parishioners. I believe you should do something similar, Miss Ella. Return home and serve gentlewomen. These seamen are not worth your efforts."

Her blood boiled. "Safe travels, Mr. Doolittle. I've never met another man who, despite reading the Bible regularly, understood so little of what it teaches. Goodbye." She let the door slam behind her.

Down in the dining room, Ella stopped to think. She came to France with two companions. The chaplain betrayed the prisoners for his benefit. But the agent who nicked Ella with her knife and then arranged for bandits to rob her had promised to help. She had to trust Rose.

As Ella walked through the winding street, lit only by the moon, she wished she waited till morning. Drunk men called to her as she neared the house that Rose told her to go to. With her head down, she almost ran into the small building without a sign.

When she opened the door, the aroma of jasmine and lavender perfume made her sneeze. Candles bathed the room in dim light, which was a good thing. Ella had no wish to see the women with bare shoulders who reclined on settees with their arms around the gentlemen. Her eyes scanned the room for the proprietress to ask where she could find Rose.

"Is this a new girl?" a man who drank with a woman at a small table asked. "I want to meet her."

He stood and stepped toward her on unsteady legs. "Let's go to a room upstairs, new girl."

Ella pressed herself to the wall. "I don't work here. I'm here to find—"

The woman who drank with the man caught his hand. "*Mon chéri*, you've lost track of time. Your wife will be angry with you. You don't want that, right?" Ella recognized Rose's voice if not her features, changed dramatically by scarlet rouge and white paste.

Rose ushered the gentleman outside and grabbed Ella's hand. Her lips were pursed as she pushed Ella into a room that contained little more than an unmade bed. After shutting the door and lighting a candle on a windowsill, she faced Ella with her arms crossed.

"I thought you would have sense to come early in the day. He was about to divulge the information I needed to learn."

Ella gaped. "Is that your mission? To get certain men to talk and learn their secrets?"

"The less you know the better. Why are you here?"

Ella shifted her feet. "Rose, you said you would help me." She told her everything that occurred since she arrived at Verdot. She even admitted her feelings for Jamie and how Vignon almost raped her.

Rose paced the room as Ella talked. Her eyes blazed and fists clenched when Ella told her about Mr. Doolittle betraying the runaways for the reward. When Ella explained about the dire situation the runaways were in, Rose raised her hand. "You can't save them all."

"But Vignon… "

"They knew what was coming if they got caught. You need to run with Jamie and Tobby before Vignon decides to throw them in the dungeon and forces you to sleep with him."

"But how can they run? They are in the infirmary. There are guards and the prison walls."

"Let me think."

Rose lounged on the bedcovers. Knowing what likely went on in that bed, Ella chose to remain standing.

After a few minutes of staring at the ceiling, Rose bolted up. "You could poison Vignon. With your medical knowledge, you could do it without being detected."

"Murder?" Ella thrusted her hand in front of her like a shield. "Absolutely not."

Rose rolled her eyes. "All right. Give him enough to make him ill for a few days. Crouching on the chamber pot, he won't be able to chase after you. Oh, you must poison the guards as well."

"Have you ever heard of the Hippocratic Oath?" Ella placed her hands on the hips. "I swore not to do harm. Do you understand how dangerous poisons are? Or even medicines in large doses?"

"I know more than you think." Rose raised her chin.

"Rose, are you in there? It's just me, Anne." A quivering voice sounded at the door.

"Ah, Anne." Rose smiled. "Would you please come in and tell my friend how well the pennyroyal tea had worked?"

A blenched woman staggered in, holding her belly.

"I'm afraid it worked too well," she murmured and fell to the floor.

Shaking her head, Ella helped Rose lift the woman onto the bed. Her skirts were covered with blood.

When Rose exchanged a glance with Ella, her eyes were wide with fright. "I gave her the pennyroyal I bought from the apothecary."

"To induce a miscarriage?"

Roses lips shook. "Yes. I've done it before. It worked for other women."

"As you see, dabbling in herbs and poisons is a dangerous gamble." Ella raised Anne's skirt to see the bleeding. "Do you have yarrow or shepherd's purse?"

Rose blinked. "What are those?"

Ella ground her teeth. Those medicinal plants likely had different names in French.

"Cinnamon? Please tell me you at least have some in the kitchen."

"That we do."

While Rose fetched the cinnamon to staunch the bleeding, Ella placed the patient's legs onto a pillow, bringing the flow away from the lower body and to the head.

Her faith in Rose was shaken. The woman, who seemed clever and mysterious at first, had nothing but wild and dangerous ideas. The patient Ella was treating had suffered from Rose's recklessness.

Rose slipped in and handed her a jar filled with cinnamon. "Will she live?"

"I hope so." Ella lifted Anne's hand to check her pulse and found a steady beat. "There's a reasonable chance she'll survive."

"Thank God. While you tend to her, I will come up with escape plan."

"I don't know, Rose. Jamie is recovering from an injury, and Tobby is only twelve. Can you conjure a plan that would help them escape without hurting anyone? I doubt that's possible."

While Ella worked to halt Anne's blood loss, Rose paced the room. Suddenly, she stopped and stared at Anne's fluttering eyes. "She has two sisters who work here. If I tell them that you saved her life, they would help us."

"Help us how?"

"You had man's clothing in your trunks. Can you disguise yourself as a man?"

Ella frowned. "I was younger when I managed to fool university professors, but I suppose I can pull it off for a short time."

"Then we have a plan."

Chapter 33

Ella climbed into the carriage and wedged herself between Anne's sisters, Jeanne and Claudine. Their tangy perfume, smelling of carnations and lilies, permeated the air. Since Ella was wearing a shirt and breeches under a loose coat, she could sit comfortably between their colorful skirts. That would not be the case if she sat next to Rose across from them because her enormous pannier took up most of the seat.

Rose turned to the window and shouted to her friend who again served as the driver. "Jacques, we are ready. Let's go!"

When the carriage jostled down the narrow road, Ella touched her breast. "I so appreciate all of you helping me."

"You saved our sister!" Jeanne said, taking Ella's hand.

"And this masquerade is fun," Claudine added. "It's been ages since I rode in a carriage." Ella insisted on a carriage not only to make a quick getaway, but on assumption that Jamie would be too weak to walk beyond the prison doors. Ella prayed he had a night of sound sleep and mostly recovered from the aftereffects of the venom.

"All this better result in a wedding in England," Rose said.

For the first time since the heartbreak Robert caused her, a hint about a marriage didn't fill Ella's stomach with rocks.

The late morning sun warmed Ella's exposed neck. As she ran her hand over the silky shirt and breeches, she thought it was better not to ask why someone left his clothing behind in the brothel and never returned to retrieve it.

She pulled the wide hat down to her forehead.

Would Vignon fail to recognize me? He is not a fool. On the other hand, the genius professor, Dr. Miller, didn't suspect I was a woman. People see what they expect to see.

When the carriage stopped by the prison walls, Rose nudged Ella. "You must help us climb out, like a male servant would."

Enjoying the freedom of movement men's clothing gave her, Ella grabbed the bag with their supplies, jumped out of the carriage, and offered her arm to the three women.

Rose and the sisters chatted and laughed as they sauntered to the gates, cooling themselves with feathery fans. Ella strode behind them with her head down.

Two guards stiffened as the women approached.

"Halt! Who's there?" one of them called.

Rose went straight to him with her ample bosom thrusted forward. "Don't you recognize us, Emile? Vignon sent for me, and I brought my friends."

Emile glanced at his partner, who'd shrugged. "We received no orders to let you in."

"Then check with your commander." Rose threw up her hands. "We spent all morning making ourselves beautiful for him. Claudine was excited to show him a trick she learned that makes men go wild. Make sure to tell him that."

The guard blushed and sped away.

Ella suppressed a giggle, covering her mouth with her gloved hand, but the movement caught the eye of the remaining guard.

"Who's he? I don't know him. And what's in his bag?"

Her spine tensed.

Jeanne raised her chin. "This is our groom, Alan. He escorts us to all our outings. And he's carrying spare clothes for us in case we must change."

"That's right. We are moving up in the world." Claudine gestured at the carriage. "We don't bother with walking through town anymore. No blisters on our gentle feet."

The guard came back running. He breathed heavily as he spoke. "Commander Vignon invites you in."

"Of course he has! Come, my friends." Rose clutched Claudine and Jeanne by the hand and turned to Ella. "You will wait in the yard while we chat with the commander."

The women, led by one of the guards, went into the direction of the commander's quarters. The other guards they passed whistled at them. While all attention was on the women, Ella crossed the yard and dashed to the infirmary.

When Ella walked in, Jamie, with only a hint of color on his cheeks, sat up on his bed. "Ella? Is something wrong?"

Perching on the edge of Jamie's bed, Tobby snickered. "Why are you wearing your hat like that? You look like a boy!"

"That's the idea." Ella grinned.

"Is this Mademoiselle Ella?" The injured guard, Gabriel, touched his bandage. "How hard did they hit my head?"

She pressed her finger to her mouth and approached Gabriel. "Monsignor, please don't give us away. Mr. Flowers, Tobby, and I are in danger. We must run."

"Don't worry." Gabriel's eyes sparkled with mischief. "I like you and your friends, and I wish you well. With my head broken, I saw and heard nothing." He turned to his side away from her and pretended to snore.

Ella dumped the contents of the bag onto Jamie's bed. A dress belonging to the largest woman in the brothel fell out along with a petticoat, a bonnet and a shawl.

Jamie's eyes grew wide. "What's all this?"

"I don't have time to explain." Ella said, taking his hand. "You must trust me. Are you able to walk to the prison doors?"

Jamie bit his lip. "I've been up earlier for a bit. It hurts to bear weight on my foot, but I can manage."

"It's perfect that you are clean-shaven. Now put on these clothes. The three of us are running away."

Tobby yelped and clapped his hands. Jamie's face, however, lost the little color it had. "But my parole. And the promise I gave Vignon."

"I doubt parole applies in this case. After what Isabelle did to you, no promises to Vignon should count."

"What about my men? I can't leave them behind."

Ella's shoulders slumped. *Jamie probably doesn't know about the mass escape, and that most of the prisoners have been locked in the dungeon.*

She grabbed his shoulder. "We must run. Commander Vignon wants me in his bed. If you or Tobby remain here, he'll torture you to make me submit to him. Once we are safe, we'll report the murders. That's the most important thing we can accomplish."

Jamie pushed himself off the bed and stood on his uninjured leg. When his face relaxed after a cringe, he lifted the petticoat. "I don't know how to put this on."

"Let me help you, my lady." Ella laughed with relief.

With chuckles and whispered curses, Ella helped Jamie dress. After giving up on the hooks in the back, she wrapped the shawl on his shoulders. Lastly, she tied the strings of the bonnet under his chin.

Tobby threw himself on the bed, holding his belly. "He makes a pretty lass!"

Ella touched Jamie's cheek. "You have those blue eyes and long eyelashes that some girls would die for. But your height gives you away. You'll need to crouch as you lean on my shoulder."

"With the pain in my leg, I can do that quite naturally." Jamie gave her a weak smile.

"You will play an inebriated woman." Ella handed him a flask of brandy she brought with her. "Drink this. The brandy will help with the pain and aid your disguise."

While Jamie gulped from the flask, Ella gathered her instruments and remedies into her medical bag and found her other belongings that were still in the infirmary.

"What about me?" Tobby asked. "I don't want to wear a dress. Digby will laugh at me if I tell him."

"You won't need to dress up," Ella reassured. "But you must do as I and my friend Rose say."

"Rose? Who is she?" Jamie asked.

As if summoned, Rose squeezed through the door in her enormously wide dress. "Ah, the masquerade is in full swing," she said studying Jamie. "Everything is going by the plan. Jeanne and Claudine have Vignon occupied and, like you British say, drunk as a lord."

"I remember you from Plymouth's jail." Jamie's eyebrows rose. "You are Ella's friend now?"

"Oh, no no." Rose waved her hand. "Don't say a word to the guards or you'll give us all away. Can you giggle?"

Jamie gulped his drink and attempted to giggle. Rose's lips tightened.

"Even worse. Better pretend that you've had too much and are about to retch. Hold your belly and moan while you lean on Ella."

"What am I supposed to do?" Tobby's eyes shined. "Do I get drunk, too?"

"Don't you dare," Ella answered. "You will hide under Rose's wide skirts."

Tobby's chin dropped. "You want me to crawl under the lady's skirts? No!"

Rose pouted. "Some would pay good money to be in that position. Come, boy. I donned clean pantaloons for the occasion."

Sighing, Tobby crawled under her skirts, which covered him.

Ella grabbed her bags and led Jamie outside, followed by Rose. As they crossed the yard, Jamie limped and groaned as he leaned on her shoulder. Ella couldn't tell if he was in character or in severe pain. Passing the sentries, Jamie groaned and clutched his stomach. The guards cringed and turned their heads.

At the prison gates, the same two guards blocked their way. Jamie moaned and doubled over.

"You silly fool, why did you drink so much?" Rose chided while fanning Jamie. She glared at the guards. "Let us pass quickly. We must take her home."

"I don't remember her with you," one of the guards mumbled.

"That's because she was rosy-cheeked and lively when we came." Rose kept cooling Jamie, using her fan to cover his face. "She's about to faint. Good thing we came in the carriage and brought a groom. My other friends will return on foot."

The guards stepped back, letting them pass.

Rose climbed into the carriage first. Ella and Jamie covered her to make sure no one saw an extra pair of legs that poked from under the skirt. Jamie climbed in next, holding onto Ella's and Rose's arms. As soon as Ella jumped in, Rose yelled to Jacques to drive at full speed.

"We did it!" Ella exclaimed when the prison disappeared from their view. "Rose, your mad plan worked!'

Rose gave her a smug expression. "I told you. And you, boy, can come out now." She lifted her skirts, and Tobby emerged.

"You both were terrific." Ella beamed at Tobby and then at Jamie.

"I didn't have to do much acting." Jamie closed his eyes.

Ella removed his bonnet and stroked his hair as he leaned on her shoulder.

"We'll take the carriage close to the woods." Rose said. "Louis will be waiting for you there. He and Jacques can carry Jamie if necessary."

Jamie raised his head. "We are going to hide out in the woods?"

"Yes." Ella smiled at him. "Then we make our way to the Channel. Once we are on the shore, we'll find a boat or some other way to get across. We may even see a British ship and get onboard."

Tobby jumped on his seat. "It could be the *Neptune*! We will be home!"

Jamie's ashen face crumpled. "I feel like I'm betraying everyone who's staying behind. Why don't we hide nearby and come up with a plan to rescue all the prisoners?"

Ella took his hand. "Jamie, we can't save them all. Rose and I thought carefully about this. About twenty men ran away the same night we found you. They killed a guard and injured Gabriel. Then they hid in an abandoned farmhouse on the outskirts of the town. Mr. Doolittle, the chaplain who came with me, found their hideaway and told the authorities in exchange for a large reward. I saw the runaways brought back to the prison. Rescuing them from the dungeon would be impossible. I saved you and Tobby because Vignon threatened to throw you in there as well."

Jamie gripped the railing on the carriage window. His knuckles turned white. "What will happen to them? Vignon will go beyond imprisoning them in the dungeon. He'll want someone to pay a higher price."

Ella fisted her trembling hands.

I better say nothing about how Vignon was beating the prisoners to confess who was their leader. And that Conor was among them.

Rose turned to the window. "This street leads to my lodging. I will leave you now."

"You are not going with us?" Ella gasped.

"No. My mission isn't done."

Ella wrapped Rose into an embrace. "I will miss you, Rose. I hope someday this war will be over, and I will visit your farm."

Rose smiled. "Good luck, Duchess. And you, boy." She tugged Tobby's ear. Then she narrowed her eyes at Jamie. "We risked much for your escape. Go back to England and don't give Ella any more heartache. Or you will have to answer to me."

Chapter 34

The fire cracked and sizzled, illuminating the forest clearing. Basked in its warmth, Jamie stretched his arms and shoulders, shaking off his grogginess. He spent most of the day sleeping off the brandy Ella gave him during their escape.

The smell of smoke mixed with aromas of pine and wildflowers, as well as the odors of two horses that were tied to the tree. Every breath of fresh air made Jamie feel stronger and more clear-headed. This morning, he followed Ella blindly, hearing nothing but her urgency to leave with him and Tobby. But before that, he didn't plan on escaping. He wanted to improve the prisoners' lives. And now that he knew about the captured runaways, his imagination showed his friends freezing on the stone floor of the dungeon.

The rustle of leaves announced Tobby returning with Jacques and Louis.

"Five rabbits were caught in the traps." Tobby held up a skinny carcass. "Jacque will cook them for our supper. Louis and I are going to check another trap. Tomorrow, we'll go fishing."

Jamie beamed at him, marveling at how well the boy understood the Frenchmen without speaking their language. "You will have much fun on this journey back to England."

"Where's Ella?" Jacques asked after the boy and Louis left.

"She went to gather some herbs and berries for tea. I don't like that she went alone, but she was determined to prove to me that she could take care of herself."

Jacques nodded and placed a kettle over the fire. "I wouldn't worry. From what I observed, she has enough sense not to go too far." He lifted a large knife and started skinning the rabbits with efficient movements.

Too squeamish to watch him, Jamie stood and took a few steps, bracing for the pain in his leg. As he shifted weight on it, he gladdened that it ached less. A large branch lay nearby, and he picked it up. Leaning on it, he walked around without cringing.

When he returned to the fire, Jacques patted him on the back like an old friend. "You will recover in no time. Eat well. I'll go to the town tomorrow, have the farrier fix my horse's shoe, and buy some food for the journey. Then we'll be ready to go."

"In that case, I'd like to come along to the town," Jamie said.

Jacque's bushy eyebrows crossed as he sliced the rabbit's soft fur. "Too dangerous. Vignon would discover by now how he and his guards were fooled. Stay away."

"I must find out what Vignon is doing to the runaways."

Jacques cocked his head, but his eyes stayed on the rabbit he skinned. "Why do you care? A beautiful girl loves you. Return to England with her and be happy."

His heart raced from hearing Jacques's words.

If only it was so easy. But I made a promise that no one would run. And a commitment to my men to make their lives better in prison. Conor, my friend. How will I leave him behind? And Ella... She confessed that she loves me. But with my illness, I can give her so little time.

"I cannot leave not knowing what will happen to my men. What will I tell their families? Tomorrow I will go to the town and learn the latest news. And find my friend, Conor Leach. He has parole and cannot run, but we must say goodbye."

Jacques's knife sunk into the rabbit. "I talked to the guards while waiting by the gates for you this morning. You will not like what you hear."

"What?" Jamie swallowed.

The rabbit's blood squirted them, staining their clothing. "After the beatings, one man took all the responsibility for the escape. Vignon plans to hang him."

"Who was it?" His gut clenched.

Please let it be Simkins. He must've made that reckless plan which involved killing and maiming the guards. Let it be that he takes responsibility.

"The young officer, Leach." Jacques wiped his hands on his breeches. "The guard said that everyone knows that he joined the runaways later, that he was among the search party that found you. Vignon doesn't care. He will hang him."

Jamie's knees buckled. He'd have fallen if not for the branch he leaned on. Jacques caught him by the waist and helped him sit and offered him a flask of cider.

When his dizziness faded, Jamie set his jaw. "My closest friend. I must return."

Jacques groaned. "After all Rose and Ella did …"

Jamie gave a curt nod. "I'll walk if I must. And, please, not a word to Ella. I'll go when she sleeps."

"Take my black horse, Cavalier Noir." Jacques scratched his head. "When you let him go, he'll find his way to me. But what about Ella and the boy?"

"I'll give you everything I have to bring them safely across the Channel."

Jacques waved him off. "We owe Ella already. She saved Louis's brother."

Jamie pressed his finger to his lips because Ella was walking toward them humming a song. She was wearing breeches and a shirt, as well as tall boots, much how she dressed on the ship. His chest squeezed as he thought of leaving her. Most likely forever.

Her cheeks and lips were smudged with something purple. Kneeling next to him, she opened her satchel and passed it to him to show. "I gathered some chamomile and wild blackberries. That should make a good tea. …Why are you staring at me like that?"

Because I love you. And leaving you will be the hardest thing I'll ever do.

"Um…You have berry juice on your face."

When he passed her his handkerchief, she smiled. "Why don't you kiss it off me instead?"

Jamie glanced at Jacques, who seemed absorbed with preparing the rabbit.

Blast it, if I don't kiss her now, when will I have a chance? We deserve a moment to cherish before we part.

Her lips were sweeter than the berry juice on them. After kissing every spot on her face, he leaned back to catch his breath. His heart fluttered wildly.

Ella's eyes sparkled brighter than stars. "I think some juice seeped on my neck. Would you check?"

His fingers loosened her collar and exposed her long neck, which indeed was stained with purple streaks. Her head rested on his chest and her hand brought his face close. As he kissed her neck, she purred like a cat who tasted creme. He was melting in her embrace.

Tobby's giddy laugh and Louis's heavy steps interrupted their caresses. They busied themselves helping with cooking the stew and brewing the tea. After the delicious supper, Tobby and the Frenchmen retired by the dying fire.

Ella, with the blanket spread over her shoulders, stared into the night sky. "Is that the North Star?" she asked, squinting at a star above her head.

"No. It's right there." Jamie pointed. "Ah, in our haste I left Caroline's telescope behind. Otherwise, I'd give it to you to see it better."

"I will present her with a new one." Ella beamed. "We should get a leave when we return to England, at least for a few days, so we could see your family."

Of course, she's looking forward to being back in England after the perilous journey.

"You are welcome to visit with my family. We've talked about you for years after you left."

Her brow knit. "You mean, we'd visit them together?"

"Yes, that's what I meant." He stared into the dying fire.

After a few minutes of silence, she pulled the blanket tighter on her shoulders. "You don't think your parents would be embarrassed by me?"

"Of course not. Why would you think that?"

Ella stared down at her boots. "Me being a surgeon. Wearing men's clothes. Living on the ship. Robert didn't want me to continue my profession. His parents would not approve of me practicing medicine, even though I saved his life. They wanted me to behave as expected of an officer's wife. Oh, and when I told Robert that my father disinherited me, he broke our betrothal. He had plenty of money but wanted mine as well."

Oh my God, she thinks I mean to marry her. His heart leapt and then plummeted into abyss. *Of course she does, after our declaration of love and all those kisses I gave her. I'd love to marry her more than anything, but she'd be a widow in a year or even less. What a rotten scoundrel I am.*

He bolted to his feet, and the pain in his leg stung him.

Ella tensed and rose as well. Her back slouched, and she hid her face behind her hands. "Forget what I said. I didn't mean to suggest..."

He pulled her hands away from her burning cheeks and brought them to his lips. After planting them with too many kisses to count, he cupped her chin in his palms. "Ella, I love you, and I love it that you have a calling. Don't you ever sacrifice your dreams, for anyone. I'm so glad you didn't marry that man, who isn't worthy of your little finger. The moment when you held that baby in one hand and your medical bag in another. I never saw anything more beautiful."

He imagined Ella hugging her rounded belly. The image was so beautiful that his heart ached.

Too bad I will not see this. Some lucky man will marry her and give her babies. He better deserve her.

"You want children?" Ella's voice quivered.

"I want you to have everything you wish for. And nothing you don't."

Her shoulders relaxed, as if weight was lifted off them. "Kiss me again."

Grinning, he kneeled and hugged her waist, pulling her to him. Her body slid next to his and nestled into his arms. When her face touched his, she gave him a long kiss that left them both breathless.

He fell on his back, and she climbed on top of him. Laughing, she relaxed with her ear on his chest.

"I could fall asleep to your heartbeat."

His breath caught. *She must know about my condition. She's a doctor and so clever. Perhaps she's being brave for me, knowing we have little time.*

He cradled her head and ran his fingers through her silky hair. "Sleep then, my love."

This may be my last night on this earth.

While Ella slumbered next to him, her head resting on his chest, he admired the pattern of the stars. An enormous painting made by the most glorious artist. There were enough to study all night and not be tired. Perhaps Caroline was out in the garden, staring in awe at the same stars. In his mind, he sent her a brotherly hug.

When the first light of dawn gave the sky rose hues, he gently slid Ella's head off his chest and hoisted himself up.

He covered Tobby, who smiled in his sleep, with his blanket. The morning breathed with cool air, and he didn't want the lad to catch a chill.

Before slipping to Jacque's horse, he planted one last kiss on Ella's wavy curls. "Goodbye, my love. Go back to England and be happy."

Chapter 35

Ella woke up to the chirping of forest birds and the smells of pine and burned-out fire. Turning to her other side, she hoped to return to her dream where she was sitting on a beach and watching two children play. A boy with dark hair and eyes, and a girl with sandy blond tresses. They were so beautiful that her heart swelled. The idea of giving birth normally filled her with horror. But seeing these lively children and herself beside them, this was something to live for. Marietta was right after all.

"Jamie!" She reached out for him.

When her arm found nothing, she opened her eyes and sat up. Louis and Tobby were pulling on their boots.

"We are going to catch fish for breakfast," Tobby said with a wide smile on his face.

Rising, Ella looked around. "Where's Jamie?" she asked Jacques, who was gathering wood to build a fire.

Jacques shrugged. "He must've gone for a walk."

"By himself?"

"You went alone last night. He's a grown man."

Unable to counter Jacques's point, she walked through the clearing, gathering berries and listening for Jamie's steps. Her eyes fell on a wild apple tree. Its fruit would be sour, but Jacques's horses may eat it. She picked two apples and returned to the clearing.

Only one horse, the brown one, was tied to the tree.

Ella dropped the apples and turned to Jacques. "Where's your black horse?"

He stared at his boots. "Cavalier Noir will return soon enough."

"What do you mean?" Ella crossed her arms. "Jamie must've taken him. What happened?"

Jacques fidgeted under her gaze. After a long pause, he sighed. "We can't drag the man with us if he doesn't wish to go. His friend Leach is to be hanged."

Her hands flew to her heart. "No!"

Jacques's gaze stayed on the ground. "He asked that I take you and Tobby across the Channel. I will keep my word and deliver you there unharmed."

Oh, Jamie. You thought I could leave without you. Not a chance.

Ella's lips tightened into a line and her teeth clenched. "I hope he hadn't paid you to drag us by force."

Jacques held up his hands. "No. He only wanted me to keep you safe."

"Then protect me on my return to Verdot. I must save Jamie. Again."

***

The knocking, coming from inside the prison walls, gave Jamie more discomfort than the throbbing in his leg. By the time he arrived back to Verdot, it was nearly noon. As agreed with Jacques, he released the horse to find its master. Then he picked up a branch to lean on as he limped to the prison gate. Upon coming there, he walked right up to the two guards.

"Did you miss me?"

Their eyes went round. "You've returned?" one of them stammered.

"Vignon hadn't ordered a search. But you better stay away," the other one added.

Jamie's jaw dropped. "Vignon isn't searching for me? Or for Miss Parker?"

The first guard shook his head. "When he sobered up from yesterday, he ordered workmen to build the gallows in the yard. Hear the hammering? That's the carpenters working. Vignon also ordered a great amount of food prepared and the territory cleaned and tidied for some kind of celebration."

Each knock resonated in Jamie's chest. "Is it true that he means to hang Conor Leach, even though everyone knows he could not be the ringleader?"

Both guards stared down and nodded.

Perhaps Vignon anticipated I wouldn't flee if my friend faced hanging.

Jamie squared his shoulders. "I must see Commander Vignon."

The guards exchanged glances. One of them gestured for Jamie to follow.

When Jamie stepped into Vignon's office, the commander was rapidly writing something at his desk. He gestured to a chair for Jamie to sit on.

"I almost called a search for you," he said without taking his eyes off the paper. "But I had a feeling you would return. Is the boy back as well?"

"Forget about Tobby. No one will ever ask you what happened to a twelve-year-old boy. It's me you want. I made a deal with you that you treat the prisoners better, and there would be no more escapes. I failed to keep my word and came to pay the price. But Conor Leach must be freed."

Vignon lowered his pen. "You want to be hanged instead of your friend."

"Yes. I want his parole to be returned. And the other prisoners removed from the dungeon."

Vignon lifted a bottle of wine. He sighed at the small amount left at the bottom, then he poured it into a goblet. "I can say no."

"Why would you?" Jamie leaned back. He did not expect Vignon opposing his proposal.

"Because the prisoners respect and follow you." Vignon sipped his wine. "I am concerned about their reaction if you are the one who's hanged. Instead, I could have you talk to them and find out who organized the escape."

"I have a guess who the ringleader was."

"Mr. Simkins?"

"Yes. But you don't want to hang him."

"Why not?" Vignon raised an eyebrow.

"No one would miss that wretched man. My death, on the other hand, would demoralize the prisoners. They would re-member the consequences of their actions. You should hang me and no one else."

Vignon scratched his beard. "I agree for a different reason. I am expecting an important guest to arrive tonight. So impor-tant that I am willing to forget that Miss Parker disappeared or the other peculiar events that occurred here yesterday. In the morning, I will offer him to watch the hanging, and I'm sure he'd be eager to witness it. Everything must go smoothly. I don't want hysterics from the condemned. Unlike the coward Simkins or unripe boy officer Leach, you will conduct yourself with dignity."

He's right about that. After all those years of waiting for my heart to stop, I am more than prepared to meet death.

Jamie rose and threw his shoulders back. "I will accept the end of my life with dignity. Your guest, whoever it is, would witness exemplary conduct at the execution."

Vignon bore his gaze into Jamie, as if sizing him up, and nodded. He called the guard to enter.

"Escort Mr. Flowers to the second level. Bring Mr. Leach there as well. And move the prisoners in the dungeon to their regular cell."

Pain shot up his leg as Jamie stood. "Conor Leach will have his parole."

"He'll have it after the execution. Until then, I will keep him locked up. I can't have him staging a rescue."

The guard's arm clenched Jamie's elbow.

"You will be hanged tomorrow." Vignon puffed his chest. "Meanwhile, you and Mr. Leach will be kept in one of our most comfortable cells, fit for high ranked officers. I want your friend to witness the execution, so he stays out of trouble in the future. Do you want to write a letter to your family? Or confess to a Catholic priest? Unfortunately, your chaplain already left town in his new carriage."

"Most kind of you, but I respectfully decline both offers." There was nothing he could say to his family without adding to their anguish. And he long gave up on praying for his recovery and a longer life and didn't like speaking to clergymen.

As the guard prompted him to go, he straightened his back and forced himself to walk with gravity in his gait, stepping hard on his throbbing leg. If only he could as easily compel his palpitating heart to slow.

Chapter 36

The cell was high up in the tower and had a window over-looking the yard, giving Jamie an unobstructed view of the scaffold being built. The hammering pounded in his head, but between the knocks, the afternoon chirping of birds pleased his ears.

The hammering will cease soon, but the singing of birds will go on.

The guards pushed Conor into the cell. His face was drained of color, and his entire body shook. Jamie embraced him and winced at the cold skin.

"It was deathly chilly there," Conor muttered.

Jamie led Conor to one of the two cots in the cell and helped him to pull off his boots. When his friend collapsed on the mattress, he covered him with two blankets. Then he stoked the flames in the hearth.

"Sit with me, please," Conor asked. His teeth rattled as he spoke, and he continued to shiver.

Jamie pulled up a chair. "How did you end up with the runaways?"

Conor touched his head, showing Jamie a bump. "After I told the British officers that you've been found, we went for a drink at the tavern. On the way, I turned to my lodging to grab my money purse with my winnings. When I walked to the tavern, I spotted Simkins. At that moment, someone hit me on the head. I woke up in the farmhouse where they were hiding. They stole my money."

"Why did you take responsibility for the escape?"

"Vignon was beating the men. Even those who were ill." Conor cringed, as if seeing the scene again. "I asked myself, 'What would Jamie do if he were here?' And I immediately knew that you would take the responsibility to stop the flogging."

"That's probably what I would do. But why did *you* do it?"

Conor blinked. "I wanted to behave as you would. When you won that fight against Simkins, I was so pleased. I decided at that moment I would look up to you."

"You saved Tobby's life. Then found me as well. Now you stopped Vignon from beating the prisoners. I'm immensely proud of you." Jamie grinned.

Renaut entered, carrying a tray with two steaming bowls of soup and a large loaf of bread. His hands slightly shook as he put the tray down at the table.

"Thank you, friend," Jamie said. "The hot soup will do Mr. Leach much good."

The young guard stared at Jamie with a somber expression. "Make sure you eat the bread as well," he said in a soft voice.

When Renaut left, Conor glanced at Jamie. "That was strange."

Jamie shrugged and gave Conor his soup. After a sip, Conor wrapped his hands around the bowl, warming them.

"It was so cold in the dungeon. But I suppose the grave will be colder."

Jamie winced. "That's an unpleasant thought."

"They are building the scaffold for me." Conor craned his neck toward the window. "I will die tomorrow."

He doesn't know I took his place.

Jamie patted his friend's shoulder and forced a smile. "You are not dying tomorrow. You have your whole life ahead of you."

"Then who? Someone will be hanged on that scaffold they built."

Jamie stood and stared out of the window. The carpenters were walking away from the finished gallows.

I can't tell him that it's for me. He'll try to talk me out of my decision.

"Why don't you get some sleep? The dungeon was likely less comfortable than this bed." He took the empty bowl from Conor.

Conor's shoulders trembled. "It was awful. No straw at all. All those men moaning and crying. The smells of human waste so awful, I couldn't breathe."

"It's over now."

After a few minutes, Conor eyelids drooped, and his breaths deepened.

The old guard, Batiste, walked in. Jamie pressed his finger against his lips and glanced at Conor on the bed. "He just fell asleep."

Batiste nodded and gestured for Jamie to follow. He brought him down the stairs to a kitchen where Renaut and two more guards gathered by the heath.

Renaut offered Jamie a stool. "Please sit. You must be still recovering your health."

When Jamie sat, the guards regarded him quietly.

"Do you want a smoke or a drink?" Batiste asked.

Jamie shook his head.

Batiste gulped from the flask. "We don't wish to participate in what's about to happen tomorrow. We have a mind to refuse performing our duties."

"Please." Jamie raised his hand. "Don't lose your livelihood because of me. Your families depend on your wages. Even if you refuse, Vignon will find men willing to hang me tomorrow."

Renaut dropped his gaze and swallowed. "Vignon is determined to have an execution because the emperor will be here. He's willing to kill an innocent man to have a show for Bonaparte."

Jamie's mouth rounded. "Is that right? Boney is expected here?"

The four guards gave him somber nods.

"I heard he's touring his empire, visiting a vast number of cities. He means to sleep in the town and visit the prison before crossing the river over the pontoon bridge," one of the other two guards said.

"The commander wants to entertain him with a feast and an execution," the other added.

"You can't trust Vignon," Batiste said. "He can decide to execute Mr. Leach as well. Or keep him imprisoned. Run with your friend. We won't stop you."

Jamie gave an uneasy laugh. "You can't just let us walk out of here."

"No. But we can let you escape. And provide you with the needed supplies." Renaut peered at him. "We think you should cross the river over the pontoon bridge. It's in the opposite direction than the gendarmes would expect you to run. Tonight, it won't be guarded."

"Thank you." he offered each guard his hand to shake.

I will make sure Conor runs. And then I will face my death in the morning.

Chapter 37

When Jamie stepped back into his cell, Conor was sitting on his bed. With his mouth half open, he twisted a thick rope in his fingers.

"You won't believe this." Conor whispered with his eyes wide. "The guard brought more logs. As he threw one into the fire, he pushed a bag under your cot. Then he pressed his finger to his lips and left. This rope was in the bag."

Jamie examined the rope. It was thick and sturdy.

"And remember how that guard said to eat the bread? Well, I broke the loaf and there was a small but sharp saw inside. Do you know what that means? They want us to run. We will get away from here, and they won't stop us."

His sparkling eyes studied Jamie. "I think we should wait until dark. Then we cut through the bars, use the rope to get down, and scale the wall. I saw storm clouds in the window.

Rainy weather will conceal us and wash away our footprints. Except I'm not sure which way it's better to run."

"Over the river by the pontoon bridge. It's the opposite direction of what gendarmes would expect."

"Good plan!" Conor bounced on the bed like a child. "I've been to that bridge. By tomorrow we will be far from this place."

Jamie gave him a smile.

I will make sure he makes it over the bridge and then I will turn back.

***

When night swallowed daylight and rain drummed on the windows, Conor climbed through the sawn bars and slid down the rope. Jamie could hardly see him in the dark or hear him in the pounding rain. A part of him wondered if he should let Conor run alone.

No, I will see him make it over the river.

After waiting for what he thought would be long enough for his friend to touch the ground, he followed. Powerful rain battered him as he descended. Thanks to the skills he acquired on the ship, his body glided with control, and he didn't get a rope burn on his hands. His feet sank into the muddy ground. Conor tried to yank the rope from the window, but it wouldn't budge.

"Let it be," Jamie said. "We won't need it." The guards would have evidence of their escape and won't be blamed.

Soaking wet and chilled by the rain, they sped through the empty prison yard, past the infirmary. No guards' voices bellowed after them or lanterns shone in their faces.

Within minutes, they came to the wall. "How do we scale it without a rope?" Conor asked.

Jamie ran his hand over the stones and almost by feel found a small gate, normally locked and guarded. As he predicted, it swung open.

Conor gawked, but Jamie pulled his arm as he ran through the gate and down the steep hill. As they descended, their boots filled with water.

"I thought there would be a beach here." Jamie yelled through the wall of rain.

With his hand over his face, Conor squinted into the darkness. "More importantly, where is the bridge?"

They waded in knee deep water, guessing which way was the pontoon bridge. When they came to an uprooted tree, Conor grabbed Jamie's shoulder. "I remember this tree. The bridge was here. The storm must've broken the chain, and the bridge was swept away by the current."

Jamie sighed. "Let's go back. You will not be—"

"Swim across, Jamie." Conor put his arm around him. "You said you are an excellent swimmer. But I'm not. You go on without me."

A rush of warmth made him forget that he was chilled to the bone. Jamie yelled in Conor's ear.

"I thought to help you cross while I stay behind. Now you are offering the same. You are truly a brother to me."

"A brother I can't stand to lose! Go!"

With a bolt of lightning, a plan formed in Jamie's mind.

"No." Jamie clapped Conor on the back. "The loss of the bridge can save us all."

***

In her soaked shirt and breeches, Ella trudged through the downpour. Because Jacque's horse had thrown a shoe, she and her companions walked to Verdot. She left Tobby and the Frenchmen in the nearby woods. The men reassured her their tarp would protect them from the weather, but as she pulled a cloak around herself, she couldn't help but worry.

When she neared the prison doors, she had to yell at the top of her lungs that she must see Commander Vignon. To her surprise, the guard removed his coat to shield her from the rain and rushed her inside the citadel. When the lanterns illuminated his face, Gabriel, her patient in the infirmary, grinned at her.

"How are you feeling, Monsignor Gabriel?" Her teeth rattled.

"Fully recovered and back to my duties, *Docteur Parker*." The guard chuckled. Then a shadow crossed his face. "I think I know why you are here."

Ella steeled herself. "Tell me the news."

"Mr. Flowers showed up and persuaded Vignon to hang him instead of Mr. Leach. The execution is planned for tomorrow morning. Unless—"

"No!" The world spun in front of her. Gabriel brought a finger to his lips, but it was too late. Steps thundered from the hall, and Vignon appeared.

With his breath stinking of alcohol, he approached her nose to nose.

"Came to see me, mademoiselle? I could use your company."

She swallowed. "Yes, I came to see you."

Gabriel coughed and stepped forward. "Monsieur, it's late. Perhaps I should escort Miss Parker to her lodging?"

Vignon's face turned red. "How dare you interfere with my business? Go back to your post."

The guard remained rooted in his spot.

"It's all right, Gabriel." Ella said. "You can go."

I knew it would likely come to this. Jamie's life and freedom are worth more than my maidenhood.

Vignon gripped Ella's wrist. Yanking her by the arm, he walked so fast that Ella's legs could barely keep up.

"You are hurting me!"

"Pardon." Vignon loosened his grip a bit. "I've had a foul evening. But I'm hoping it is about to change."

When they entered his quarters, he dismissed the guard. After pulling Ella inside, he threw a few logs into the fireplace. Ella removed her wet cloak and warmed her hands.

Vignon poured a glass that had such a strong scent that Ella wrinkled her nose. "Drink and take off your wet clothes."

Her shoulders tensed. "I would prefer tea to warm myself."

"I don't care what you prefer. I'm tired of waiting, of pleasing. Ever since I was named a commander of this prison, I anticipated this evening, and all for nothing."

Ella blinked. "What do you mean? I..."

"I don't mean *you*, of course!" Vignon gulped his drink. "The Emperor Bonaparte! I've hoped, I prayed for him to come here and notice my diligent efforts. A smile of his lips would've been the greatest reward for me."

"Napoleon is here?" Ella asked, her mind buzzing.

Vignon must be planning for the emperor to see the execution. Perhaps I could throw myself at Napoleon's feet and beg him to pardon Jamie and the other prisoners.

Vignon paced by the fire. "I bowed so low that my back ached. I spoke the words I prepared all day. The emperor passed me like I wasn't there. Didn't bother to turn his head for a single glance. Yelled for his dinner to be brought to his room and went straight to bed."

She batted her lashes like her friends did when speaking to gentlemen they wanted to charm. "I cannot believe Napoleon is here. I'm curious where is he is staying."

Vignon drained his drink and stared at her. "You wish to warm the royal bed? My cot is not good enough?"

Ella cringed, but Vignon gave a chilling laugh.

"Enough games. I know what you are up to. You came here to beg for Mr. Flowers's life and offer yourself in exchange. Now you hear that the emperor is nearby, and you decided to sell yourself to an even more powerful man. Turns out you are a whore like the two you sent me yesterday."

His hand swung and hit Ella's cheek. Pain shot from her mouth to her ear. For a moment she was a younger girl, struck by her cruel father. The scar on her neck, inflicted by him in a drunken rage, burned.

"Did that hurt, *ma chérie*?" Vignon said in a mocking voice. "You hurt my pride, and that's much more painful. I'm no longer in a mood to give you pleasure. Shrieks of pain will be music to my ears."

His hands reached for her bosom.

Stepping back, Ella sunk her hand into her pocket and gripped Jacques's dagger. The robber reassured her this would be the best weapon, better than a scalpel she intended to bring. She pointed the blade at Vignon's neck.

"Don't forget I'm a surgeon and know exactly where to strike so you die instantly," Ella hissed. "If you attempt to call the guards, I will do just that before they get to you."

"You are mad!" Vignon's body shook. "You will be executed for my murder."

"Then I will share my beloved's fate. But unlike Jamie, I will be tried before the judge. And before I'm executed, I will reveal the hideous crimes you and your daughter committed." She brought the blade closer to the pulsing artery on his neck.

Vignon trembled. "My daughter! What will happen to her if you kill me?"

Isabelle belonged in the insane asylum, but despite the murders she committed, Ella's chest wrenched. Pure horrors went on in such places.

Taking advantage of her pensiveness, Vignon lunged at her and pinned her to the table. The dagger fell out of her hands.

Vignon picked it up and hid in on his belt. "There was your mistake. You hesitated, thinking of Isabelle. I will not be so merciful."

He punched her in the abdomen, making her double-over with a scream.

"Vignon, open the door, you scoundrel," Conor's bellow came from beyond the door. "Or we are breaking it."

"If that was Ella screaming just now, I swear I will kill you." Ella's heart leapt at Jamie's voice.

Vignon turned to the door. "What are those two doing here?!"

Using the distraction, Ella's hand searched for something heavy. When her fingers found the candelabra, she grabbed it and swung it at Vignon's head.

Vignon stared at her wide-eyed, then fell back like a chopped tree.

"I'm here," Ella yelled and unlocked the door for Jamie and Conor.

Jamie's hands wrapped around her. "I see that you are, but you shouldn't be."

Conor bent over Vignon. "He passed out. Impressive work, Ella." He opened a drawer, where he found Vignon's pistol and loaded it.

"Yes, most impressive, my love." Jamie caressed her wet hair. "But you shouldn't risk yourself for me."

Ella breathed deeply to steady her rattled nerves. "As you can see, I wasn't waiting for help. I was trying to rescue you two. But how are you here?"

"I'll explain later. We have a plan that could save all the prisoners and us." Jamie stared at the adulations of the commander's chest. "Unfortunately, we need him for this plan. Ella, would you be able to wake him?"

"I will keep the pistol pointed to be sure he won't try anything," Conor added.

Ella found a jug of water by the bed and poured the contents on Vignon's face.

"Ahh, what's this?" Vignon gasped and raised his head. His eyes bulged as he stared at the pistol in Conor's hands. "I didn't hurt her, I swear."

"Miss Parker gave you a mighty smack. I hope that taught you to stay away from her," Jamie said.

Ella crossed her arms and shot the commander a smug look.

"Yes. I swear. I won't touch her ever again."

"I'd give you a few more punches, to be sure you've learned your lesson, but we have a need for you. Although your need for us is even bigger," Conor added.

Vignon rubbed his head where Ella hit him. "I don't follow."

"The pontoon bridge broke and was washed away. Your emperor won't be able to leave in the morning."

Ella's jaw dropped. She guessed their scheme.

Vignon grabbed his chest. "Is it true?"

Jamie nodded "If the bridge were still there, Mr. Leach would be on the other side by now. But you have a severe problem. How will you inform Bonaparte with his entourage that he is stuck on this side of the river?"

Vignon sat up, holding his head. "I must... The guards will rebuild it. They must start immediately."

Jamie raised an eyebrow. "You don't have enough men for the job. Also, do they know what needs to be done?"

"You suggest..." Vignon massaged the spot where Ella hit him. "... to use the prisoners?"

"The British sailors are excellent men for this work. Mr. Leach and I are the officers you need to organize them."

Vignon slowly rose to his feet. "Yes, yes. Let's go right now. I will let your men out to work." He removed the key ring on his belt. Conor raised the pistol, while Jamie grabbed the keys from him.

Jamie peered into Vignon's widened eyes. "Now, I need reassurance. The execution you planned..."

"No execution, Mr. Flowers. No one is to fear for their lives." Vignon shifted his feet. "Can we go now?"

Jamie didn't move. "You will not interfere with our commands."

"Yes, of course."

Ella placed her hands on her hips. "Men are to be fed well. They will take breaks to rest and drink water."

Vignon bobbed his head.

"You will bring Napoleon to see our work." Jamie raised his chin. "And you will persuade your emperor to officially release all prisoners toiling on the bridge."

Vignon hung his head. "Yes. Rebuild the bridge. I will do as you say."

Chapter 38

Jamie and Conor were up to their waists in the river along with the prisoners and most of the guards. Only the sickest men stayed behind in Ella's care; the rest, seized by the excitement of seeing Napoleon and hopefully earning their freedom, volunteered to rebuild the bridge.

At first, Jamie proposed to find the boats that the current carried downstream and link them together again, but the seamen suggested a better plan. They passed several stout chains across the river and collected the largest and the least damaged boats. Then they passed those boats across on an improvised chain-ferry. Everyone, even Simkins and his friends, did their fair share of labor.

"Keep up the good work," Jamie yelled. "Soon we'll take a short rest."

Jamie glanced back at Ella on the shore as she set up a late breakfast of bread, cheese, and slices of ham. Her men's clothes dried, and once again she appeared stunning in those breeches. Like the sun that warmed up the earth after the storm, a content smile lit her face.

She jumped up and glanced behind her. A short man, dressed in a surprisingly modest-looking uniform of a green coat, white breeches, black boots, and a two-cornered hat, walked toward the river. Only a few gold buttons added a touch of finery to his clothes, but there was no doubt in Jamie's mind that this was the French emperor Napoleon Bonaparte, accompanied by Commander Vignon and two soldiers of the Imperial Guard.

"Keep the men working," Jamie said to Conor and stepped to the shore. Simkins trailed him with his eyes glued to Napoleon. A few guards tensed and followed as well.

"Go back to work, Simkins," Jamie ordered, but the seaman stayed with him like a wide-eyed shadow.

"As you can see, the prisoners are almost finished with rebuilding the bridge," Vignon spoke to the emperor in his oiliest voice.

Bonaparte's face was passive as he watched the British sailors. Then his head swiveled toward Ella. Jamie bristled as the emperor ogled her.

The emperor gestured for her to approach. "Madam, how are you here? Is your husband a British prisoner?"

She glanced at Jamie for a moment and smiled. His breath caught. But then she turned back to Napoleon and made a graceful curtsy despite her unfeminine clothing. "Your Majesty, my name is Ella Parker. I am a surgeon who came here to care for my sick countrymen."

Napoleon raised an eyebrow. "These men are fortunate to be in your care. Is there anything you wish to ask of me?"

A smile lit Ella's face. "My wish is for them to be set free and reunited with their families in England."

The emperor furrowed his brow and clicked his tongue.

In that silent moment, Jamie's heart thundered like a drum.

"That's quite a difficult request, madam."

Ella fidgeted as if unsure what to do. Then she clenched her hands together. "Surely, it's nothing less than these men deserve for rebuilding the bridge. They've worked most of the night and this morning."

Napoleon made a throaty chuckle. "I was only teasing you. I will sign the order. All men working on this bridge are to be set free."

"Thank you, Sire. *Merci*." Ella curtsied again, beaming.

Napoleon waved to the sailors. Then he gestured to one of his men, who brought him a silver box. The emperor snuffed a pinch of tobacco.

Simkins woke up from his trance. "Ask him for some tobacco for us," he yelled to Ella.

Ella stared him down while Jamie balled his fists.

That fool will spoil everything.

"What did this man say?" Napoleon glanced at Vignon.

The commander's face reddened like a cooked lobster. "He said he wishes for a snuff of tobacco from you, Sire."

Napoleon chuckled again and, holding his box, offered Simkins to take some. Vignon shook like he was ready to swoon.

"The French emperor is setting all of us free!" Jamie yelled to the men. His words were met with a boom of cheers.

***

Ella's hand squeezed Jamie's as they watched Napoleon and his Imperial Guard get across the pontoon bridge.

This is quite a moment, she thought. *I wonder if it will be written about in historical texts.*

"Are we truly free to go home?" Conor asked.

"Yes. Bonaparte signed the papers for release of all Verdot's prisoners." Jamie showed Conor the document.

"Then what are we waiting for? Let's go."

"Several men became ill in the dungeon," Ella said. "I will nurse them until they are fit to travel."

Jamie touched her arm, giving her a sweet sensation. "Then we'll stay as well. Those who want to leave earlier may do so."

The former prisoners crowded around them. Many were rubbing their limbs after doing strenuous work. They chatted with each other, but their glances were fixed on Jamie, as if waiting for his instructions.

He raised his hand, and they quieted. "Men, you've done well today. I'm proud of you. As you heard, Napoleon set us all free. I suggest you stay in groups and make your way to the Channel, where you can cross to England. For those who have injuries that prevent them from walking, I will hire a carriage. Miss Parker, Mr. Leach and I will stay with the those who are too weak to travel and care for them until they are fit to go home."

The men cheered. Jamie dismissed them and intertwined his fingers with Ella's as they walked back toward the infirmary. Ella was thinking of her patients, the medicines she needed to treat them.

"Miss Parker! Help!"

The voice sounding from the yard was so high-pitched and frantic that Ella didn't recognize it. She dashed forward, with Jamie and Conor speeding behind her.

With a grimace of anguish, Vignon stood in the middle of the yard. It took her a moment to realize that the scream belonged to him. His shaking hand pointed to the scaffold. As Ella neared it, her blood chilled. A long-haired woman in a white shift hung in the noose. Her face was gray, and her purple tongue fell out of her mouth.

"Isabelle! She killed herself!" Ella cried. Her palm flew to her mouth. Jamie's arm wrapped her shoulder, but his eyes were fixed on the ground, as if he couldn't bear to look at the dead woman.

Conor exhaled with a hiss. "That could've been me," he whispered and covered his face.

Ella's stomach twisted. "I made her face the truth of her crimes. But I didn't wish such a death on her after all her suffering."

"Don't just stand there!" Vignon bellowed, waving his hands toward Ella. "You are a doctor. Save her!"

Her shoulders slumped. "There's nothing I can do. She's dead."

"Nooo!" Vignon ran up to the scaffold. With a slice of his knife, he cut the rope and caught his daughter's body in his arms. Tears ran down his face as he lay her down on the grass and shook her.

Ella approached and lifted Isabelle's hand. There would be no pulse, but she wanted to show Vignon that she tried. Feeling the cold skin, Ella shook her head. "She's gone."

"She is free of her suffering," Jamie said. His eyes were brimming with tears.

Vignon clutched at his chest and backed away. Color drained from his face. He pivoted and ran inside the citadel.

Conor, Jamie, and Ella stood frozen, recovering from the terrible scene. Then a boom from a pistol shot made them shudder. Her heart in her throat, Ella sprang in the direction Vignon ran. Jamie's and Conor's hurried steps stomped behind her, followed by a couple of guards.

Blood seeped from under the door of Vignon's private chamber. Ella tried to open but it was locked.

Conor told her to stay back and kicked the door open with his foot.

The broken door fell open. Inside, Vignon's dead body slumped in his chair. The pistol laid at his feet.

Chapter 39

With her hand in Jamie's, Ella admired the vivid colors and fragrances of the meadow. Conor strode in front, swiveling his head to spot any danger. Tobby stayed close to him. The boy seemed to grow several inches in the couple of weeks he hid in the forest with French outlaws. Three former prisoners Ella nursed back to health, Culpepper, Jacobs, and Price, brought up the rear.

"Strange to say this, but I'm glad the carriage broke down," Ella said. "This way, we get to see the lovely countryside."

And I can savor every moment of this journey with Jamie.

"I agree." Jamie's dimples emphasized his smile. "Except, I'm worried if we'll make it to the nearest town before nightfall."

Ella watched for Jamie's limping and didn't see it anymore. He appeared healthier since she met him in Plymouth six months ago. His shoulders spread wider, and his biceps bulged from under his shirt. There was confidence in his step that he lacked before the journey.

"We can sleep in the woods!" Tobby jumped with excitement. "I will set traps and catch some rabbits for dinner like Jacques and Louis taught me."

"We sure made strange friends in France. We left Verdot two weeks ago, but I miss them already." Jamie said. "Prison guards and outlaws."

"A female agent and prostitutes," Ella murmured under her breath to make sure Tobby didn't hear her. "Shockingly, I consider them friends as well."

Conor snapped his head back and scoffed. "How come I didn't meet them?"

"And don't forget Napoleon," Jamie added with a wink. "Since he released us, I call him a friend. At least until we reach England."

"Are we close to England?" Tobby's voice pitched. "When will I see Digby and the other ship boys? I must tell them all about France."

Conor halted and raised his finger. "Quiet! I heard something."

They froze and listened. Ella squeezed Jamie's hand, concerned about the danger Conor sensed.

A grin spread on Jamie's face. "Ah, I hear it too. And I feel the change in the wind."

"You sound like a sailor," Ella remarked. The far-off sound of crashing waves reached her ears. A hint of salt wafted in the air.

Her skin tingled. "We must be close to the Channel. I smell the sea air."

"That's what freedom smells like," Jamie answered.

The sun set before they reached the shore. To Tobby's excitement, they decided to spend the night in the woods beyond the meadow. Tired after the long day of walking, everyone fell asleep after a simple dinner of fish caught by Tobby and the seamen.

When Ella woke up, stars lit the sky, and the snores and deep breathing of the men mixed with the sounds of the forest. She sat up and shook herself to make the remnants of her dream let go of her.

Her hand reached for Jamie. Feeling his body next to hers, she shimmied closer to get warm and rested her head on his chest. His heartbeat was steady and strong, but for a second she thought she heard a murmur. She listened again, but this time she didn't perceive it.

I wish I had something to aid my hearing. My professor, Dr. Miller, somehow detected heart murmurs even when I or other students couldn't. Not that we ever admitted our shortcoming. Most of us competed for his apprenticeship and always agreed with him.

Frustrated by uncertainty, she ran her fingers over Jamie's heart to feel for a murmur, a technique her mentor Dr. Pesce taught her. She didn't notice anything unusual.

Why am I worried? He doesn't show any symptoms of an illness. And he survived the hardships of prison and the snake bite.

Jamie stirred under her, and his eyelids flew open. He regarded her as she smiled into his eyes.

"Can't sleep, my love?"

"No. I'm too excited. Do you think we could walk to the Channel, just the two of us?"

He scratched the stubble on his cheek. "Are you thinking to go for a night swim?"

"Yes. Like I wanted on that seaside holiday when I met you. We never got to do it."

Conor groaned nearby. "Why are you two chatting in this late hour?"

"We are going for a swim," Jamie said. "We'll be back soon enough."

They hiked toward the sound of the water and reached the beach sooner than they predicted. The moonlight reflected like silver ribbons in the water, and the site made Ella giddy. The wind lifted her hair, and she twirled like a little girl.

Jamie came up to the water and dipped his hand. "It's cold for a swim," he said when he returned.

She wrapped her arms around his neck. "Your kisses will keep me warm."

Her heart fluttered like a swallow when he lifted her into his arms and spun her around.

We are free to do as we wish. No one can stop us.

Her body relaxed, anticipating the pleasure of his kisses. After waiting for the first one too long, she leaned toward his lips.

Instead of a kiss she longed for, he set her down.

"What's wrong, Jamie?"

His face tensed. "I hear someone."

Perplexed, Ella listened. Someone's quiet wailing, muffled by the wind, came from a short distance away.

Ignore it, Ella wanted to say, but bliss was gone. Neither Jamie nor she would ever walk away from a cry without investigating.

"Who are you? Do you need help?" he yelled in French.

"I've been robbed. I'm starving!" A man's voice whimpered back in English.

"I know that voice," Ella groaned. "If it's who I think it is, he has plenty of body fat to avoid starvation."

They found Mr. Doolittle a short distance away, sitting with his head in his hands, and his shoulders shaking. As they drew near, the chaplain dropped onto his knees. "Miss Ella! And you, Mr. Flowers. You must be an answer to my prayers."

"What happened to your fine carriage and horses?" Ella asked.

"Robbers! The same ones who attacked us on our way to Verdot. They stole everything. After a tiny sip of comfortable life, I'm poor as a church mouse again."

"Poverty is a virtue for a man of God," Ella reminded him. "You sent me to a convent and wanted me to give all my assets to the church."

She hid her smile, but she was glad for what had occurred. Mr. Doolittle did not deserve to profit by betraying the runaways. Conor or Jamie could've paid with their lives because of his snitching.

Jamie gave him a hand to rise. "I'm sorry you were robbed, but you seem unharmed. We'll lead you to our camp and share what's left of our supper. Tomorrow we will find a boat and cross the Channel."

In the morning, Ella woke up to the smell of fried fish. Despite her hunger, she let herself keep her eyes closed a bit longer and remember last night, before Mr. Doolittle appeared. Her body became limp and warm as she saw herself in Jamie's arms.

He fills me with happiness. He is everything Robert Weston was not: caring, accepting, humble, and honest. He isn't after my money. I want to marry him. However, I desire a unique proposal moment, unlike the one I had with Robert.

When she opened her eyes, she found all the men gathered by the fire, holding sticks over it to fry their fish.

"Save some for me," she cried when she saw Mr. Doolittle stuffing his mouth with two small fishes at a time.

Conor laughed. "Don't worry, we have plenty more."

She studied piles of whiting and mackerel large enough to feed all of them. "Tobby, did you catch so many?"

Tobby blew on the stick and took a large bite. "I wish. Conor brought these before I woke up."

Ella's neck swiveled to Conor, who grinned with pride. "I didn't know you are such a skilled fisherman, Conor."

His smile widened. "I'm a man of many talents."

Jamie rolled his eyes. "He bought this from the local fisher-men."

Conor bumped Jamie on the shoulder. "If you are impressed with the fish, wait until you hear this. For a small fee, they agreed to transport us across the Channel in their boat."

Everyone whooped and cheered at that news.

Jacobs peered into the sky. "When do we go?"

"Early in the evening, after they are back from the market," Conor said.

The sailor scratched his neck. "Let's hope the weather stays calm. I feel the rain coming."

True to Jacobs's prediction, the sky grew cloudy in the afternoon and the clouds obscured the sun. With hope that the rain would be mild, the group gathered their things and walked to the beach. Conor led the way. Ella followed, holding her medical bag in one hand, and Jamie's hand in the other.

The anticipation of arriving in England made her heart dance. Despite the sailors' frowns at the sky, Jamie's hand in hers made her feel safe.

The drops of rain hit them when the boat glided into their sight.

"Should we wait for morning?" Jamie asked.

"But we are so close," Tobby whined. "I want to go."

"I agree with Tobby," Conor said. "If the fishermen can take us today, I say we go."

Jamie kept his gaze on the sailors. "We need your expert opinion."

Culpepper shrugged. "Their boat looks sturdy. And it's only rain."

"Who knows if the weather will be any better tomorrow?" Price shrugged.

Jacobs stayed silent.

They met two French fishermen, by appearance a father and a son, at their boat.

"What do you think of this weather?" Jamie asked.

"We've come out fishing in such clouds. I see no danger," the older one said.

With their words and the confirmation from the seamen, Ella gazed into the distance with a smile. *Soon we will be home.*

The fishermen pushed the boat into the water. They hopped in, followed by Conor, who lifted Tobby inside. The three seamen jumped in. With water getting into her boots, Ella ran next to Jamie, who gave her a hand to jump in. Mr. Doolittle was last, with several people helping him in.

The fishermen and the sailors lifted the oars and rowed in unison. Fresh wind hit Ella's face. The smell of the sea made her lungs expand. Despite the falling rain, her excitement made her almost oblivious to it.

An hour later, the sky turned black, and the wind whipped their backs. They doubled-over as rain soaked them through.

Fear gripped Ella as she scanned everyone's faces. The seamen and the fishermen exchanged worried glances. Jamie, who took his turn with the oar, chewed his lip. Only Tobby remained smiling as he gazed in the distance.

Her knuckles turned white as she gripped the side of the boat. "Is the rain getting worse?"

Culpepper and Price nodded. The younger fisherman retrieved several cups to bail water that was gathering at the bottom of the boat. With his eyes wide, Mr. Doolittle clasped his hands to pray.

Their small boat tossed from side to side at the mercy of the elements. The wind and current were carrying them toward England, and they could do little more than follow Mr. Doolittle's example.

Her eyes went to Jamie. Despite the rain hammering him, he rowed without missing a beat. He gave her a reassuring nod.

"We'll get home safely, my love."

He's staying calm in a storm like a seasoned captain, Ella thought with pride.

"Look!" Tobby pointed into the distance. "A light!"

"Good eye, lad!" Jacobs yelled. "It's a lantern of a ship!"

Ella uttered a prayer of thanks. Whether English or French, a vessel would aid a fishing boat caught in severe weather.

"What if it's the *Neptune*?" Tobby's voice rang in the hammering rain.

"Careful!" Conor yelled. "Sit down!"

Ella's head whipped to Tobby, but his seat was empty. A splash pierced the darkness.

"He fell overboard!" Ella bellowed.

In one movement, Jamie threw off his jacket. "I love you," he mouthed to her before jumping into the churning water.

Chapter 40

Tobby's arms flailed above water. The current carried Jamie forward, but it swept the boy even faster.

"Hold on, Tobby!" Jamie made powerful strokes toward the boy. Water stung his face, burned his eyes. Shouts reached him, but the wind roared over the words, making them undiscernible. Every fiber of his being concentrated pushing himself to swim faster. His limbs moaned and threatened to lock up from the cold, but he pushed on despite the pain.

The only muscle in his body he could not trust to persevere was his heart.

After many agonizing strokes, his hand grabbed onto Tobby's shirt. The boy's eyes were wide with panic. His trembling arms clenched on Jamie's neck, pulling him down.

He could drown me.

Jamie suppressed the impulse to shake the boy off him. To-bby clung for his life. He would let him hold on as long as he could.

A wave rushed over him, and water filled his nose and ears. His lungs yearned for a breath, but with Tobby's grip on him, he couldn't emerge.

The boy must live even if I die. It's a good thing I told Ella that I love her. I wish we had more time, were his last thought when darkness overtook his senses.

***

Ella kept afloat with one arm under Jamie's armpit, another holding onto the ropes of the cork life buoy. Jamie's body was limp, and his head down. With the waves crashing against them, she could not tell if he was breathing.

Jamie, I swam after you in this weather. I pulled you up to air. You must live.

Tobby was next to her, holding the life buoy with both hands, his teeth rattling loud enough to hear over the wind.

"Hold on, Tobby. The boat is almost here." She tried to sound calm for the boy.

Splashes of oars sounded closer. The fishing boat would get to them before the ship that threw them the life buoy. In the downpour, Ella could just make out the three masts with most of the sails reefed, and the gun ports. A sloop of war, like the *Neptune*.

The boat came closer; hands reached and pulled Tobby out of the tossing waves.

"Ella, give me your arm." The voice was Conor's.

"Grab Jamie first. He's unconscious."

Conor's eyes, illuminated by the lantern next to him, widened. His hands, as well as those of the seamen, reached for Jamie. Once his limp body was in the boat, Ella grabbed Conor's arm and let him lift her up.

When her feet touched the bottom of the boat, she crouched next to Jamie. Her fingers searched for a pulse. They couldn't find it.

Her heart sank into the depth and her lungs refused to inhale.

No, he cannot be dead. My hands are too numb to feel any-thing. That's why I can't find the pulse.

She was about to position her head on Jamie's chest to listen for breaths and his heartbeat, but a voice from the ship, ampli-fied by the bullhorn, startled her.

"This is Captain Grey of the *Neptune*. Take the rope we will lower to you."

Tobby squealed. "I was right. It's our ship!"

A collective exhale of relief came from the seamen. Mr. Doolittle folded his hands in a thankful prayer.

Her eyes met Conor's widened pupils. "Conor, go up to the deck first and tell them that Jamie needs urgent help. They'll need the boatswain's chair to bring him up."

She checked Jamie's heartbeat but could not hear it. The world shuddered.

I can't let you die, Jamie. I want you to live, to marry me, to be the father of my children.

Putting to practice the theory she described in her medical school dissertation, she fisted her hands and pushed on Jamie's chest, trying to keep the blood pumping through his body.

Please, let this work.

Ella's muscles strained and screamed as she pushed on Jamie's heart, pausing to give occasional breath into his mouth. Tobby's whimpering sounded near her head. She was vaguely aware of the men leaving the boat. Someone lifted Jamie into the boatswain's chair and pulled her on as well. Her eyes saw nothing but Jamie's unmoving chest.

The moment her feet touched the deck, she dropped to her knees and continued pumping Jamie's heart. The tense faces of her assistants, Tyler and Sully, loomed above. Her hands, weary from swimming, somehow found the strength to keep working. Sully and Tyler offered to take over, but she shook her head, afraid they wouldn't administer the compressions properly. Not that she knew how to do this. Surgeon John Hunter's theory on reviving drowning victims served as excellent research for her dissertation, but she never applied it until now.

"Jamie, after all we've been through, I can't lose you," she muttered.

She inhaled a lungful of air and blew it into Jamie's mouth.

Chapter 41

Jamie's lungs constricted and bitter water rushed into his mouth. He spat it out and coughed. Someone rolled him onto his side and struck him on the back, causing him to cough up more water. When he managed to gulp salty air into his irritated throat, his stomach heaved, and he vomited a puddle of water. Crushing weight lifted off his chest, and sweet air filled him.

He didn't need to open his eyes to know that the hands caressing him were Ella's. When her kisses covered his cheeks, he reached for her. Her hands grabbed his and rubbed some warmth into them. Water dripped from her clothes and hair.

"Doctor Ella, I will prepare a tobacco enema," someone said. Jamie's eyes snapped open.

"Tyler, didn't I tell you that it does no good?" Ella shook her head at her assistant. "We'll warm Jamie with blankets and hot liquids. Make them ready in the sickbay and get the stretcher."

"Can I give him brandy?" Conor loomed above him, drinking from a flask. He lifted Jamie's head to drink, but more vomit spilled from Jamie's mouth, hitting Conor's boots.

"Sorry," Jamie muttered.

Conor laughed as if he heard the funniest joke. "Did you hear that, Ella? He spoke!"

Ella's fingers ran through Jamie's wet hair. "My love, we are on the *Neptune*. We are going home."

It dawned on him that he was lying on the deck. Ella and Conor huddled next to him, and many concerned faces loomed behind them. A breeze blew through his wet clothes. Drizzle, a mere remnant of the prior storm, grazed his face.

His mind was sluggish as he willed it to remember what happened. The images of his desperate swim to save Tobby gave him a slight boost of energy. "Is Tobby all right?"

"Yes. He's at the sickbay, cared for by Sully, my other assistant. He'll be fine." Ella smiled.

Her head turned to Captain Gray, who approached through the crowd of men parting for him. He bent over Jamie. "Doctor Parker, did you manage to bring my servant back to life?"

She rose. "Aye, sir. But he needs rest."

"I will resume my duties tomorrow, sir." Jamie murmured.

Captain Grey laughed. "I'm not sure what duties to give you at this point. From the little I've heard you deserve a promotion. But first you must get better."

With fatherly concern in his eyes, he clasped Jamie by the shoulders and helped Tyler move him onto the stretcher.

Before they brought him to the sickbay, Jamie's eyelids grew too heavy to keep open.

***

With her limbs heavy with weariness, Ella staggered to her cabin. Her will to save Jamie helped her endure the cold, but when the immediate danger passed, her body shuddered from the chill. She changed into a wool dress and threw on a shawl. Still cold, she wrapped herself in a blanket, dropped onto the cot, and let herself catch a breath.

I almost lost Jamie. In this war, we can die at any moment. But while we are alive, we must give ourselves a chance to be happy.

Someone knocked on her door. "I brought you tea, Ella." The voice belonged to Conor. "Is it all right if I come in?"

When she let him in, Conor's hand slightly shook as he passed the steaming cup to her. He was wearing dry clothes that were too large on him, likely borrowed from someone. "I just saw Jamie at the sick bay. He's fallen asleep."

"Good." She took a careful sip and placed the cup on the table to cool a bit. "He needs rest more than anything."

He dropped his chin to his chest. "Thank you what you did. For saving his life."

"Why are you thanking me?" She raised her eyebrow. "You know how I feel about Jamie. Besides I was doing my job as a doctor."

"I should've gone after him. But I'm not a strong swimmer."

She clapped him on the shoulder. "Then it's a good thing you stayed in the boat."

"Do you believe he will be fine?" His eyes studied her, making her fidget. "Ella, please tell me the truth."

She wanted to reassure Conor and herself.

"He will recover in no time. From what I've observed, his constitution is remarkably strong."

Conor's shoulders relaxed, and he released a long breath. "He risks his life so readily. I even had this mad thought that he believes he'll die soon, perhaps from some incurable disease, and wants to be remembered as a hero instead. But if he's ill, you'd know, right?"

"Of course. That *is* a mad thought. I've examined him many times. He never complained about any pain or discomfort. And he survived many hours in the tunnels and a viper bite. If he were of weak health, he'd surely perish. He is an extremely unselfish and brave person and cannot stand by when someone is in trouble. Which is why we love him."

"I lost a brother. And today, I thought I would lose another." His eyes glistened, and he turned away. "I'm not crying. Something in my eye."

She put her hand on Conor's shoulder. "Like me, you've lost people you loved. It's terrifying to make yourself vulnerable. Jamie could've drowned. I could've died as well. But since we survived, I will not waste another day being afraid. I want to live life without boundaries I or someone else imposed on me. These limits are just another prison. I choose to be free."

A smile spread on Conor's lips, and he unrolled his shoulders.

Chapter 42

Through his sleep, Ella's voice whispered in his ear. "Jamie, I love you. Love you more than anything. I want us to get married. I even want your children. I still want to be a surgeon, but I could be a wife and a mother as well. You said you want me to have everything I want. With you, I can do more than if I stayed alone. We will be so happy."

What a wonderful dream. He was afraid to move and make it dispel.

When the smell of porridge tickled his nostrils, he opened his eyes. On the cot across from him, Tyler propped Tobby up for breakfast. The boy waved energetically to Jamie.

"Good morning!"

Jamie grinned. "How are you feeling, Tobby?"

"I'm hungry. This porridge seems awfully good right now."

Jamie's stomach rumbled, and he accepted the tray from Tyler with eagerness.

After he had eaten several spoonfuls, Tyler nodded approvingly. "Dr. Ella will be happy to hear that you have a healthy appetite."

"Where is she?"

"Finally resting, I hope." Tyler rolled his eyes. "She spent all night by your bedside. Not that there was any need. You slept soundly."

It wasn't a dream. Ella whispered her innermost desires as I slumbered. Marriage, children, pursuing her profession.

His heart leapt with happiness. But as it palpitated, his fears grew.

"What's wrong?" Tyler asked. "Are you feeling ill? Should I get Dr. Ella?"

Jamie lowered his bowl. "Tyler, would you do me a favor? Would you listen to my heart and tell me if you hear a murmur?"

Tyler bent to his chest. "Hmm. I don't have the best ear for this. Did someone tell you that you have it?"

"Dr. Miller."

"Oh." Tyler listened some more. "Now that you mentioned it," he said when he straightened, "I believe I heard it. Such an esteemed physician is unlikely to be wrong. But I don't know what it could mean. Did you discuss it with Dr. Ella?"

"Yes." Jamie glanced at Tobby, afraid that Tyler would say something to alarm the boy. "Don't worry about it. Ella said ... that it's nothing."

Except it's everything.

By the afternoon, he was restless from wallowing in bed and brooding. When Conor strode into the sickbay, Jamie was pondering his actions once they reach the port.

"When will we arrive to Plymouth?" He asked Conor.

Should I write to my family? I missed them terribly and have much to tell them, but would my letter give them false hope? Afterall, my heart is still damaged.

Conor perched on Jamie's bed. "We were blown off course, but if my calculations are correct, we are about to see England on the horizon."

Tobby clapped his hands.

"I'm sure you are correct." Jamie grinned at Conor. "But are you going to tell the truth to Captain Grey about your lack of naval experience?"

"I already did." Conor hung his head. "He was furious. But when I told him about everything that happened to us since, especially the part when I took responsibility for the escape and was going to be hanged, his anger ebbed. He said I've grown much, and in my actions, I resembled my father. I wish I knew more what he meant."

"I'm sure your father will tell you someday." He clapped his friend's back. "Would you help me go up to the deck? I'd love some fresh air."

"I'm happy to lend my shoulder, but I must ask Ella. Otherwise, she'll have my blood."

Throughout the day, Ella appeared in the sickbay several times. Her eyes stared like she wished to tell Jamie something important, but she asked only about his health.

Tobby bounced on his cot. "Ask if I can come as well."

Conor left and soon returned. "Um... she said I can bring you to the deck in twenty minutes."

"Why in twenty minutes?"

"I did not ask."

Tobby slid to the edge of his cot. "What about me?"

"She said you can come after."

"After what?"

Conor threw up his hands. "I'm only a messenger."

***

In her cabin, Ella rummaged in her trunk. She owned two gowns for special occasions, but she wished to find something else to wear. Those dresses she wore during her courtship with Robert Weston, and she preferred not to revisit the memories they brought.

Why does it matter what I wear? Jamie already said that he loves me more than life itself.

Her hands found something silky. She pulled out a violet gown with delicate lace. It took her a minute to remember that this dress was a gift from her friends at the party they threw for Matilda. She hastily put it on and fixed her hair.

My dear mentor and my friends will be with me.

She could almost see Veronica and Henrietta cheer, as well as Matilda's eyebrows rise. Marietta whispering, "It's all worth it."

With her heart fluttering, she came out to the deck. The wind played with her hair, and her skirt flowed. The crispness of the air made each breath invigorating, and the colors of the sea intense.

This moment couldn't be more perfect.

Warmed by the sun, she leaned on the railing and watched Jamie take careful steps toward her with one hand on Conor's shoulder. Conor was speaking, but Jamie's eyes stared into hers as if she was the only person there. She wanted to hold the gaze of those cornflower blue eyes all her life.

"How are you feeling?" she asked Jamie probably for the fifth time that day.

"Never better. You are so beautiful."

Nervous energy spread through her.

"Land ho!" the lookout yelled from above.

"I was right! It must be England." Conor jumped with his fist in the air.

Finally taking his eyes off Ella, Jamie grinned at his friend. His cheeks regained some color.

Conor ushered Jamie to the railing next to Ella. "I brought him like you asked. Now I must get to the quarterdeck and help get our ship to harbor."

When he left, Ella took Jamie's hand. He was about to say something, but she was quicker to speak.

With her heart beating like it wanted to escape her chest, she voiced the words she thought of last night, when Jamie was recovering from near death.

"Jamie, listen to me. There are many boundaries on women. Concerning profession. Or a place in society. A great number of other things. They are like a prison with no walls. Since I left home, I broke many rules. I'm about to break one more. And believe me, it will take much courage."

Jamie's palm sweated as he held on to her hand. "What are you planning, my love?"

"Only this." Ella got down on one knee. "James Flowers, would you take my hand in marriage? Would you be my wedded husband?"

His jaw dropped open.

Ella laughed. "I know this is shocking. But I'm not an ordinary woman. As you are aware."

As seconds passed, and Jamie hadn't moved, an uncomfortable sensation clenched her throat. When her knees began to throb, she stood. She was suddenly aware of many curious eyes on them. Seamen staring, whispering to each other. Likely judging her or gossiping about her broken betrothal with Robert.

"Why are you hesitating? After all we've been through, you must know your heart. We pledged our love to each other. More than once."

"I'm sorry," he whispered. "Ella, I am so sorry."

She jerked away as if from a slap. Her skin was aflame.

He rejected me. I broke all the rules, asked him to marry me, and he rejected me.

The world shuttered around her, but she forced herself to gather the remains of her dignity. She raised her chin and held her gaze. "Don't ever talk to me again, Jamie Flowers. I am done with you."

As she marched away with her head high, she caught Jamie's expression from a corner of her eye. His hands grabbed the railing like he was about to fall. She never saw anyone looking more miserable.

But she walked on.

***

Will Jamie survive? Will Ella forgive him? Find out in Book 4 of Hearts and Sails Series.

Jamie's and Ella's first meeting happens in the prequel Hearts by the Sea. Read a free book!

Also by Alina Rubin

A Girl with a Knife—Hearts and Sails Book 1

Women could not be surgeons. She did it anyway.
After the heartbreaking loss of her mother and a cruel attack by her drunken father, Ella Parker decides that dishonesty is fine when it serves her needs. At a time when wealthy young ladies do little more than embroidery, Ella escapes her luxurious but lonely life, disguises herself as a male medical student, and finds her footing in the university.
But when she brilliantly saves a patient and gains the approval of a famed professor, she must choose between truth and lies, and distinguish between real and false friends, before her pretense is discovered.

***

No Job for a Woman—Hearts and Sails Book 2

She sailed against the current.

As a woman in 1810 England, Ella cannot find a job as a doctor's assistant. In a life-or-death emergency with a mother in labor, she oversteps her boundaries and risks arrest. Determined to practice medicine, she decides to join her mentor on the *Neptune*, a warship heading for open waters. Following an accident, she is quickly thrust into the role of ship surgeon, and her skills are put to the test. Hoping to fit in with the all-male crew and make friends, instead, Ella creates chaos and suspicion among the superstitious sailors. Lieutenant Jack Wyse, though charged by the captain with protecting Ella, is keen on making her lea ve.After a fierce battle, Ella saves the handsome officer, Robert Weston. Her commitment to her profession is tested, however, when he asks for her hand in marriage. But are Weston's intentions sincere, and would he allow her the freedom to pursue her calling?

Ella must decide where she belongs before her future sails away from her.

***

New Series with Familiar Characters!

Abigail's Song—Hearts and Harmony Book 1

Can music heal a broken heart?

Cast out from her home after her mother's death, orphan Abigail Jones wanders around her English town on Christmas Eve of 1809. Desperately trying to suppress her cough—the same that killed her mother—Abigail begs for coins on the freezing cold streets. With the help of the medical student, Oli Higgins, she recovers and avoids being sent to the cruel orphanage. Oli then reveals his secret: he is hiding his Jewish identity and his birth name, David Fridman, to pursue his chosen profession.

He brings her into his devout, loving Jewish home. Over time, she embraces her found family and discovers her talent for music.

When she grows up, Abigail is caught between two worlds; not Christian enough for the Gentiles, but as a non-Jew, she has no hope of marrying David, the man she dreams of. While she is recovering from a deadly illness, David's brother Moishe inspires her with music to rise from her sickbed and to begin her journey of converting to Judaism.

Her attempt to capture David's heart fails when his true love appears in town. Heartbroken, Abigail hastily accepts another man's marriage proposal and plans a double wedding with David's bride. On the big day, guilt and misery drive her to take drastic actions.

Can her family save her?

Friends Don't Let Friends Read Boring Books!

Thank you for reading A Surgeon and a Spy!

Leaving a review is like recommending a book to hundreds of friends. Please share your thoughts at:

Amazon

Goodreads

BookBub

Join the crew! Be the first to know of new adventures by subscribing to the newsletter at alinarubinauthor.com

I love hearing from my readers! Please connect with me!

Instagram: Alina.Rubin.Author

Facebook: Alina Rubin Author

Email: alina@alinarubinauthor.com

Historical Notes

Much of what's known about the lives of British seamen imprisoned in France comes from their personal journals. The account I've read was by Seacombe Ellison, Master of first grade, and was called *Prison Scenes; and Narrative of Escape from France, During the Late War.* Ellison spent time in two French prisons: Verdun and Bitche. If those were listed on a site where prisoners could rate them for cleanliness, comfort, spread of disease, etc. Verdun would be a four-star luxury and Bitche a one-star hellhole.

In his journal, Ellison describes his numerous attempts to escape. While at Verdun, he and his friends went to the nearby town and purchased tools and supplies. They couldn't just walk away from the town: that would violate their parole. Instead, they went to the tavern and broke furniture and dishes until the owner called the authorities. A gendarme wanted them to leave quietly, but the seamen demanded to be taken to Verdun citadel. The prison commander didn't want them, so again they had to insist on the punishment. Locked up in a cell, they finally attempted their escape but with disastrous consequences: the rope they climbed broke, and a couple of people broke their legs. And this was only one of the wild stories Ellison depicted.

While Ellison's account was colorful, I didn't get a full picture of French prisons until I found Michael Lewis's book *Napoleon and his British Captives*. This book gave a comprehensive account of the locations, conditions, and a comparison of the written accounts. Best of all, the author described all the escapes, successful and not. One man escaped by hiding under the skirts of a Frenchwoman and her maid. An officer swam in the river and was believed to have drowned, except his friend waited for him downstream with a set of change clothes. Another man bought a cap off a Frenchman and joined a search for himself. Five-year-old boys escaped by scaling walls without a rope. A wealth of ideas to weave into fiction.

I had the research needed to write the novel. The logical plan was to select a French prison, send Jamie and his friends there, and design their method of escape. Except I couldn't choose between Verdun, Givet, Bitche, or other locations. The setting would be key to what would happen after the escape, whether they would cross Rhine to reach Austria or Russia, or go toward the Channel, bound for England. At Verdun, Jamie and Conor would live in the town and enjoy amusements; in Givet they would be locked up in a cell. The pressure of choosing the 'right' prison for the story paralyzed me. The way out was to create a fictional prison that would suit my story. I designed it to combine the characteristics of other places: privileges for the officers, like in Verdun. A pontoon bridge, similar to one at Givet. The tunnels were my own invention. The story came together.

Jamie's benevolent deeds during his imprisonment were inspired by the life of Rev. Robert Wolfe. The reverend lived in France with his family when the authorities detained him and sent him to Verdun on parole. This was done to British men living in France to prevent them from joining the fight against Napoleon's army. Instead of staying in the town in comfort, Wolfe volunteered to go to a much harsher prison, Givet. There he started a school for children and adults, organized the work to fix a dilapidated hospital, and befriended both the prisoners and the guards.

The scene about Napoleon freeing the prisoners who rebuilt the bridge is based on historical events. The emperor arrived at Givet in 1811, ignored the local dignitaries, and went straight to bed. During the night, the heavy rain poured, and the pontoon bridge broke and was swept away. About thirty British prisoners restored the bridge. Napoleon watched them work in the morning and gifted them freedom. Even the episode where a cheeky sailor asked for snuff was noted by several sources. My only invention was how many men gained their freedom and how long it took. It was a lengthy process to complete the paperwork, and only around a dozen prisoners were ultimately released.

Some notes about historical medicine:

Ella's study of surgeon John Hunter's works enabled her to bring Jamie back to life after drowning. He recommended mouth-to-mouth resuscitation and heart stimulation back in 1776. Otherwise, the doctors of the time administered tobacco enemas or hung the patient upside down.

The first record of a mother and a baby surviving a cesarean section goes back to 1500s Switzerland. There were also accounts of travelers visiting African countries and witnessing the indigenous people performing the surgery. The British doctors often dismissed those accounts. The first successful cesarean in the British Empire was conducted by Dr. James Barry sometime between 1815 and 1821 in South Africa. Dr. Barry was a respected physician and a surgeon, trained in Scotland and tending to soldiers and sailors. Only after the surgeon's death, people learned a scandalous secret. Dr. Barry was a woman, Margaret Anne Bulkley. Her story inspired my ideas on how Ella received her medical education.

When researching how doctors diagnosed heart disease before stethoscopes and x-rays were invented, I learned of an incredible doctor, Helen B. Taussig. Because of an ear infection that resulted in deafness, Dr. Taussig developed a method of using her fingers to feel the heart rhythm and find issues. Her achievements in pediatric cardiology saved numerous lives.

I hope you enjoyed these notes and feel inspired to do some research on your own. Historical medicine is incredibly compelling and often makes me thankful for modern innovations.

Acknowledgements

The first fragments of story came to me in October 2020, when I was an accomplished writer of heart wrenching IT compliance documents. That day, I was working on an exciting spreadsheet. The work captivated me, so much that my brain kept giving me helpful hints such as, *check if your friend has posted a new cat video* or *look up the weather for tomorrow even if you're not going anywhere.* When I disregarded those suggestions, my brain did something I couldn't ignore. It played a song in my head.

The song my brain played was by a Russian guitar duo Ivasi and called *Did the Frigate Sink (Погиб ли тот Фригат)*. Suddenly I needed to hear that song and do some urgent research. What frigate is this song about? Is it a true story? And did that frigate sink? After some googling, I learned that the song wasn't based on any real ship. I also came across a video where the song played in the background of scenes from a movie. The glimpse into that film hooked me: sailing ships, battles, and two young officers who were obviously best friends. I needed to know more.

With some digging, I learned the reel was from British mini-series *Hornblower*, which first aired in 2000. I became obsessed with that show. (Just to clarify for fans of *Hornblower* or Ivasi, there's no official connection between the song and the mini-series, but someone created a video combining the two and posted it to YouTube.)

After watching the series twice, stories started coming to me. Visions of ship battles, prison escapes, and a brave young woman doctor who saves her friends when they become injured. On February 26, 2021, I said to my husband, "I think I'm supposed to write a novel." He replied, "That sounds like time better spent than watching tv."

From that day on, I stepped on a journey no less exciting than what my characters sailed through. Exactly a year later, I published *A Girl with a Knife*. Three years and four books later, I said goodbye to the wonderful world of IT compliance and became a full-time fiction author.

A Surgeon and a Spy was the first story I wrote, but the only thing that the first draft and the final draft have in common are the names of the two main characters. I'm so glad I showed the first draft to three people, and I thank them because they played key roles in my author journey. The first was my dearest "found sister" Inessa Levin, who cheered for me and told me to keep writing. The second was my beta reader, Becky Paroz, who told me my book has "bones of a good story," but needs to be more believable and based on history, not just my imagination. The third was editor Kirsten Rees, who told me that my manuscript had great potential but wasn't ready for professional editing. She pointed me toward writing classes and critique groups. As a result, I learned the craft and built a series. The story of Ella rescuing Jamie from an enemy prison became Book Three. I'm delighted it's finally ready to meet its readers.

This book had been greatly improved with the help of excellent beta readers. Rachel Callaghan, Michelle Ross, Lindsey S. Fera, and Kester Bathgate, thank you so much for your suggestions and eagle eyes. Special thanks to LJ Dix for helping me write my first fight scene.

I must thank Rochelle Zappia for giving me an idea to put a male character in a dress, as a balance to Ella wearing trousers. This sparked the manner of Jamie's escape.

Thank you to my editor and fellow historical fiction author Marthese Fenech for all her hard work on this book. You were a pleasure to work with in every way.

Next, I want to thank my wonderful readers. Your support, reviews, and emails warm my heart. All the best to you and keep reading! Special thank you to my superfans Michelle Ross, Helen Kopner, Inessa Levina, Cynthia Florsheim, Michael, Jamie, and Karina Rubinshteyn.

Thank you to the wonderful communities of Paper Lantern Writers, Harvest Moon, Inner Circle, and All-American Speakers for your help and support. A special thanks to Tami Palmer and Kim Kleeman.

Teachers are never thanked enough. Thank you, Mr. Kevin Hickey, Mrs. Barbara Fryzel-Marquette, and Mrs. Barbara Schuman, among many other wonderful teachers from Prospect High School.

Thank you to my dearest Elanna who makes me so proud. And thank you to my husband Vitaly. It takes much love to support a spouse who leaves a steady career to embark on the volatile paths of publishing and entrepreneurship.

Until the next adventure!

Alina

About the Author

Alina Rubin is a best-selling author who celebrates heroines with strong voices and able hands. Amidst the pandemic, she authored her debut novel while working in IT. Her characters took her on a journey beyond her wildest dreams. She's an accomplished speaker and an owner of Hearts and Sails Author Services.

Alina's debut novel, *A Girl with a Knife,* has won the Illinois Soon to be Famous Author Competition. Her book series is set in the Regency England era, but her characters are more likely to suture wounds and climb rigging than dance at a ball. Since publishing, Alina has been interviewed by Glenview Off The Shelf TV program, Ukrainian-American Magazine, History through Fiction, and many other programs and podcasts. She's also a member of Paper Lantern Writers.

Alina obtained a B.S. and M.S. degrees in Business and Information Technology from DePaul University. She lives in Chicago with her husband and daughter. She enjoys yoga, hiking, and traveling.

Follow her blog and sign up for her newsletter on her website alinarubinauthor.com

www.ingramcontent.com/pod-product-compliance
Lightning Source LLC
Chambersburg PA
CBHW062112290726
48975CB00001B/198